# ROAD STORIES

# ROAD STORIES

NEW WRITING INSPIRED
BY EXHIBITION ROAD

EDITED BY MARY MORRIS

THE ROYAL BOROUGH OF
KENSINGTON
AND CHELSEA

DREAM

EXHIBITION
ROAD SHOW

First published in 2012
By the Royal Borough of Kensington and Chelsea for ROAD SHOW
Project conceived and produced by Di Robson Events and Arts Management (DREAM)
Typeset and designed by Will Webb Design www.willwebb.co.uk
Paper sculptures by Mandy Smith
Photography by James Medcraft

Printed and bound by CPI Group (UK) Ltd, Croydon CR0 4YY



A CIP record for this book is available from the British Library

ISBN 978-0-9549-8484-7

ROAD SHOW has been commissioned by the Royal Borough of Kensington and Chelsea in partnership with the Exhibition Road Cultural Group and Westminster City Council to contribute to the celebrations for the 2012 Olympics.

2 4 6 8 10 9 7 5 3 1

IN MEMORY OF RUSSELL HOBAN

1925 – 2011

# Contents

Exhibition Road has long been a place for people to be inspired by, to dream about and discover for themselves.

Prince Albert's vision was for this quarter of London to be devoted exclusively to science and the arts. Today Exhibition Road is home to the world's leading institutions in science, natural history, art and design, culture and music.

*Road Stories* was commissioned by the Royal Borough of Kensington and Chelsea to capture the wonder of Exhibition Road. The writers of this collection of short stories have been inspired by the people and places that make up London's cultural heartland.

With the public space on Exhibition Road now reopened, I hope that by reading these stories you will be encouraged to come and be inspired yourself.

COUNCILLOR SIR MERRICK COCKELL,
LEADER, THE ROYAL BOROUGH OF
KENSINGTON AND CHELSEA
JUNE 2012

The Great Exhibition of the Works of Industry of All Nations in 1851 created an extraordinary legacy for Exhibition Road. It is a great meeting place of science, knowledge and creativity. Our particular challenge in making the Exhibition Road Show in 2012 was to reflect and celebrate this extraordinary place. Commissioning this collection of short stories has allowed us to recruit other distinctive and wonderful voices to this challenge. I'd like to give our thanks to all the writers in this volume and to our editor Mary Morris who has served this task so brilliantly.

DI ROBSON
DIRECTOR
EXHIBITION ROAD SHOW

When Charlotte Brontë attended the Great Exhibition in London's Hyde Park in 1851 she was overwhelmed: 'It is a wonderful place – vast, strange, new and impossible to describe. Its grandeur does not consist in *one* thing, but in the unique assemblage of *all* things ... It seems as if only magic could have gathered this mass of wealth from all the ends of the earth – as if none but supernatural hands could have arranged it thus, with such a blaze and contrast of colours and marvellous power of effect.' These words are equally fitting to describe the Exhibition Road of today: its glorious architecture and collections, the learning and scholarship and innovation of its institutions – indeed its very name – a legacy of that international celebration of culture and industry that so captured the imagination of Victorian London 160 years ago.

Commissioning a story collection to celebrate the newly refurbished Exhibition Road was a challenge. With so many world-famous artistic, scientific and academic organisations in an area a mere kilometre long, any attempt to reflect all that Exhibition Road has to offer in nine short pieces would be doomed to failure. And so rather than assigning a specific destination to a specific author, I offered them all a broad brief: they were to find inspiration in 'the collections and life of Exhibition Road's most famous institutions, colleges and parks, or the lives of the area's residents'. For any writer, finding a richer source of ideas than this particular road would surely be difficult.

Inspiration, as it turned out, was not wanting, and the resulting collection of stories is as varied and surprising, as thought-provoking and playful – and as international – as I had hoped it could be. The characters you'll find within these pages might hail from Lahore, Yemen, or Mysore, from our own century or other centuries, but all have something very specific in common: they are transported, sometimes literally, by this place of beauty and discovery and history – this treasure trove in the heart of our capital city. And we are transported with them. As Ali Smith's wonderful story concludes, in Exhibition Road 'There will always be something you know you're missing out on, there'll always be something you'll come back to.'

It is a particular privilege to have in this collection a story by the much loved, and much missed, Russell Hoban. He delivered it, typewritten on his trademark yellow paper, very shortly before he died, and it's as redolent of his curiosity, originality and sense of fun as anything he wrote. It is to his memory that this book is dedicated.

MARY MORRIS
EDITOR

# Gold Medal Day

KAMILA SHAMSIE

She lived in a flat on Exhibition Road.

'You must get so many visitors,' people would say.

She wasn't the one with the visitors. It was the Science Museum, the Albert Hall, the V&A, the Natural History Museum, Hyde Park, Kensington Palace, even the Ismaili Centre – which hadn't been there as long as she had – which attracted the visitors. She was the afterthought.

Some people at least had the decency to call well in advance so that she might at least think that they were coming to Exhibition Road only to see her. The really polite ones visited her before they went to the museums or parks, though the children always kicked their heels against her sofa and looked beseechingly at their parents in a way that made it clear that this visit to the ageing lady was the concession that had been extracted from them in exchange for a dinosaur or a galaxy. The ones who arrived with bags from the museum shops, always late because no one ever correctly predicted the length of time they'd spend there, were served tea and cake on the Woolworth's crockery instead of the John Lewis. She was a woman given to meting out the kinds of insults that no one else would notice, because her fear of driving people away was equal to her inability to let a slight, real or imagined, pass.

But the ones who made her furious to a degree that required a punishment beyond second-rate crockery were those who rang her bell and said they were in the neighbourhood and thought they must drop in, and fifteen seconds after she'd ushered them through the door were asking where they might find the loo (they were all of that variety of Pakistani who would never use a public loo when a more exclusive option was within walking distance). But she could do nothing to express her fury: what if they left? So she'd smile and say how lovely to see them, and when they stood up to leave she'd say, 'So soon?' and then she'd wag a mock-admonishing finger at them and say, 'I'm going to believe you only came here to use the loo,' a remark so searing it forced the visitors to stay for at least another hour to prove it untrue.

She never visited the museums or parks herself. She used to, once. When she first came to live here in 1970, a young bride from Lahore, everything about this street was dazzling with possibility. Music! Parks! Dinosaurs! And best of all, in the V&A, the most beautiful Gandhara sculptures. On quiet afternoons, she could stand and stare at them for long uninterrupted stretches of time and imagine herself back in the Lahore Museum, a student at Kinnaird College. Then she'd remember – no! She was here, in London, a wife

– and that would be all right; that would be more than all right. Everything she'd given up – the beautiful tree-lined canals, the gracious pace of living, the vast network of friends and relatives, the ribald humour of women who'd known each other long enough to make 'propriety' irrelevant – seemed insignificant compared to this life of freedom and blessed anonymity where no one could tell her what to do except an indulgent, broad-shouldered husband.

What had changed? How had that girl who used to spend at least two afternoons a week walking through her neighbourhood museums become this woman who hadn't stepped through the door of one in … decades? Yes, decades. That torso of the seated Buddha, with its exquisite drapes and the nipples jutting out beneath (impossible that the whole thing was carved out of stone and not composed of flesh and muslin), well, she couldn't even remember the last time she had seen it. There'd never been a decision – no more! I'm leaving – no firmly closed door, no packed suitcases. Nothing like that. It had simply happened that something which had once been a part of her life now no longer was. No good now trying to find that one moment when everything changed; day by day in this city of seeping cold and strangers, change simply kept happening, all around you, all the time. And if you tried to stay still in it, you became outdated, unwanted.

Then, one afternoon in April – the kind of afternoon which turns London into the world's most beautiful city, everywhere cherry blossoms and wisteria and a madcap desire to absorb every ray of the sun before it disappears again – one of her great-nephews came to visit with his fiancée. She barely knew this great-nephew; he hadn't been to London since he was a small child, but she liked him for his well-cut suit (none of that jeans and T-shirt nonsense) and the fact that he introduced her to his fiancée as 'the most independent, and stylish, woman in our family'. They had called in advance; they had no paraphernalia from the neighbourhood; they had brought her flowers: she served them tea and cake on her Noritake plates. They didn't seem to notice, but she didn't mind.

– You've been here a long time, the fiancée said.

– Longer than you've been alive!

– I used to spend a lot of time here, in my student days. I wish I'd known you then. It would have been nice to have had someone in the neighbourhood who I could take out for a cup of tea in the evening.

Oh, the fiancée was sucking up, of course. The family's feeling was that she wasn't 'good enough' – no background to speak of – so it would do her status no end of good if she could win one of the elders onto her side. But knowing this didn't make the remark any less charming.

– You were at Imperial?

– No. But I spent a lot of time at the Royal Geographical Society, for research.

The Royal Geographical Society. That was one she'd never visited. At school she'd hated geography: all those facts and figures about rainfall and crops in places she didn't know, where she would never feel the rain on her face, or play hide-and-seek in the fields, so what did it matter how much rain fell or if the fields were of maize or sugarcane? All that remained to her now of her geography lessons was the term 'boll weevil'. She had named her two pet rabbits 'Boll' and 'Weevil', she remembered now. Poor rabbits. One had its ear completely bitten off by the neighbour's dog. Was that Boll or Weevil? She had heard the commotion and come out into the garden, and there it was, one rabbit, hunched in the grass, with a pink stub where its ear had been. It showed no real sign of distress then or later, but it was a strange relief to her when it was squashed beneath the wheels of a car not long after.

Her great-nephew was speaking now, leaning towards his fiancée, asking her something about the Royal Geographical Society and women. So transparent, these young men attempting to act interested in the things that mattered to the women they were wooing. Soon it would end. 'It's just a lump of stone,' the man would eventually say, though he had once exclaimed with delight at the seated Buddha.

The fiancée – what was her name? what was his name, come to think of it? – was animated now, talking with more enthusiasm about the research of her student days and her impending fellowship in America than she'd put into discussing the plans for her marriage just a few minutes earlier. Imagine, going into a marriage with this other world of passion, this idea of what you wanted to do other than be a wife. Wouldn't that just create a wedge between the couple, or was it possible it might prevent him from ever saying to her 'It's been years since you said a single sentence of any interest'?

– Only seven women have ever received the Gold Medal from the Royal Geographical Society. Seven since 1832. Can you imagine?

– The Gold Medal is?

– The highest award given by the Society. All the great explorers received it: Stanley, Livingstone, Scott, Aurel Stein, Hillary. And only seven women.

The man tried to look appalled, although he was most certainly thinking – as she herself was – that the only surprising part of this was that seven women had received a medal from a society for exploration. Walking down a street on your own: for a woman, this was exploration. Yes, it was. She had lived for nearly a month in this flat before she had managed to leave it while her husband was at work. She'd never forget the thrill and terror of realising that she was the one who had to decide what to do, where to go. She had walked north just a few paces, and the park was just there, just a minute away, but she'd have had to cross the road. No. She had turned round and walked halfway down Exhibition Road. Everyone was staring at her. It was the sari, it was the colour of her skin, it was the fact that she looked so terrified … she walked home as quickly as she could. But a few days later she found herself recalling the feeling of possibility she had experienced when she'd first stepped out onto the street. London! It wasn't so warm today; she could wear the long coat, which went down to the ground and covered the sari completely. And she'd wear the hat that her husband had bought for her, and keep her head bent, and her hands in her pocket, and no one would know she didn't belong. What a triumph that day had been. In some ways, yes, the best of her life, even though by the end she was almost fainting in the long winter coat. And how proud her husband had been when he came home and she told him what she'd done. He had swung her around in his arms, and taken her to the Savoy for dinner. A Gold Medal day.

– And the first woman to receive the Gold Medal – Lady Franklin – it wasn't because of any exploring she'd done, but because of the pointless expeditions she'd financed to discover what had happened to her husband. He was the real explorer of the pair – he disappeared somewhere near the Arctic.

– And what had happened to her husband?

– He was eaten by his crew!

– Seriously, babe?

'Babe'. What a way to refer to the woman you were about to marry. What was wrong with *jaan* – 'my life'? Perhaps that was considered old-fashioned now. She looked above the couple's head at the painting of an Alpine landscape that her husband had given her on their first anniversary, as a reminder of their honeymoon.

After the relative and his fiancée had left – they let slip that they had tickets to something at the Royal Albert Hall, which made her regret the Noritake – she found herself thinking about this Lady Franklin who sent out expedition after expedition to try and find her missing husband. She was still thinking about her the next day when she found herself walking, for the first time, to the Royal Geographical Society. She didn't know exactly what she wanted there. Though she enjoyed the travel photographs she left feeling unsatisfied.

But later, when night settled in and the street lamps spotlit the blossoms as though they were an exhibit, she pulled her laptop out of its hiding place and switched it on. She never kept it in view when her visitors came by; she knew families used it to stay in touch without ever meeting, and this was not something she was about to encourage. But it was a miracle. She could watch old PTV dramas uploaded onto YouTube, pay her bills, order her groceries, read all kinds of gossip about her favourite actors and even those she despised … there was no end to its wonders. Because of it, some days she didn't even notice that she hadn't actually spoken to another person from morning to night.

She typed 'Lady Franklin' into Google.

Many hours later, 'in the time between the nightingale and the rooster', as her husband used to say some nights when asked when he'd return, she sat down to write:

*Do you know about Lady Franklin? Her husband was an explorer: John Franklin. She was thirty-four when they married in 1828. I thought twenty-three was very old for marriage in 1969: can you imagine how much older thirty-four must have seemed in 1828? In 1845 the British government asked him to lead an expedition to the Arctic. She stayed behind.*

*The expedition set off in May 1845. The ships were seen two months later by a passing crew. No one ever saw any of them again.*

*When two years had gone by without a word, Lady Franklin asked the government to send out a search mission. Eventually a search party was assembled. Lady Franklin even wrote to the President of America asking for help and he directly asked Congress to give any assistance possible. Can you imagine? Your husband disappears and you write to the American President!*

*But perhaps writing to the American President didn't seem remarkable to her; she was, I think, that sort of woman, and besides, America wasn't America then. Though what would she have done if he'd left rather than disappeared – would she have pretended for months that no such thing had happened? Is not knowing easier than knowing things your heart can't understand? Between 1850 and 1875 Lady Franklin sponsored seven expeditions herself to look for her husband. In 1859 the sixth of those expeditions, led by Captain McClintock, discovered that Franklin had died in 1847.*

*The Royal Geographical Society gave out its two gold medals – one to McClintock 'for the skill and fortitude displayed by him and his companion in their search for records of the lost [Franklin] expedition and for valuable coast surveys' and one to Lady Franklin 'for self-sacrificing perseverance in sending out expeditions to ascertain the fate of her husband'. They must have thought the medal marked the end: perhaps the medal was their way of telling her it was time to stop. But Lady Franklin hadn't finished. She was convinced something remained to be found – written records, diaries, journals, buried somewhere in the Arctic ice. How is it possible that she could have believed … oh, but we'll believe anything rather than let go. We'll wait and wait, holding on to hairstyles and clothes and household objects that once drew forth a smile or a compliment.*

*In 1875 she sponsored the last of 'Lady Franklin's expeditions'. She died that year before the ship returned, unsuccessful.*

*How am I supposed to feel about her? More men and ships were lost searching for her husband than were part of his expedition. Isn't there a point when you say, 'Enough'?*

*But here is an important thing to add: she didn't just sit at home, waiting for news of the ships she waved goodbye to. She didn't spend her entire day making sure everything was as he liked it – the forty-watt bulbs, the bar of Imperial Leather, the curtains rather than blinds, the heavy gilt-framed paintings – so that if he walked back through the door after years away he'd understand immediately that this, only this, was home. No, she didn't! She travelled around the world herself. Once she went to the northernmost of the British Isles, to get as close as she could to her missing husband. Some writer called Jessie Saxby says, 'She stood on the Out Stack and said, "Send love on the wings of a prayer," quite silent with tears falling slowly and her hands stretched out toward the north.' This sounds made-up to me. But was it Jessie Saxby or Lady Franklin who was guilty of inventing it?*

~~*Your wife*~~
*Saqina*

When she had finished, she opened her desk drawer, took out some papers from an envelope and signed them. Then she placed them, and the letter, in a fresh envelope. It occurred to her only now that it had been years since the solicitor called to say she needed to sign. How long? She considered. It had been fourteen years since he'd left. Fourteen years: the length of time between Franklin's departure and McClintock's discovery of his death. The solicitor's phone calls all blurred into each other. It might have been three years since the last one; it might have been five; it might have been more. So, either the French woman had stopped wanting to be his wife or he was dead. She waited to feel delight at the first thought, an ache at the second.

– Well, well, well.

The room echoed her surprise back at her.

For a minute or two, there was nothing. And then a wild glee came upon her. Now her life would change! She knew it. Everything would be different. She looked around, frantic. Her glance came to rest on the Alpine landscape. Kicking off her slippers, she stood on the sofa, lifted the hanging wire off its nail and there: it was done.

She placed the painting on the floor, turned towards the wall. She had never, ever, ever liked it.

Now there was a nail visible on her wall, and a square of paint several shades darker than the rest of this sun-drenched room. (Oh, it was morning.)

She would get dressed, and go out, and she would find a painting that she wanted to look at every day. And she'd buy it.

# A&V at the V&A

## ALI SMITH

Whenever A and V went to the V&A they always ended up going off in different directions and losing each other. The days of mobile phones had made this a problem much more easily solved (though reception could be patchy in certain parts of the V&A). Anyway they were on their way to the V&A now and had been arguing already on the Tube about whether to take the tunnel or the road. Then, walking along the road – V had won – they began another argument. This one was about the first time they had ever visited the V&A together and when exactly this had been.

See, I don't remember that at all, A said.

We *did*, V said, really early on. When we first knew each other. But it was in the days when you were still being very Scottish about things and full of righteousness –

You think those days are over? A said.

– Ha, V said, listen, because when I said I wanted to show you a funny mechanical man being eaten by a tiger you went off on one about how savage it sounded, how like Victorian England, how like imperialism, how you'd no wish to see something like that.

Whenever they went to the V&A or even talked about visiting the V&A they invariably ended up arguing about something, maybe partly because A had had a kind of a fling (ten years ago now) with a rich Kensington girl who'd lived not far from the Conran Shop. There had been a nice deli near this girl's flat and V often taunted A about the burnt broccoli that this deli had sold and that A had particularly liked. It was one of V's subtle ways of getting at A while remaining humorous and benign; it was affectionately done, and in any case the fling hadn't come to anything, had fizzled out well before any difficult verbs were involved. But even so, this would be one of the reasons A was so forcefully disagreeing.

I like Tipu's Tiger, A was saying now. I always have. I liked it as soon as I saw it. It's ingenious. It's a brilliant satire on colonialism and on industrialism. I've always thought that. But I definitely didn't see it till, like, 2001.

Here A faltered slightly, perhaps because 2001 was around the time of the rich girl.

We *did*, V said.

A was blushing. But a blush was on its way to V's ears too, with what felt like ferocity. What A didn't know was that as recently as last summer V had come to the V&A alone on one of its late-open evenings, to meet a beautiful yellow-haired woman, the kind who turns heads in the street, who when you go to lunch with her gets brought desserts free by smitten waiters in cafes or restaurants, who goes through life casually trailing behind her, like an expensive scarf bought in a shop like the one at the V&A, these and all the other perks of this kind of beauty. They'd had a drink (there was a bar and a DJ – that was what the V&A was like now, nothing like it had been, or any museum had been, when V had been a child); they'd looked at some medieval and Renaissance things in the newer gallery where the light, regardless of what time of day it is, is steadily like Italian summer daylight; they'd gone downstairs and seen some much more ancient stuff made of gold and wood and clay; then they'd drifted out across the late-evening park towards the city, with all the birds on the lake gathered in a secret piece of bird theatre now that the dark was coming down and most of the humans gone.

It wasn't the fact that A didn't know about this, though, that was making V blush. It was the memory, prompted by coming to the V&A again for the first time since, of that beautiful woman's indifference and distraction. They had seen the exhibits and crossed the grass and passed the night birds and it had been as if that woman hadn't actually seen any of it, as if it were all a stage-flat she was passing in front of on her way to some other life entirely, V tagging along, slightly behind, breathless, slightly off to the side.

Luckily A was still holding forth righteously about their own far past:

Because I'd really have remembered something like that, I remember really clearly all the places you showed me in London, all the things we went to see when we were first together, the South Bank and the Hodgkin pictures at the Hayward, and you showing me the Pre-Raphaelite girls coming down the stairs in the National Gallery, but not the V&A, I don't remember the –

Well, maybe we didn't actually go, V said. Maybe it was something I thought we'd do and then told you about and then we didn't do because you said words like savage and imperial.

OK, A said. Well. Maybe.

Now A was off on another tangent, talking about how the thing about the V&A was that it didn't matter where you were in the building, you always had a feeling that there was something you weren't seeing.

Like there's always some secret wing of the building that you're missing out on, A said. Like somewhere there'll be a statue of the Buddha that'll change your life when you see it, or, if you just turn the right corner, a perfect tiny bottle the size of a thumb and shaped like a wise man, that when you see it means you'll understand something you haven't yet understood about life. Or a tiny pair of pink crinkly shoes so small they look like they'd never fit a human foot, that when you see them will let something inside you know how the whole world works.

While A talked on about how, currently, there was meant to be a huge beautiful Madagascan spider-web gold shawl in the V&A, how it was said to be huge and beautiful but how it sounded, to A anyway, like spider slave labour, V walked along not listening, thinking about the ten minutes that night last summer when the beautiful woman had been taking a call on her mobile in the lobby and V, waiting and polite, had wandered into the new gallery and seen an old Crucifixion figure, a relief, was it? (in the artistic sense of the word anyway), on the wall.

The Christ had had a huge hole in his side, a wound that actually looked like an extra ear. That's clever, V had thought, an ear into the body like that, the appearance of a God with extra unexpected hearing. The figure had also had a hole right in the centre of the chest. The card on the wall next to the figure had said on it: *Christ's wounds were a focus for devotion. His side wound was especially venerated, and in prayer it was evoked as a refuge for sinners. The hole in the chest of the figure probably housed a relic.*

A refuge – as if you could actually crawl, for safety, inside a wound. But it was the Christ's face in relation to the wounds which had really caught V's attention. The face was full of blank anguish and sadness; all the same the artist had made it look like the Christ figure was holding his side open rather jauntily. The act looked almost camp.

Maybe that was the best way to deal with pain. Maybe it was the only generous way. It would take some doing, to have human form and be so holy – and so holey – all at the same time. The artist had also remembered the nail holes in the hands, and then there was this extra hole, large and circular and untraditional, in the chest, from which the ribs radiated outward. For relics. It looked like it had been made by machine rather than by art. But somehow it made the rest of the piece acceptable, it made the figure even more able to house things other than itself.

Remember? A was saying by V's side.

Sorry? V said.

Made of logs, A said. In the new courtyard. And more and more people, every time we tried to take our photo. So every time we got ready to take one, someone else came in.

I don't remember that at all, V said.

You *do*, A said. You *must* do. I don't know, seven or eight years ago. You stood in it and you said: *We could live in this. We could be really happy in a house like this one.*

Did I? V said.

And then we went through to look at the room that the artist had taken a plaster cast of, that artist who fills things with plaster, the one who did the whole house and then they knocked it down, A said.

I remember seeing *that* here, V said, the light switches and the skirting boards all white. And do you remember – d'you remember – after the Ossie Clark exhibition when you bought the replica shirt?

At this both A and V started to laugh. They stopped walking because they were laughing so much and they stood just laughing in the street in the noise of traffic. They laughed until they actually had to hold on to each other.

People walked past them.

Oh God. So much money. I know, and we had hardly any. In the wardrobe. Still in the wardrobe. Well, the nipples. Your mother. Never mind my mother, your father. Worth what it cost just to see. Didn't wear it again.

But oh, the moment of buying it. And you'd been so unwell for so long. And your shining face when you did, V said. It was the start of a new time, that shirt.

I'll get it out this summer, A said. I'll wear it anyway. I'll wear it to all the family parties for the next ten years.

It's such a fantastic shirt, V said. If you don't, I will.

No, it won't fit you, A said.

You didn't even know who Ossie Clark was, V said.

Yeah, well, you and your childhood on the doorstep of the National Theatre, A said, you and your adolescence at the threshold of culture, you and your *Pravda*, your Julie Covington and David Essex live on stage in *Evita*.

You and your 'The Kilt is My Delight', V said. You and your Highland Museum with the stuffed stag and the stuffed wildcat.

I hope you're not dissing my childhood, A said. And the stuffed wildcat kittens and the mannequin from Burton's Menswear dressed in clan tartan in front of the black-and-white picturewall of the clan burial stones at Culloden Battlefield. Tragic.

In all the ways, V said.

You better not be dissing the museum culture that made me, A said.

Was the wildcat in a glass case? V said. Were its ears flat or pointed?

Of course it was in a case, A said. It's still in a case. You can't touch the wildcat.

How old were you? V said.

Eight, twelve, seventeen, forty-three, A said. It's still there. They kept it when they upgraded. That means more than just me loved the wildcat.

I like to imagine you at all those ages, seeing it through the glass, V said. Take me to see it next time we're up.

Funny, A said. Because that's what I do every time I come here, I think of that thing you told me about when you were seventeen and they let you into the special room somewhere in this building to see the William Morris wallpaper for the research project.

Snakes and grapes, V said. Large grapes, small snakes.

You alone in the room, A said, in this exemplary museum, with that precious wallpaper, touching it anyway though they'd told you not to, to feel the emboss, see what it felt like.

But I was wearing the gloves, V said.

That's what you're like, A said.

Which? The touching the paper or the wearing the gloves? V said.

Bit of both, A said.

I still dream of that wallpaper sometimes, V said.

I still dream of that wildcat sometimes, A said.

They had reached the steps of the V&A. It rose above them like a – a what? Cathedral? Grand hotel? Train station? Museum?

We are such stuffed wildcats as dreams are made on, V said, and our little life is rounded with a sleep.

Yeah, A said, well. At least I can honestly say that no dream I've ever had in my life has involved wallpaper.

Snakes and grapes, grapes and snakes; tiny shoes that show what humans are happy to do to their own feet; clay; cloth; wood; gold; a transparent 100 per cent silk shirt; the plaster cast of a gone room; a wise man in the shape of a bottle; the gods; the holes in the gods: it was all ahead of them and all behind them. They went in arm in arm through the big doors. They kissed each other on the cheek. Then they did what they usually did and went their separate ways for a while. V turned right and strolled through to have another look at what was there and what wasn't, and A went straight ahead, maybe to the shop or maybe to the corridor beyond, the galleries of histories of everything from dust-fleck to architecture; or maybe to look again at the man being eternally eaten by the tiger, the machine of nature, the nature of the machine; or maybe just to sit in some of the afternoon sun in the courtyard, who knows? Here in this place named for lovers, this museum of historic fidelities, there'll always be something you know you're missing out on, there'll always be something you'll come back to.

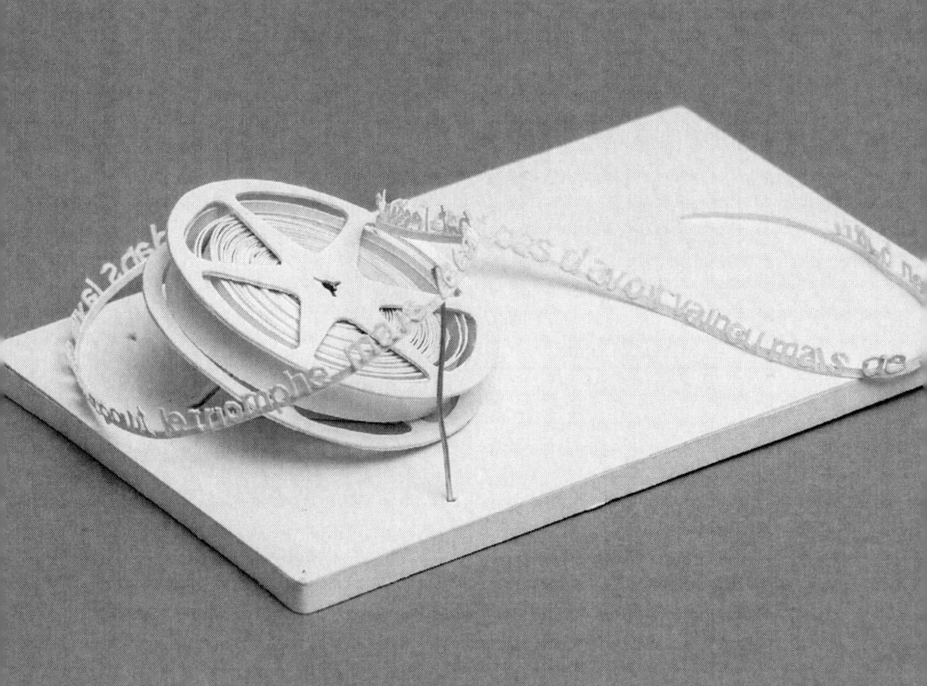
d'avoir vaincu mais de

# Meet the Monster

CLARE WIGFALL

That spring of 1812 is when the rumour first blisters their attention. Over cigars and port wine, it flirts at the earlobes of the Geological Society Fellows, as yet unverified. A remarkable discovery. Indeed? Made by a girl. A girl? Indeed, a girl! A twelve-year-old girl. An uneducated carpenter's child. And where, pray? Lyme Regis. The towering Dorset coast, where the cliffs are ever crumbling into the sea. Boulders of limestone and slabs of shale hailing incessantly from the cliff face. Tides that can sweep in between a blink. And amidst all this, the girl, out each day with her hammer and chisel until –

Such an astonishing find. A marvel. A mystery. A miracle. A monster!

'Why,' he grants, with eye-swimming incredulity, as he travels homewards that evening, 'this could change the world.' Alone in his carriage, Professor Campbell McManus laughs out loud at its potential immensity.

He sleeps not a wink. His thoughts are abuzz. Rising in the insipid puddle of a damp grey dawn, he asks his footman to pack a travel bag and catches the London to Exeter stagecoach.

He must see for himself if this beast is fact or fiction. He must see it with his own eyes if he is to become a believer.

'Spurling's Curiositiyes' is painted in a childish hand above the door: 'Fossils for Sale'. Standing outside, in a narrow pitched street in this small seaside town, seagulls reeling in the air above, he surveys the signage to confirm he's reached his destination, then knocks. A neat rap upon the wooden door. 'Miss Spurling?'

'Quack quack,' comes from within; a young voice, strong and fearless. This is unexpected; McManus's face takes on a perplexed little frown. There follows, 'Snap snap!'

The professor falters. 'Excuse me?' he calls out. When there is no response, he pushes the door gingerly.

'Gnash gnash,' the voice now growls.

Cautiously, he peers into the dark and cluttered interior. The walls are lined with ten-a-penny fossils – the snakelike coils of ammonites, horny devil's toenails, fingers of pale belemnites, trilobite carapaces. 'Miss … Spurling?'

'ROAR!!!' the girl thunders, and lets out a peal of laughter upon seeing the grown man jump.

She is squeezed deep inside an enormous rib cage. It crowds the small front-parlour shop, the massive ribs suspended from a thick vertebral column running above like a curtain rod – perhaps indeed it is a curtain rod, he can't quite see in the dim light. A fishy tail disappears into the back room and a long snout of a toothy head, four foot in length at least, leers at him with a crocodile smirk and huge dull bony-round eyes the size of saucers.

By contrast, the girl's eyes gleam opal-bright in the near-darkness. A female Jonah in the whale! Thrusting her boot heels against rib bones she clambers out towards him, her skinny arms levering open the mouth so that she can corkscrew her torso through the beast's long jaws. She tumbles to the professor's feet, her skirts catching with a tear against the fearsome battalion of teeth.

In all his life, he has never before encountered a creature quite like this.

Practically feral, is the thought that passes through his mind. Her skin is sun-browned and chafed by the wind. Her hair is frizzed by sea mist. He thinks he sees a flurry of midges dislodged as she smoothes out her matted tresses. Her features retain the malleable innocence of childhood. The quick eyes are dark and glossy. Delicate and slender-boned, she stands no higher than his breast pocket. As she finds her footing on the floorboards, she gives a smile and curtsies. 'Miss Anna Spurling, at your service, sir.'

He is speechless.

'Have you come to meet my monster?' she enquires coyly.

That night in the local inn he opens his journal and dipping his quill in a bottle of ink writes: 'It would appear that Miss Spurling has uncovered a beast unknown in our present world. Is it possible this could be a species that has *passed out of existence*? Is such a notion conceivable? The creature has the characteristics of a fish combined with those of a lizard, and is nearly seventeen feet in length. Miss Spurling has likened it, not unfairly, to a crocodile. However, its size is far greater than any crocodile known to roam this earth and it has not legs but vast paddles. The erstwhile eyes display a distinctive bone-like casing I have not witnessed previously – perhaps for protection in deep waters? – and look to be at least the size of a side plate. The countenance is disconcertingly eerie. I estimate that over two hundred razor-sharp interlocking teeth line the long jaws – not a creature one would wish to meet on a dark night!' Here he draws a sketch of the beast.

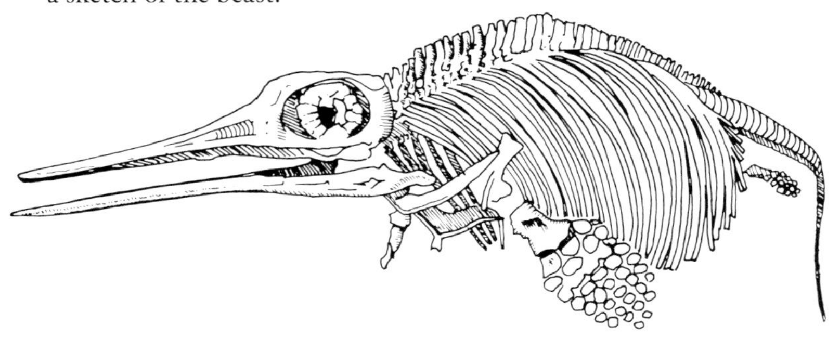

'The remains are remarkably preserved and would appear to be exceedingly old, older perhaps than any history our society can account for.' He lifts his quill, then a moment later continues with renewed determination: 'I believe it is possible that this discovery will cause us to rethink everything we know.' With such intensity does he underscore the 'everything' the point of his quill catches the page and ink spatters across the paper.

Professor McManus had considered sketching in Miss Spurling, curled within the rib cage as he had first found her, but subsequently banishes the idea, aware that he might wish to share the diagram with his colleagues at the Geological Society. Instead he writes, 'The young Miss Spurling is herself a curious creature. Intelligent, spirited, eager for knowledge. She inherited her fascination with fossil-hunting from her late father and continues the pursuit now to aid her family's meagre income. What she lacks in formal education she more than makes up for in her uncomplicated zeal for discovery. Her curiosity about palaeontology – this new science of ours – and our study of the Earth's strata is most engaging. Our conversation was peppered by her questions, which I answered as fully as I knew how. She has promised to lead me tomorrow to the site of her discovery.'

It storms that night. He fears the wind will shake the shingles from the inn's low rooftop. Rain pelts against the window and rattles the glass in its frame. Beneath the blanket, he shivers and tosses awake in the moonlit room. A persistent trace of a dream only recently departed lingers as he struggles to place himself. He had been swimming – or fighting to swim more like – along the sandy bottom of the sea. Arms reaching and clawing through water thick as mud, his legs kicking frantically. He was dressed in his academic robes and the heavy swathes of fabric weighed down his limbs. Somehow his boots and stockings had been lost, and at his bare ankles and toes he felt the nip and snap of two hundred tiny teeth.

He rises feeling unrested. Puffy-eyed and unsettled. The wind is still gusting clouds fast across the sky. Sleetish rain slants through the air. He fears he has caught a chill in the night and wishes he had brought a cashmere neckcloth in place of the silk one he now ties before the low mirror.

Miss Spurling is waiting on the shore, skipping from foot to foot. She wears a deep-brimmed bonnet tied beneath her chin and a thick woollen cloak. On catching sight of him, she grins. Dimples pucker her cheeks. 'Professor,' she waves animatedly, 'such good fortune, no?!'

'Fortune?' Only a pace or two away now.

'This weather!'

He pulls his tweed topcoat tighter around himself and frowns uncomprehendingly at the glowering sky.

'The storm, the storm! Think, Professor, of the treasures it will have battered down from the cliffs. Please, let us be off – no time to waste.' She turns on her heel and scampers away across the sand, her cloak trailing behind her. Casting another rueful glance heavenwards, the professor has no alternative but to follow.

They head east and leave the town and the long stone jetty of the Cobb behind them. They leave the calm sands and the bathing machines and head out to where the beach turns rocky. The gulls clatter noisily in the air above. She leaps, sure-footed, across the stones, pausing here and there for him to catch up. A couple of times he slips and his boot splashes in a rock pool. He narrowly misses twisting an ankle, feeling oafish in her company. Once, as he lowers his glance to focus upon a particularly taxing necessity of footwork, he could swear that as he looks back ahead he catches her turning a cartwheel. Above them, dark clouds menace.

'That's where we be heading,' she announces, lifting an arm to point. From her wrist hangs a small fabric bag containing the clink of her tools – her pick, her hammer, several brushes, a chisel. 'Past the Black Ven to the Church Cliffs. That's where I did find the monster.'

His eye scans the line drawn by her finger, past an ominously dark cliff of black slippery sand to where the rock face turns a pale blue-grey. A weathered parish church perches atop the cliff, the gravestones of its long-past parishioners spilling over the edge. He looks to the ragged rocks where he and the girl are headed. There appears the very real risk of landslides. Of falling debris.

'And what if the tide should come in?' he questions, a part of him beginning to wonder if it is madness to be placing his trust in one so young. She would appear to be immune to the perils of the landscape.

'That's why we have no time to dally,' she responds, springing once more away. 'Tally ho!'

Funny, doughty little being, he thinks, and despite himself, he can't help but smile.

It is widely acknowledged – and indeed a notion of which others widely approve – that before the season is out Professor Campbell McManus will ask for the hand of Miss Hester Quince. At twenty-one and agreeably fair of face, she has come of legal age this spring and will bring with her a handsome dowry. Miss Quince is an accomplished watercolourist, excels at lace fancywork, dances more than passably, and it is reported that she is remarkably talented on the descant recorder. Discreetly, her father has been informed of the professor's ambitions and has indicated that he will pose no objection to the match.

Thus, concerned by his unexplained absence from more than a week of his usual London engagements, Miss Quince is delighted to see that Professor McManus has come to the dance in Mayfair this evening. Oh joy, to set eyes upon his familiar chestnut whiskers, his dear winged nostrils and sweet heavy eyebrows! Her countenance brightens, her voice lifts, her laughter lilts in a way she has been informed is most beguiling.

'Miss Quince,' he says with feeling, and taking her hand he invites her for a waltz.

As they turn to the music, most prettily she remonstrates with him for quitting town without warning.

'A remarkable turn of events made my hasty departure unavoidable,' he tells her, his tone eager. 'A discovery has been made on the East Dorset coast.'

She raises her eyebrows. 'A discovery?'

'The remains of a most extraordinary creature,' he whispers.

She gives a delicate gasp.

'I've returned with a case of specimens I must take to the Geological Society first thing.'

She blinks her long lashes at him and smiles. Such earnest ambition in a man is really most endearing. 'Oh, dear Professor,' she says affectionately, jiggling the blonde curls at her temples. 'You and your old rocks and bones. What are we to do with you?'

His steps pause, freezing their dance amidst the mêlée of rotating bodies and swirling silk gowns. 'But these are not merely "old rocks and bones", Miss Quince. This creature could rewrite history.'

Miss Quince is feeling distinctly uncomfortable. She wishes he would resume their waltzing. With a gay smile, she manages to dismiss the concerned glance of a passing dancer.

His grip on the pale flesh above her glove is tighter than she would desire.

'This creature –' he says with intensity. 'This creature could prove everything we have believed about the world's creation to be false. A simple child can see that.'

Her attention is snatched back at this, drawn from the genteel act of keeping up appearances. Only now does she look truly at her companion. Beneath his frustration, a menacing undercurrent is discernible, anger almost. It is an emotion so foreign in his countenance that it shocks her as profoundly as his words have done. 'If I have understood your meaning, Professor,' she cautions in a trepid undertone, 'I think you should halt yourself.'

'But I have seen the evidence! It exists!'

Her blue eyes widen. She retracts minutely, but his grip on her arm is tight still.

'"In six days the LORD made heaven and earth, the sea, and all that in them is, and rested the seventh day": indeed, thus we have it explained to us in all simplicity. Yet surely, Miss Quince, you must be able at least to entertain the possibility of an alternative?'

She shakes her head hesitantly. 'It is not our place to question the Lord's word,' she breathes, with quiet dismay.

'But surely life is there for us to question. The universe is there for us to question.'

She frowns, her lip quivers. 'Oh,' is all she says, and then again, her distress a little more acute, 'oh,' and in the next instant, Miss Quince swoons and falls limp in his arms.

A woman beside them lets out a shrill cry. The waltz halts with a discord of horsehair on string. The crowd flusters about them. 'Her salts!' someone cries. 'Give her air,' shouts another. 'Check for a pulse!' ejaculates a bosomy matriarch. 'Water!' 'Brandy!'

Later that evening, he regrets not having had the opportunity to talk again with Miss Quince once she had revived. There was nary a moment for privacy. His last sight of her was that of her chaperone ushering her from the room swaddled in blankets, her little face peaky, her eyes still wide and startled, the blonde curls trembling.

The wooden case of Lyme Regis specimens sits on the carpet in his study as if in reproach. Large, dark, heavy, crouching; a Pandora's box he is suddenly afraid to open. He retires to his bedchamber and pens a concerned note to Miss Quince to catch the morning post. In the moments before he falls into a deep and dreamless sleep, he recalls a conversation that had taken place on the Lyme beach only the morning prior.

'Well, perhaps –' his young companion had ventured, as she chipped at a slab of limestone, '– perhaps the Bible is simply wrong? If what you say about time and place, and about the layers of the Earth, if all that be true, well,' she released a dismissive puff of breath, 'if you were to ask me, this world we know would seem an awful lot of work for just six days of accounting.'

He had drawn in a breath. 'Miss Spurling,' he had smiled, half wanting to lay a protective hand upon her cloaked shoulder, 'I venture you should keep such notions to yourself. Such ideas will not be taken well by everybody.'

'Imbecile,' he tells himself now, cringing at the events of the evening. 'Foolish imbecile.' He is, he registers, a man who does not heed his own advice.

Only minutes later, however, he gives a small snort of laughter into his pillow. He has recalled the response of Miss Spurling to his caution: 'Well, if they don't like it, more fool them!'

He knew, of course, that the contents of his wooden case would cause a stir at the Society. For a not inconsiderable fee – 'I've a mother to support, you will remember. A mother who is for the most while confined to her bed with the mopes' – Miss Spurling had allowed him to package up the head of her creature. He has the intention of returning for the body once he is better equipped for its transportation and availed of more substantial funds to persuade her. The huge bony skull of the beast astounds his colleagues, with its pointed snout, grisly interlocked teeth and the enormous sockets of its strange saucer eyes, silent and unblinking from an unknown past. As the professor himself had recognised from the outset, this formidable discovery would inevitably give rise to mounting conjecture.

In spite of this, he feels that his own exhilaration has dissipated. When the time comes to log the strange creature in the Society's folio of discoveries he feels an unease, queerly bereft of pride to see his name marked down as its discoverer. As a passing fancy, he considers whether he should request that Miss Spurling be accredited in the record, but more sensibly concludes that it would be unseemly to have a female marked in the register.

And yet his thoughts turn to her more than occasionally. To his own embarrassment, he conducts conversations with the girl in his head. He thinks about the things he would explain to her and how eager and open she was towards becoming educated in the wonders of the natural world and its history. He even toys with the thought of inviting her to London and presenting her to the Society – that would shake them up! – but then dismisses the idea for the foolishness that it is. An untamed creature such as her would rail against the confines of a Regency drawing room.

In the coming weeks he extends his notes and makes careful etchings of the four-foot head and all the other curios he had brought back with him to London. He considers writing a paper on the significance of the find, but time passes and somehow he never quite gets round to it. This is distinctly unlike him. Presently, life would appear to weary the professor. The city seems oppressive. He finds himself longing again for clear seaside air. He has the desire to open his lungs and let out a bellowing roar that feels trapped inside him.

Professor McManus has met Miss Quince more than once since, and their conversation has been quite cordial enough, although he has noted the absence of their former intimacy. She has been sufficiently discreet not to mention again the conversation of that 'unfortunate night', and his gratitude for her tact is considerable; mere recollection now of the insensitivity of his conduct towards her leaves him flushed with shame.

The season however is coming to a close, and Mr Henry Quince has begun to wonder whether and when his footman will again present him with McManus's calling card. With the engagement not yet made formal, there is no legal action he can take on his daughter's behalf. At least he can console himself that she is still young and there is yet hope for her. But this business has cost her a season and such an incident – the unexplained fading of a suitor's affections – can spoil the bloom of a young lady's prospects.

The irony, as McManus is all too aware, is that the notion of taking a wife had begun to appeal to him. He acknowledges that he has a longing for companionship. He had daydreamed of simple pleasures – strolling with his wife in Hyde Park or sharing breakfast with her each morning. He had toyed with a curiosity towards the children who would no doubt have ensued. He had even begun looking at villas in south London that he might have purchased to house a family. He is weary these days of his cramped, once-beloved rooms in Bloomsbury Square, dusty with books and fossils and stones – all his 'old rocks and bones', as he will recall to himself now and again with a rueful smile.

He has a dream that, for weeks now, has been recurring. In the dream, he is in his bedchamber (that same bedchamber where in reality he is at that very moment asleep). He is lying beneath the quilt, and a slim female, Miss Quince, appears out of the darkness. She is dressed for sleeping, in only her chemise. The fine linen marks a ghostly white in the dark room. The garment is loose-fitting to her bare knees, with lace about the low neck. Without a word she simply climbs beneath the covers and curls herself like an ancient ammonite alongside him. He feels her body weigh down the mattress; he can sense the warmth of her skin against his own. Lying beside this woman, he does not move a muscle nor say a word. Against his shoulder blade he feels her warm breath as it traffics her lungs, and keenly he listens to it slowing as she falls to sleep.

When he wakes from this dream to acknowledge the cold chill of the empty mattress beside him, McManus senses each time an ache of remorse.

He cannot say with certainty when the transformation occurred, but there was a night, lying wakened in the early hours, when he realised that the young female climbing into his dream was no longer Miss Quince.

And then a letter arrives by first post. He pushes aside his breakfast plate to examine it. The paper is of poor quality, the address written in a crude, ink-splotted hand. With impatience, he breaks the seal:

> *Come quik, profesar! I hav fownd another monstar!!!*
> *Faithfelly, Anna Spurling*

Scanning once more through the brief communication, he lets loose a deep exhalation of relief. Finally: news to break the torpor that has beset him. He feels charged with a sudden crackling energy. A new monster! She has found a new monster! 'Make haste,' he calls to his footman, raking his chair back from the table, 'I must travel to Lyme forthwith!'

This time he does not find her entombed in the belly of a giant beast, although the alternative is no less eccentric. When he reaches the low wooden front door with 'Spurling's Curiositiyes' lettered above, he again knocks neatly, on this occasion with more confidence.

'Come in,' calls a thin muffled voice.

She is squashed inside a huge glass bottle, like a scientific specimen. The impression is one of witnessing an impossibility. The funnelled neck of the bottle is narrower than her skull, her torso, her hips.

'Professor McManus, at last!' she exclaims excitedly, then smacks her lips up against the dusty glass and blows out her cheeks like a sucker fish.

It is the second time she has rendered the professor speechless.

'You are wondering how I inched my way into this vessel,' she mouths from within. It is a large bottle, but not so large that she might fit comfortably. Her limbs are bent and folded in around her body. As always, her eyes are bright with merriment. 'Like a ship in a bottle, Professor McManus! Now, will you please close your eyes –'

When he reopens them, she is standing on the floorboards before him. The glass vessel is empty.

It is some conjuring trick. He knows it must be. He knows there must be illusion involved. But he has no means of explaining to himself the bizarre antics he has just witnessed. He had forgotten indeed how fanciful, how peculiar, this child could be.

At that, Professor McManus does something he hasn't done for a very long while. He holds back his head and lets out a long roar of laughter.

The monster is too large this time, she tells him, and too tightly encased in the rock for her to transport it back to her front parlour. It will take the strength of several men to move it.

She will take him to see it. Let them go now. He needn't even take off his coat and hat – keep them on, it is awful chilly on the shore at this time, and there is a thick low fog this morning. When they reach the beach, she grabs a stick and begins to sketch her discovery.

With eager anticipation, he watches her mark out her monster in the sand. A long, snakelike neck … four monumental paddles … a spine that reaches the length of near three full-grown men at least.

'And it is this size?' he asks incredulously, shouting against the wind. 'So large?'

She gives a vigorous nod. Hair whips back and forth across her face. 'With shocking teeth!'

As he surveys the girl's drawing, and considers this new terrible beast that he is shortly to encounter, Professor McManus realises that in this moment he is quite sublimely happy. It is such a change after the inertia of his recent months in London. The sea wind is blowing about his ears, clearing space in his head once again for the thrill of maverick thought.

'Miss Spurling, I have a great deal to thank you for,' he shouts, feeling invigorated by her company. 'A very great deal. You –' He pauses, unsure how to put it into words. 'You make me look afresh at the world, my eyes wide open with the wonder of a child. You place within my reach fantastic possibilities as yet undreamt of. You – You – You make me feel alive!'

She looks at him as if he were a simpleton, then jams her stick into the sand beside her illustration. 'Come. Before the tide catches us.'

Turning, she sets off across the shore. Her boots make deep footprints in the wet sand. 'Come,' she calls again. Her figure is receding into the low fog; evaporating it seems, diluting. There before his eyes, she vanishes. Her second conjuring trick of the day.

For a few moments, he remains where he is, boots sinking in the sand as her disembodied laughter, shrill in its childishness, trails back through the opaque air to where he stands alone. With resolve, he places one foot ahead in the well of her footstep, and then another. He puts his top hat beneath his arm and begins to run, confident that each step is taking him closer to unsolved truths, to miraculous possibilities. He follows the strange young girl into the fog. Running with her towards an unknown monster.

*This story has been inspired by the life and achievements of Mary Anning, a young girl from Lyme Regis who, in 1812, at the age of twelve, was the first to discover the fossilised remains of an ichthyosaur. She continued hunting all her life and went on to discover a plesiosaur as well as the first pterodactyl known to science.*

*I learned about Mary Anning on a visit to the Natural History Museum in London, where a portrait of a grown Mary Anning, posing on the Lyme Regis foreshore with a rock hammer and her little dog Tray, hangs at the end of the dinosaur display. I was interested (and made a little indignant) by the fact that Anning, like other women such as Mary Mantell, finder of the first iguanodon tooth, was never welcomed into the scientific community of nineteenth-century Britain and received little official credit in her day for her most monumental of discoveries, simply due to the fact that she was neither wealthy and well-educated nor, more importantly, male.*

*I have twisted truths here for the benefit of my story and for this reason have renamed my young heroine. Professor McManus is an entirely fictitious character, although he is perhaps a composite of a number of worthy academics who befriended the young Mary Anning.*

*Clare Wigfall*
*Berlin 2012*

# Improving the Image of Destruction

IAIN SINCLAIR

*'The ancients,' said Socrates, 'were uncomplicated, and if a certain rock was known for telling the truth, they would listen to it.' John Michell*

Now even the squirrels eat muesli, or don't, or have moved on to more enticing diets. In Hackney, they can afford to spurn the health food option. A conical mound, like vitamin-enriched sawdust, has been set out for the flying rats of the inner suburbs. Then ignored. As I bend forward to stare intently at the paving slabs, the river-patterns of crack, the persistence of weeds and mosses, a creature with a hooped spine bounds forward with a rippling motion, one of those concertina sets of metal rings that snake down childhood staircases. All the discrete points through which the rusty animal passes are preserved in the mind's eye, wavelike, serpentine. And this episode, the accidental morning rodent, confirms the motif of my walk: a mindless flow against unarguable obstacles, the great rocks and stones that hold down the neurotic spread of our city.

This was my idiot-simple proposition, psychogeology. The beach beneath the pavements. Twenty thousand streets under the sky. The rocks of the geological collection at the Natural History Museum in Exhibition Road, South Kensington, were calling me in. I would come to them, across London, connecting with, recording, investigating – and listening to, that above all – a chain of glacial erratics, Aberdeen granite lumps, public art boulders, rubble, kerbstones, unnecessary cladding, erased memorials, and demolished terraces with the split heads of Coade stone effigies. The stone in our blood, the lime mortar in our bones, takes sustenance from that chain of ancient volcanic and glacial detritus left behind or exposed in public parks. Fossils swim through ocean beds of Portland stone churches and encrust the statues of proud dignitaries. Crude megaliths, pulsing with faint prelapsarian signals, sprawl in shallow grassland declivities. Disregarded by tourists and speeding urban commuters, they bask in the achieved invisibility of things that have always been there with no requirement to make themselves known. Until they are trapped, captured on film, measured and catalogued, removed to the benevolent reservation in Kensington, where crowds wait in an orderly mob, to be granted privileged access. This chambered, post-cultural reservation of rocks was where I was headed on a frisky, blameless morning, under a clear sky and that unwitnessed caul of stars without number.

They call it the Snake Park. And promote it, in a tidy enclosure beneath an elevated railway, alongside all the other parks by which London is now defined and divided: retail parks, theme parks, business parks, car parks. Where a decision has been taken, to trim budget by abandoning grass-cutting operations, a post is driven into the ground announcing: 'Wilderness Zone' or 'Nature Reserve'. There are two kinds of wilderness and you do not want to be caught in the wrong one. An approved wilderness will be demarcated by an orange mesh fence. It looks like a few yards of captured meadow, but is spared human intervention. This is the quotation wilderness, a mental conceit; a framed folk-memory intended to alleviate the brutality of permanent building works, holes in the road, strange muddy wounds allowing the curious a glimpse beneath the surface membrane of London, the dull clays and chalks that sprawl in a promiscuous tangle above bubbling, spitting magma. The bad kind of wilderness is also known as 'wasteland', as in: 'The Lower Lea Valley was a wasteland. There was nothing there.'

The Snake Park had been here for a number of years; several generations of infant liberation and juvenile japes. Then, like the railway above, it fell from favour. It remained, on its own terms, occasionally visited, often padlocked under threat of improvement. My interest today is in the snake itself, the votive beast, a humped and heavy-headed artwork in painted concrete. It lies, glutted, replete, jaws gaping, nodding in the direction I must travel, south-west.

A snakestone or serpentine-stone is an ammonite, the heat-print of a creature translated into more permanent form. A solid photograph on which to break your toe. The classic ammonite is coiled like the horn of Ammon, the Egyptian ram god. This snake has a Mexican or Mayan quality, skin shimmering with tesserae, ceramic and glass fragments implying movement, a slither and stretch to excite the small children who clamber on the long arched back or dive beneath the hungry belly. The decorative surface carries the life force, responding magnetically to the rattle of passing trains. The stone is slack, cooked up, impure, sand and slurry, offering no connection to the geological trail I am trying to establish, my star-path across the covered fields of London.

A lively local, a lady with a small white dog, is in conversation with an elderly Muslim man wearing a sweat-stained lace skullcap. 'When they get palpitations ...' She prods the supine dog with her stick. 'Heart problems, just like us. They cough.'

She pokes her pet again, aiming for where the troubled heart might be. The pooch spews up a hairball. He wheezes. But he couldn't, in all honesty, be accused of a cough. *She* coughs, by way of example. He raises a paw. In silence.

The old man, tilting to the west, dragging a stiff leg, eyes me with suspicion, when, resting on a cold metal bench, I sketch a few preliminary observations. How sinister they seem, those brass stirrups hanging from the tree to entice undersize climbers. How strident the mechanical voice anticipating the arrival of trains. 'Crystal Palace. Highbury.'

Very soon, another ageing man in an ageing city, I am advancing backwards into a pattern of street names I inscribed years ago, with no sense of their meaning, but with an irrational belief that they were somehow connected. I half-remember lines written by another person, myself, aged thirty-three. 'Reels in the Blake skein ... Orsman Road ... Whitmore Road, Hoxton Street, the Latter-Day Outpourings revival.' *Orsman Road.* The Muslim, after his ritual conversation with the dog woman – I imagine it happening every day, same words, same time – has an established direction of travel, tacking through crowds of preoccupied pedestrians to the pencil-thin mosque.

Orsman Road, deserted but carrying an ominous freight of memory, was not my first choice. Permissions, along the canal, were again suspended. More developments, more non-elective futurology. A barrier to which have been attached notices proclaiming the erroneous information that the canalside cafe with the celebrated coffee is still open for trade. And that its bicycle-repairing neighbour is eager to service punctures or to adjust gear ratios. The ink on the laminated notices has run. The businesses in question are shuttered. Nobody is enraged. We encounter the fence; we nod. This is London. A boy with prominent ribs and dirty pink trainers photographs the smeared notices for his portfolio. Then knuckles his groin and snorts.

In my case, on my geomorphic walk to Kensington, the banishment was a blessing, redirecting me to the legendary Orsman Road. I associate this tight tributary, overseen by defunct or revamped warehouses, with shamanic practice, horse sacrifice. Men stitched into reeking horse hide. That amputated Cockney 'h' triggering thoughts of a severed head, guillotine slicing off the first letter, the veins and threads of a thick equine neck. Godfathering my perverse quest.

Here is a bucket-like container known as a skip. Here is a display of rock and rubble. Broken buildings and dug-up pavements are geological by-products returned to their original unexploited form. Odd words, like *skip* with its Scandinavian origin, older than Ikea, sit comfortably with odd stones. Stones, in all shapes and sizes, split, cut, smashed, are a mute alphabet. They are not telling us anything; they talk to themselves in their own language. A forgotten language constructed from bursts of signal and flare. One stone to another. Grain to grain. Crystal to crystal. In Trinity College, Dublin, where I was a student, the term skip was applied to college servants. Dictionaries of etymology suggest an ugly colonialist derivation: 'skip-kennel'. Dog of the slums. Gutter-jumper. Native. Doing what has to be done in a Viking seatown. Let them suck stones in their porridge, the masters. Let them break teeth on pebbles painted to look like eggs.

Behind and above the skip is a warehouse I have visited on several occasions, the reserve collection of the Museum of London; superseded ethnographic and anthropological displays. Horizontal totem poles stacked like lumber in a canalside woodyard. Cabinets of ticketed Aboriginal and Inuit skulls waiting for candles. Whole streets, blitzed in war, or torn down to improve the image of destruction, are stored within the vaults and galleries of this covert building.

I thought of a documentary I had glimpsed, the night before, in a fast-food joint. Parrot-fish are capable of chewing into rock with their powerful jaws, munching coral and shitting sand. Those picture-postcard atolls with their virgin beaches, beloved of cartoonists, pimped in honeymoon brochures distributed by merchant banks, surveyed by atom-bomb tests, are the waste of dredger-mouthed fish. The new restaurant alongside this spoilheap of cargo-cult trade goods and unexploitable street furniture is offering, as its speciality, 'stone-baked pizza'.

What I am attempting to trace is the line, laid out like a Richard Long sculpture, of granite kerbstones, heavy, grey and sepulchral, cold to the touch, leading me westward, and faithfully shadowed for mile after mile by thick yellow streaks, a sludge of paint as an over-emphatic subtext: you cannot park here. Georges Perec taught us how to read such streets: 'Underneath, just underneath, resuscitate the eocene: the limestone, the marl and the soft chalk, the gypsum ... the sands, the rough limestone ... lignites, the plastic clay, the hard chalk.'

This area, its obscurity threatened by development, was made from river terrace deposits, after the diverting of the Thames. The zone of Hackney Gravel through which I was now advancing was known to geologists as 'Artificially Modified Ground', a surface 'wholly or partially disturbed by human activity'. Its symbol on the chart was a cloud of bar-code rain, a box stretching from London Fields to the boundary with Islington.

As I approach the Gainsborough Studios complex, a trim young woman in red passes in the other direction, conducting an intimate, domestic and admittedly one-sided conversation with a tongue-dangling greyhound. The old film studios, now a Germanic courtyard development, are dedicated to, and dominated by, a vast boilerplated head of Alfred Hitchcock. The metal from which this hieratic totem has been assembled stays close to its origins in the earth, the heated stone. Spindly leaf patterns play across the protuberant lower lip and the well-fed cheek flaps of the eminent director. The scale of the thing, the swollen giganticism by which all cultural references are now made, acts like an iron-cored meteorite on our individual compasses. We warp and bend, absorbing all the back-catalogue film references encrypted within this hidden courtyard: the vertiginous rear windows, the grassy knoll from *Torn Curtain*, the magnetic pull taking us away from *North by Northwest* to the gravity of the waiting rocks in their cases in Exhibition Road. Was Hitchcock just a head? You have to imagine the rest of the man, the great belly, the belt worn tight to the breastline, buried deep in the clay and silt of a Pleistocene bed.

In Shoreditch Park is an object that balances the Hitchcock head, a free-standing megalith as hard-travelled as the sarsen stones of Stonehenge. And as mysterious. I recognise the carved intruder as part of a chain of stones, set in parks and beside housing projects between Shoreditch and the Thames at Shadwell. You could see them as glacial erratics abandoned by the retreating ice. Or as follies laid out, at enormous expense, for a corporate project whose purpose has never been revealed and which is now quite forgotten. This igneous rock was the immediate inspiration for my walk to Kensington. It shines with discriminations of feldspar, quartz and mica. And is dressed with manmade holes which give it a cartoonish, anthropomorphic quality.

Who would leave such a thing in such a place? The natives, sweeping through on their preoccupied trajectories, ignore its immense and shamed bulk, as they scamper to secure a Boris bike from the set of hitching posts. The stone has been labelled by John Frankland, the artist responsible, as BOULDER. But if you think that word suggests a random obstacle, the Shoreditch Park erratic is no such thing: it's intended, blasted from a Cornish quarry, heaved, manhandled, hoisted and transported like a chained captive to its secular resting point in a public park. The holes you might take for sculptural embellishments or Bronze Age workings are nothing of the sort. They are aids for climbers. The rock is here for urban recreation: a hundred tonnes, four metres high and soliciting engagement. A tricky ascent, graded V4 in the advisory booklet, is known as 'Inner City Riots', a prophetic stab in the dark. Athletes travelling to Shoreditch to take up the challenge are advised not to leave any valuables in their parked cars. They will arrive, as if in the Lake District or North Wales, in a motor vehicle. And they will be reminded, in the brochure, of where they are. A criminous backwater where potential upheavals can be conquered by crabbing over a standing stone. 'You are in London,' says the artist, addressing his boulder as much as the casual visitor, 'and not in Cornwall.'

A marble bench from which to view the rock has been embossed with the words NEWTON STREET, as if in homage to William Blake's naked youth, stooped over his compasses, against the teeth of a stone circle. Shoreditch Park, today, is a pure geometry of shadow-lines – human, light pole, tree – making alignments with the stolen boulder. Patches of black lichen are like smears of squashed bug, like dried heart-blood sweated from deep within the stone. Lesser rocks, chipped or carved, surround the monolith in an unconvinced scatter.

The Newtonian compasses have been primed; I will follow their dictation to that minatory workshop on Shepherdess Road, H. Bestimt & Co, Feather Merchants. Dark stairs at the rear, rooms let out to single gentlemen of a retiring disposition. I came here, once, with my young son, to deliver a book. He never forgot it, the reek of scorched feathers, plucked birds, wings pegged out to dry. A fine dust waiting to lodge in the cracks of your skin, the corners of your eyes. If the chain of orphaned rocks had no weight and floated down on the landscape like loaves of Magritte bread, then the feathers were as heavy as steel. Plumage House, they call it.

The small park, on the other side of the road, a ghost of demolition, felt like a burial ground. It contained a group of granite coprolites, sculptural interventions in the form of carved sheep. Spiral horns butting out of stone. I noticed a walker come away from the path, to piss like a horse in the sheltering bushes. Trail-marking, I suppose, for future reference. Vegetation, dense and tangled, was pierced by columns of weak sunlight. The man, duty done, stood unmoving as I walked away. A German described the risks of being drawn so deeply into the act of gazing at a jungle. 'Stay still for five minutes and the plants will eat you.' Keep moving, stone to stone, and one of those boulders will absorb you entirely. You become the thing that you imagine.

Even the paper hoardings on City Road, near the inlet of the City Road Basin, reference geology as a selling point, a style issue. 'Designer kitchen with granite worktops', they assert, will feature in every virtual flat in this photographed but unbuilt canalside development. You can see, looking across the water, that not only does Hawksmoor's obelisk at St Luke's, Old Street, hang on its relationship with the shape of the narrowboat basin, but it predicts an alignment with the tower of St Mary's Church in Upper Street, Islington. The advertising hoarding is no help, suggesting, as it does, that we are in an occulted city under the laws of the voodoo of capital. Estate agents hold the key but it is only available to bona fide investors. A rectangle has been depicted as a labyrinth of unreadable black shapes: 'A Bar Code app is required to read the above Code'. To add to the confusion, my geological chart warns of shifting gravel beds, areas in a lurid yellow, like quicksand, and incense-bearing clouds of ecclesiastic purple, the silts of Enfield and the gravel of Finsbury and Boyn Hill.

At the crossroads of the Angel, stone is mere cladding, a quotation. I found myself, in a sentimental gesture, echoing Scott Fitzgerald. The way that walkers, from time to time, need to touch and stroke and pet the stone, graze a knuckle. 'He felt suddenly of the texture of his own coat,' Fitzgerald said, 'and pressed his thumb against the granite of the building by his side.' The angels of Islington are hobbled: wings of granite, limbs of marble. Loose Grecian wraps around unsexed goddesses who perch, flightless, on plinths in shady parks, under moulting plane trees.

Housmans Bookshop is a necessary pit stop, before the calamity of the great metropolitan stations, the cliffs of brick under permanent revision. King's Cross was formerly a site of memory, the war dead, the fire victims, those killed in bomb blasts: names engraved on marble. Much of this matter has now been sent away, into storage in Acton. The wrong geology for an age of pastiche. I pick up a book, on grounds of size, weight (lack of), and title: *An English Figure (Two Essays on the Work of John Michell).* I felt that this might be the right moment to reconnect with the author of *The Old Stones of Land's End.* Michell, whatever is said of him, did not feel the need to blast lumps out of Cornwall and to transport them back to Notting Hill to prove a thesis.

The British Library, relocated from its established nest in the British Museum in Bloomsbury, has taken some account of its position on our geological track. Sands and gravels, London clay, they are exposed in the perpetual trenches dug by utility companies. The approach to the Library is a provocative confusion of art and artifice, the sacred and the profane. A sunken amphitheatre, dressed with stones on plinths, is a site of authentic attraction for urban dreamers, coin-tossing gamblers, resting pilgrims. Many of whom will advance no further towards the doors of the Library. This forum, with its sculptural interventions, open-air cafe and hedged enclosures, is enough: a retreat trading on its proximity to the walls of books, the multiple voices at play against the contrived tranquillity of a place of passage.

The local sculptor, Antony Gormley, a hierophant of grand corporate developments, has given the small amphitheatre (a teasing recollection of the Irish and Scottish drinking schools who met in a declivity one of the survivors, John Healy, called 'The Grass Arena') some necessary gravitas. Eight rocks assigned to eight planets encircle the sprawled visitors. Pressed into the stone, or emerging from it, are hands and limbs. Like prints of the future dead. Or stopped citizens of a city overwhelmed by a volcanic eruption, bathing in hot lava, and lingering ever afterwards as images fixed in the cooling grain of igneous rock. These sophisticated trophies, floating between the status of museum-quality geological specimens and a prescient anticipation of future catastrophe, have an evident relationship to the humbler sheep-stones of the little park off Shepherdess Walk. The art aspect rubs off, the rocks hold their position on the flight path of a potential drift through London, leading inexorably towards Exhibition Road.

An Irish writer who always kept pebbles in his pockets, flattened schist, ovoid serpentine, fled disgrace (after soliciting it for so many years) by enduring a downriver exile in Silvertown. He saw his nocturnal train ride, overground, then under, to South Kensington, as a stretching of that precious silver, by rail, towards the silent rocks in their glass cabinets. Subterranean snail tracks. The total anonymity of his position as a night watchman chimed with his notion of what a writer's life should be. One of the senior curators, so he told me, cycled through the silent galleries when the crowds had gone. He held loud conversations, in Latin, Greek, old Cornish, Norse, as was appropriate, with favoured stones. When, inevitably, the old dusty museum was challenged to justify itself and to pay its way, they dedicated a chunk of the budget to art promotions. A troop of nude figures, white, plastered in gypsum, living plaster casts, statues liberated from their perches, roamed the corridors. The writer took his cards and returned to Dublin.

Dominating the British Library terrace, and facing firmly east, is Eduardo Paolozzi's three-dimensional rendering of Blake's *Newton*. In the lee of the Novotel, the bronze giant stoops to his compasses, like an unclothed supplicant attending to his football coupon – which is appropriate; the artwork is sponsored by Vernons, Littlewoods and Zetters, the pools conglomerate. As at Shoreditch Park, the combination of boilerplated figure and captured rock (in this case the necklace of small Gormley boulders) confirms the significance of the site. But, if I were to make the transit to the sphere of influence of Kensington, away from this reef of railway stations and the approaching concrete launch-ramp of the Westway, I would have to attempt a forced detour into older gravel deposits from the Pre-Anglian epoch. Marylebone represented a surface shift: less granite, more marble. Sleeker surfaces dressed with blue plaques, memory prompts no pedestrians troubled to read.

At what point, precisely, do the stones of Kensington replace the boulders of the East London gravel beds as the dominant influence, the force warping my magnetic compass? Not yet, not here, where the pressure is off and dignified grey buildings are protected by discreet security, winking cameras and window boxes and plump chauffeurs waiting in black cars outside cancer clinics.

In Woburn Place, right opposite the plaque for W. B. Yeats, is a newsagent's shop with a copy of *Frankfurter Allgemeine* on display. The front-page spread, today, features a black-and-white photograph of a naked man – Newton released from his bronze armour – posing against an insecure heap of boulders. I have no idea what the story is about, but it confirms, once again, my direction of travel: unmapped ignorance. The creamy limestone of the middle Jurassic age, quarried from Cotswold hills, is drawing me, unconsciously, to the west. Like a poultice against infection. Against the residual West End fear of a wind from the east, bringing poverty and disease. Portland Place, with its BBC bastion and its reservations of tame architects, is also Portland stone. Eric Gill chopping the male member to dimensions acceptable to Lord Reith. The muscular Edward Bainbridge Copnall, shirt off, beret on, takes his chisel to an hieratic relief figure symbolising *Architectural Aspiration* on the facade of the RIBA building. There is now, distinctly, as much geology above ground as below: the thin granite margin of the kerb, the cut blocks from quarries on Portland Bill (decorated with Jurassic oysters), paving slabs of Mansfield stone (from Nottingham and the Permian age), sandstone slabs from the suburbs of Edinburgh. A catalogue as eccentric as the great human shoals competing for space on pavements and in gutters. There are slumbering, flowing, deeper layers of clay, sand, chalk and shallows of drift-geology exposed by those casual archaeologists, the Irishmen with picks and shovels, drills and dredgers.

Drifting with the faint south-westerly pull of the Kensington reservation, the deliciously sliced rock samples in their display cases, I find myself on Weymouth Street. STONE HOUSE announces a dazzling brass plaque, being polished at this very moment by a man in a brown suit. An elegant, stepped, flower-bedizened enterprise, like a faux-thirties hotel from an Agatha Christie television adaptation, dealing, behind the intimidating foyer, with some form of biotech research and sinister marketing. I thought: vivisection. I thought: John Cowper Powys. I thought: *Weymouth Sands*. Powys, of all English writers, loved his stones, the animist philosophy, the unconscious surge of life to be found in reaching for and touching a shard on his track. Preoccupied, alarmed and excited by the imagined tortures and perversions of science within protected buildings, Powys ritualised a counter-current by fixing 'one of those geographical points on the surface of the planet that would surely rush into his mind when he came to die'. A bench, a bent nail, a lichen blot, they contained 'the concentrated essence of all that life meant!'

Property developers, not much interested in geology or deep topography, have issued their own bulletin on Weymouth Street from what might be described as an anti-Powys perspective. They see this seductive tributary as consisting of 'eighty-nine properties, seventy-eight homes'. The average 'asking price' – you asking? – is £1,550,924. The great advantage of the street, so the promoters suggest, is that the nearest petrol station is only ten minutes away. There is a convenient orthopaedic hospital on Bolsover Street, but you will have to endure the noise of ambulances.

Manchester Street and Manchester Square remind me of the strange psychogeographical doodlings of the Spitalfields hermit David Rodinsky. Rodinsky annotated his friable copy of the *London A–Z*. One of his routes carried him to this point. I walked, as nearly as I could, down the fading biro track, but never established a motive for his projected (or remembered) journey. I was tempted to inspect the Wallace Collection, standing proud to the tree-enclosed square, for paintings that featured significant rocks. But the presence of a young European woman, posing, so much a quotation from an artwork I failed to identify, long legs and country-splashed wellington boots, threw me off balance. And I photographed, in compensation, a ram's-head embellishment in Bath stone. The poet Ed Dorn, lodging here in the mid-seventies, was captured on camera in the square gardens, alongside Marianne Faithfull and the rest of the Dunbar family tribe. He reports, with relish, that a key to this enclosure cost two guineas: 'that denomination a remoter clue than it once was'.

Marble Arch was such an obvious portal on this expedition that I was tempted to leave it out of my narrative, but passing through, as one might have passed, by John Nash's original intention, into Buckingham Palace, opens a direct route to Exhibition Road. The geological gravity – and the gilded frivolity – of the Albert Memorial and the Albert Hall hurry my tread. Hyde Park wraps walkers in meadowland, aborting plans, revising destinations. They wander in delirious circles, before giving it all up and flopping on the grass.

The Serpentine Gallery triggered a memory flash of the performance artist Brian Catling, in residence, circumnavigating the paths and pavilions before tapping neurotically at the glass, a pebble in his mouth and his eyes bathed with thimbles of ink. Inside the current gallery was a photographic print of Hackney flats by Tom Hunter, a mirror image of my starting point, letting me know that my journey was almost done.

The queue on Cromwell Road, outside the Natural History Museum, is substantial. And growing by the minute. Has there been a sudden convulsive urge to visit the stones? What looks like another transported monolith, peaty, iron-enhanced, and erected to stand against the artificial towers of Alfred Waterhouse's Romanesque depository, is actually a tree, 'older than the dinosaurs'. A fabulous stump extracted from rocks with a birth certificate going back 330 million years. This withered tusk, exposed like a Tyburn sacrifice, outranks the Victorian museum, where a crowd of the indifferently curious cluster and mob.

The only viable strategy was a retreat to Exhibition Road, now fenced, excavated, brutalised. Teams of sponsored improvers were 'Transforming London's Cultural Heartland', by undertaking the sort of activities that deny a zone its geological pedigree. Visible rebranding, by way of clawing away the surface, trenching, scraping, erecting granite bollards and avenues of orange cones, distorts the older identity, long-established patterns of flow and access. London clay, from the ocean bed of fifty million years ago, is easy to tunnel. Tiled passages run away to other collections and educative gatherings from the era of empire. Sound reverberates from packs of children enduring cultural improvement with varying degrees of grace and acceptance.

If you come in at the door closest to the former Geological Museum, you bypass the restricted admittance policy of Cromwell Road. J. E. Gray, Keeper of Zoology (1840–74), believed that exposure to this overwhelming abundance of specimens and categories, the ever-expanding treasures and taxonomies of the museum, drove curators and keepers mad. The vast building turned humans into ghosts. And ghosts into stones. It wasn't the room of geological maps and charts, the one with no official opening hours, that I was seeking. Nor yet the exhibitions of sea lilies and aragonite. Nor moon dust scratched from the blind eye of our nearest neighbour. Something more insistent was dragging me in, a density of reference more convoluted and complex than anything encountered on my walk. Something unearthly but utterly present: *a meteorite*. Admiral Peary dragged, at great cost, and after several fruitless attempts, just such a brute, thrumming with ferrous memories, from Greenland to New York. With this difference: he chased rumour, snow weapons tipped with material grudgingly excavated from this extraterrestrial boulder. The Cranbourne Meteorite of Exhibition Road appears to have been here forever, before the first brick was laid; so that the London of the walkers, the ones whose peering faces were now reflected on the dusty glass of the protective display case, retreated, layer by layer, away from the killing indifference of the captured specimen. Here was a tumour we could never extract, older and more savage than the London Stone from which all distances were once measured. The surface of the meteorite was indented with pressings and finger marks, as if earlier guardians had tried to claw their way inside, to reveal a locked secret. Rocks fly, humans crawl. Out in Stratford, the furthest easterly point on my necklace of accidental boulders, was an anonymously crafted memorial, about the size of the meteorite, dedicated to Gerard Manley Hopkins. That small boulder, or grey lump, unlike this one in Kensington, has a message on an embossed panel. A fragment of text. The meteorite sucks words in, solicits narrative, and offers nothing in return. The Hopkins rock pays tribute to a drowning, 'The Wreck of the *Deutschland*'. Five Franciscan nuns lost at sea.

> *Rhine refused them. Thames would ruin them,*
> *Surf, snow, river and earth*
> *Gnarled: but thou art above, thou Orion of light.*

# The Photograph of the Prince

ABDULRAZAK GURNAH

'There are grandchildren who are still living,' she said. 'They should not do this without asking them. It can't be that hard to find them, but I expect they did not even try. I know one of his grandchildren ... should I go to the reception desk and tell those women there? Then I could put them in touch. These are family matters, they should not exhibit pictures without permission.'

She said *permission* with a disapproving pout of her lips, frowning irritably. She spoke softly but her voice was stern and scornful. She meant it, and I was surprised at her vehemence. It did not make her face any less attractive, but it did slightly sour its loveliness, that hint of spite. We were looking at a photograph of an Indian aristocrat, or what looked like an aristocrat: a young man, robed and sashed, with burning eyes and that self-important tilt of the chin you see in images of the most paltry sultan or chieftain, even when, unlike this young man, they might only be dressed in a thin piece of fur, draped over one shoulder. I drew closer to the text beside the photograph, and read the subject's name, Raja Deva, and his story: he was a prince in a district of the kingdom of Mysore who had abdicated on a visit to London and refused to return. The photograph was an item in an exhibition of the work of the British photographer Emily Harewood at the V&A. The second paragraph of the text was about where she was in her career when she took the picture (in her thirties and with her own studio in Brighton) and what equipment she used (Sanderson ¼ Plate hand and stand at exposure 1/50th and f/10) and the printing details (gelatin silver printing-out paper). The text drew attention to the sharpness of the image and the striking way it captured the light in the subject's eyes. The photograph had been taken in the conservatory of Emily Harewood's friend's house in Banbury in 1909, where the prince was also visiting. The husband of the friend had been the prince's housemaster at Harrow School during all the time he spent there. It was the only known photograph Emily Harewood had taken of an oriental subject, her pictures were mostly of architecture and landscapes.

I waited for her to explain why permission would be needed from the grandchildren to exhibit the photograph. The prince seemed willing enough, was conventionally regal in his pose and looked striking, with those shining eyes. In photographs of other sultans and chieftains, the eyes often made you quail, such fierce agony blazed out of them. I imagined that the raja would have been pleased at how princely and handsome he looked in this one, despite the oddness of the robes and the turban in the pallid light of the conservatory. If there was mockery in the picture, it was the mild, habitual pretence of taking seriously the deluded self-importance of a subdued chief. If there was satire in it, it was the self-satirising oriental making himself accessible to the presumptions of his hosts: what an exotic and gleaming little jewel I am!

I would not have expected an Indian prince from Mysore to have such tight curls and such full lips – so full that he could have passed for someone from the African coast, a Somali or Bajun or Zanzibari. At that time, I did not know with any precision where Mysore really was and how unusual or otherwise such features were among its people.

In the end I asked her to explain. 'Why do you think they should ask for permission from the grandchildren to exhibit something like this? Do you find it mocking or intrusive? It's just a picture of a man dressed up for a portrait, isn't it? A crumb of history, a little item in a photographer's life-work. And the raja looks as if he is enjoying making an exhibition of himself. Anyway, it's also about knowledge, about what can be known, about a glimpse of a moment. I think that's what photographs do really well, give you an unexpected and intimate understanding of something or someone you knew nothing about a moment before. It's a kind of knowledge in itself, not a replacement or an illustration of another way of knowing: do you see what I mean? Why should we wait for permission from families to look at pictures like that, taken a century ago?'

Her gaze stayed on me for some seconds, and in the silence I understood that I had been lecturing. I thought she would say something, but after that long moment she turned to the photograph and pointed to the first paragraph of the text beside it, to the story of the prince, to the line about his abdication. It was an abrupt, exaggerated gesture, a kind of riposte. 'It's not true, that story,' she said.

'How do you know that?' I asked, making sure she understood that I was curious and not challenging her.

'Because he was my great-grandfather, and I know the real story,' she said, in her eyes a look of amused and vindicated satisfaction, and I guessed she was pleased with the way I had picked up my cues and allowed myself to be brought to where she intended. She broke into a smile that lit up her eyes and made her skin glow, a sudden and brief delight that had something passionate in it, and which made me realise how much I was in love with her. I laughed too, without knowing why. Those were early days between us, and every now and again this realisation of the love I felt would take me unawares and would fill me with desire.

She walked on to the next item while I stayed a moment longer with the prince, unable to decide whether to like him or not. There was so much confidence in his bearing, as if he were thoroughly satisfied with the melodrama of his costume and his presence, yet the look of arrogance had a brazen assurance that hinted at the histrionic: an uneasy and slightly blustery swagger. I guessed he was in his late twenties, a prepossessing man who stood there as if he thought himself attractive and pleasing. She looked nothing like him. He was short and muscular, or perhaps a little fleshy, it was hard to tell with all the robes and sashes, while she was slim and quick in her movements. Her features had an angular elegance, like those on a coin, although perhaps her lips hinted of the prince, especially when they pouted irritably. Her complexion had a trace of south in it. When I caught up with her, she was absorbed with the exhibits, and I did not think I should interrupt her. This was our first visit to the museum together, at her suggestion, and I had not yet learned whether she liked to talk about what she viewed or preferred to be left alone. In any case, I think she wanted to defer the telling, to let the story turn tense with expectation. It worked on me because I knew she would eventually tell me more, and I relished the waiting.

We went back to my apartment afterwards because she shared a flat with two other women, whom I had not yet met, and they had an agreement not to bring men friends home.

'I took you to the museum to see that photograph,' she said when she was ready.

'I can't wait to hear the story,' I said.

'He did not abdicate,' she said. 'He was abducted, more likely. Let me start from the beginning. Once upon a time, in a kingdom in the east, there was a prince who would not obey the rules of the conquerors and protectors of his land. It seems he did not fully understand what a British protectorate was, so he was removed and another prince who understood his true position was put in his place. To show his admiration for his benefactors, the new prince sent his thirteen-year-old son to a public school in England. That son was my great-grandfather. His nickname at school was Moonbeam. Not very original, but it could have been worse.

'He loved it here: the clothes, the games, the tuck shop. Then about three years later his father died suddenly and he was hurried home to succeed, before any other upstart could cause trouble. It was Easter when he left, he loved that time of year, and he was sad to leave England and all his friends. He was too young to be a proper prince, so until he could succeed properly the British agent had to be his guardian. It sounds a reassuring and modest little title, doesn't it? Agent. The agent thought it was too modest, and changed it to regent. It didn't matter what he was called, he made all the decisions anyway. He had done so even when my great-grandfather's father had been alive, but now he did not have to bother to explain himself, even as a courtesy. My great-grandfather was surrounded by British advisers who paid themselves well, lived in large comfortable houses, wore gorgeous uniforms with buttons of gold and carried silver-mounted swords. They gave themselves grand titles when really they were not much more than clerks, and you can just imagine how overbearing they must have been. Some of them didn't like that my great-grandfather had gone to Harrow School in England. They spoke about him in a high-handed tone of voice: as everyone knows, an English education only turns an Indian into a pompous snob and gives him alarming ideas above his station.'

'How do you know all this? Who said this and who said that, who wore what?' I interrupted, not because I was suspicious of the details – they sounded familiar enough – but because I wanted to understand how to take what she was telling me. Was she quoting or imagining? But she waved me down and pressed on.

'The British agent – oh, I should say regent – controlled everything, even the spending of the household: can you imagine? My great-grandfather could do none of the princely showing-off his subjects expected of him, and everyone knew it was because he was powerless in the hands of the British administrators, a little oriental puppet prince who had to do what he was told. He tried hard to flatter the regent and the advisers, to like him and them, to make them like him, but it did no good. He arranged banquets and concerts for them, sent them gifts, that kind of thing. At times, the regent did not even bother with the public show of respect that was part of the colonial charade. When the prince secretly ordered an English gilded carriage so he could ride in the splendour expected of a raja, the regent had it returned to the makers. The prince desired a car but the regent said the treasury was empty, yet *he* rode in a car and lived in luxury. My great-grandfather wrote to the India Office in his perfect English to complain about his treatment, to request that he be allowed to come to England to make his case personally to the foreign secretary. He received polite rebuffs, sent via the regent, to whom he was told to address all his concerns. He had rows with his advisers, great shouting rows. It made everything worse, and the regent, who was really in charge, just tightened the rules and wrote secret reports about his juvenile behaviour, his "tantrums", as he called them, even hinting that perhaps he was not fit to take over when he came of age. The foreign secretary murmured reassuringly to his agent, reminding him that the lad was only just out of school and should be gently coaxed to understand his true position. Rumours started among his nobles, too, that he was really not fit to rule over them, because he was descended from escaped African slaves who lived in the forests.'

'What escaped African slaves who lived in the forests?' I asked, the words out of my mouth involuntarily at this unexpected development. How much of this was I expected to believe? She gave me that long look again, as if considering whether to ignore me, get irritated with me or enlighten me. Then she smiled, and I saw that she was enjoying the telling, the withholding and the release of small, unanticipated details.

'There were African slaves in India, there are forests in India, and slaves always escape, don't they?' she said, patient with my slowness. I found out, when I checked later, that the largest population of African-descended people in India, the Siddhi as they are called, live in the territory which formed the old kingdom of Mysore. And Goa was just the other side of the border, where the Portuguese had brought in Mozambican slaves over the centuries, some of whom escaped into the kingdom of Mysore and did indeed hide in the forests. But I didn't know that at the time, and found the idea of African slaves in India implausible. After all, they had millions of their own people to enslave, they had no distant territories to turn into blood-soaked plantations, and, if anything, thousands of their own people became little more than slaves in the Caribbean, Fiji and Mauritius after the Abolition. But it turned out that they too had their Africans, just like everyone else.

Yet I still wanted to know how she knew all these details.

'Isn't it obvious?' she said, laughing outright at my witlessness. 'From my grandmother. It was family history.'

Then she put out her hand, and when I took it she pulled me gently towards her, and for a long time we did not talk and did not give any thought to the prince and his troubles. I don't think I would have been capable of any kind of thought when she took me in hand like that. Even the memory of that afternoon registers as a kind of charged emptiness, as if I was absent from myself and in some other state. Long after that we went to the cinema (to see a Woody Allen film, which we both hated) and then for a meal in a cafe that was so noisy with conversation and laughter that we could hardly hear each other. Just before I fell asleep, as I went over the day, my thoughts did return to the prince, and I imagined that confident-looking young man in the photograph standing before the British regent, in his gold-buttoned uniform and his silver-mounted sword and a bristling copper-coloured moustache, trembling with rage and shrieking foul-mouthed public-school abuse at his tormentor.

'You said the abdication was a lie,' I said, when the prince next came into our reckoning.

She was happy to see me so eager for the story, and I could see her toying with the idea of another deferral, but then she relented. 'Eventually he came of age, but by then he had been coaxed into realising his true position and understood perfectly how powerless he really was. He found ways of working with his British advisers, even though some of them laughed at him to his face and their wives mocked him with exaggerated courtesy. He obeyed their rules and tried to find ways to gain what advantage he could for himself, and his advisers exchanged smiles and pretended not to notice. It was like being a boy at school again. He longed to return to England for a visit, he had so many happy memories of his time here, and he had kept in touch with some of his school friends and his housemaster. In the end, the regent, who – now that the prince was of age – gave himself the title of chief adviser of the district, allowed that there was enough money in the treasury to let the prince come for a visit, and he came to England as a private person accompanied by one secretary. He was not to make any undesirable contacts, and guess who would be the judge of that, and he was not to seek an interview with any member of the India Office. He knew they were just bullying him, but he had no choice. He did as he was told. He met his friends and visited his former housemaster, who had invited him to spend a few days at his home in Banbury. It was while he was staying there that he met and fell in love with my great-grandmother, who was the daughter of one of the master's friends.'

Ah, I thought, he fell in love.

'You should know my great-grandfather was already married and was father to a son and daughter. As soon as he was recalled after his father's death, and even before he arrived home from England, a marriage was arranged and executed by proxy. The grandees of his kingdom did not want him bringing back any fancy ideas from England. He was sixteen years old. He returned to find a bride who was thirteen years old waiting for him, a shy and ugly child whom his British advisers forbade him from disavowing. But when he met my great-grandmother it was real love, and no one could talk him out of it. That was the man you saw in that photograph: a man in love, who had taken to visiting Banbury regularly to meet my great-grandmother. When he refused to obey his adviser's demand that he give up this inappropriate affair, and made a fuss about his sovereign rights, he was called to the India Office and made aware what those rights consisted of. He was given a statement which he was required to sign: it announced his abdication, with immediate effect, because of ill-health. A settlement would be made to him under certain conditions: he was to leave England as soon as possible, he was never to return to India, he was never publicly to say or write anything about the terms of his abdication. If he refused any of these conditions, there would be no settlement and he would run the risk of detention for sedition against the agreement he had made with the British government when he became the prince of his kingdom. He should also know that it was not only the British government that insisted on these conditions but his own notables, who considered it inappropriate for him to continue as their prince, for reasons he probably very well knew. In the meantime, accommodation had been arranged for him and he would be escorted there immediately after signature, and would stay there until arrangements for his embarkation to his chosen destination had been completed.'

She delivered this last part of the story in a fleshless official voice, acting out the part, and it did capture something of what I imagine would have been the icy courtesy of the imperial bully. 'Where did he go?' I asked.

'Paris, at first, until his lover joined him, and then they moved to Nice. They had a child there in 1912 – my grandmother. Before the year was out, the prince died at the age of twenty-eight, I don't know what of, and the settlement the British government had made to him ended. So my great-grandmother came back to England with her little baby, and her family took her back in.

'So you see,' she continued, after leaving me for a moment to reflect on what she had told me, 'they shouldn't just put the picture there like that, with that horrible little untruth attached to it. How often do you think they do that, write these little lies in that knowing way? They don't have the right to steal people's lives and then exhibit them like that – like entertainment pretending to be knowledge. Don't you agree?'

I didn't, at least not where it concerned the matter of *rights*. I sympathised with her outrage at the way bland simplifications obscured an uglier truth, but that was how the story of empire was always framed by those who partook of it and those who celebrate it now. The story is not intended to explain how so much of the world collapsed so completely in the face of European designs to subdue it, but to turn that rampage into a romance and an obligation arising out of natural superiority. There is no need to see our full ugliness at all times. So the prince abdicated and was not abducted. It was too late to change that language now but we can learn to read what it hides. But I didn't see that anybody had the *right* to suppress anything it was possible to know. I didn't say this to her, I just nodded. I was afraid it would come across as harrumphing high-mindedness.

'I want to see that photograph of the prince again,' I said. 'Shall we go back to the museum this afternoon?'

'I can't,' she said. 'I have to go and see my mother.'

'Your mother? I thought you said your mother lived in Australia.'

She looked at me as if I had said something completely incomprehensible. 'What made you think that? My mother has never *been* to Australia. Oh, I know, did I say that she was thinking of visiting a friend who lives in Australia? She's been saying that for ages.'

'So she's back … I mean, she's here. I'd love to meet her,' I said. She looked thoughtful, frowning a little, as if what I was saying was puzzling to her. 'Why?' she asked.

I shrugged, but I did not say anything more, since she did not seem to like the idea. No doubt my suggestion was clumsy enthusiasm – to ask to meet her mother when it was not yet clear how serious we were with each other. I got carried away by the moment. Perhaps it would have sounded like an intrusion. I wanted to meet her because of the prince, to see whether she looked like him, to talk with her about that photograph, which she was sure to have seen. Perhaps I should have understood something from that exchange, but I did not. I was not aware at the time how often I was biting my tongue, how pliantly I retreated from challenging her. It was the first time that there was such a discrepancy between what I remembered and what she said she had told me. I had a vivid memory of her telling me about her mother moving to Queensland to join her elder brother who had emigrated there, yet she dismissed that memory with such casual certainty that I did not protest. I so much feared losing her.

But there were other moments, other mistaken recollections on my part, it would seem. What I should have understood, which it took me a while to do, was that what she told me was not always reliable. At first, I thought simply that there were variations in the telling, a detail remembered in the wrong sequence which changed other details down the line. But after two or three of these I became attentive, especially when the discrepancy was as pronounced as that first one. ('No, my mother has never been to Australia' rankled for a long time afterwards.) Then one day I found out that she did not share a flat with two other women with whom she had an agreement about not bringing men home. She lodged with a woman and her young son from whom she rented a basement room. We went there one day to leave her heavy office bag on the way to the South Bank, and I waited outside, as I had been instructed to, while she went in through the basement door. Her landlady, who was an attractive and glamorous-looking woman, appeared at her front door, which was some steps up from the road, and called me in. I followed her into the living room and saw that she would have had a good view of us arriving together and then me waiting on the pavement while she went down the steps into the basement. She introduced herself as Nicky and began to chat as comfortably as if we had known each other for a while, telling me about her son who was upstairs practising for a guitar exam, can you hear him? She said she had heard so much about me and I felt my face growing warm. Nicky had a bottle of wine in a cooler on a tray with one other glass, as if she was expecting a visitor. There must have been internal access from the basement because she came up as we talked and joined in the conversation, helping herself to the wine in my glass.

As we walked to the South Bank, she told me about Nicky, who worked in films, and her adorable son, Stephen, who was as clever as he was lazy and who was bound to sail through life. Nicky was waiting for her lover, Jeremy, who was coming for dinner. He was married but they had been lovers for years, and Nicky was quite happy for it to continue like that. When I asked about the flat share with two other women, she frowned in a puzzled way and looked surprised. She seemed displeased, and in the bustle of getting to the South Bank she allowed my question to pass without reply. The following day, back in my flat, I returned to the question and persisted even when I could see that she preferred not to be forced to answer. Our conversation was slowly developing into a quarrel but I felt I had to continue with it, to understand something of the need for these inventions. I would have hesitated if I had known that I would lose her as a result. I did not understand until it was too late that she was tiring of me, and perhaps was looking for a humane way of making her escape. I asked her if the Indian prince, Raja Deva, really was her great-grandfather, and she laughed at me.

'No, but I knew a girl at school who told a story like that. I thought you'd like it,' she said, and I thought she was laughing at me for my gullibility. I don't know why I was stung by this, but I was, as if she had discovered an addiction and was mocking me for it. 'You love those stories of colonial boorishness, don't you?' she said. It was then that I spoke to her with unnecessary cruelty and forced her hand with my brusqueness.

'Why do you tell so many lies?' I asked. 'How can you expect me to believe anything you say?'

'You don't have to believe anything I say,' she said. Then she stood up and left the room. When I followed her into the bedroom a short while later, I saw that she was packing the few things that she had left behind from previous visits and was getting ready to leave. It was too late to stop her, although I apologised and even pleaded in the end. She did not say anything as she moved about the flat, gathering her bath bag, her handbag, her coat, perhaps relieved at last to make her escape. In a matter of minutes she was done, and her last words were to tell me she did not want to hear from me, ever, because she had never met anyone who was as arrogant as I was.

I did not try to get in touch with her because I thought I had seen enough to understand that I would be incapable of holding my own against the fantasies she wilfully inhabited and abandoned. She was too much for me. After she left, at times I woke up with the sensation that she was there in the room with me, but that if I spoke she would vanish. I would lie in the dark listening, waiting to feel her weight on the bed, waiting to feel her hand on my chest, fearing that if I put on the light I would see something grotesque sidling up to me.

I saw the prince again a couple of days ago. I was reading an online article about women photographers in Sussex and remembered Emily Harewood, so I searched for her. There was a page on her with a photograph of her studio in Brighton and some of her work. One of the photographs was that of Raja Deva, followed by his dates: 1886–1912. He would have been twenty-six when he died, not twenty-eight, and whether the story of his abdication for love was true or false, it was almost certain that he would have died with a broken heart. I looked at his fleshy smugness in that photograph and could not decide whether I liked him or not.

# An Eye That Sees

HANAN AL-SHAYKH

TRANSLATED BY WIAM EL-TAMAMI

A voice rang out, loud and tuneful, through the Victoria and Albert Museum. The visitors froze, puzzled – they had never heard such a strange melody. They reacted as though a bird had just landed on their heads.

It was the attendant. He stood in the middle of the gallery, his eyes closed, his head swaying from side to side, his hands clutching his heart as though afraid it might fly away. Usually a shadowy presence, a figure of unobtrusive authority, suddenly he appeared before them as a man of flesh and blood.

*

In his early days at the job, Tareq had heartily greeted each visitor as they entered, and had taken it upon himself to accompany them as they wandered around the gallery. But before long his supervisor had asked him to keep his distance: people had complained of feeling followed, monitored. He was to stay in his corner and only intervene if there was a specific reason: to ask someone to lower their voice, silence their mobile phone, refrain from leaning against the exhibits or put away their sandwiches. On the whole he complied, except for the odd moment when he couldn't resist telling an old man that he reminded him of an uncle back home, or remarking on the coldness of the weather.

When he had first come to Britain, ten years before, Tareq would invariably introduce himself by telling the story of Tareq ibn Ziyad, the general who had led the Islamic conquest of Andalusia, and after whom both he and the mountain of Gibraltar were named. Years of seeing eyes glaze over went by before he finally understood that the British didn't care, and he stopped taking such pride in his name.

In the face of this indifference he tried to content himself, instead, with the fact that his one dream of a life in Britain had, at least, come true. He had grown up hearing his father and the village elders speak with envy of those who had left Yemen and made a life for themselves in Europe or the Arabian Gulf. Time and time again, he heard them say, *a young man who stays in this country won't find a thing to eat but flies; won't even find a shroud to cover him when they lay him to rest in the earth.* Tareq had escaped this fate. He had left his job at the Yemeni airline in Sanaa after talking to a customer who boasted to Tareq that he could earn in just a few days in the UK what amounted to Tareq's monthly salary in Yemen. The last ticket Tareq issued was his own.

After a great deal of effort he had managed to secure the necessary papers and was awarded leave to remain in the UK – and permission to work. He began drifting from job to job – from a metals factory in Sheffield to a hospital in Hackney – until his Egyptian flatmate suggested he try his luck at the V&A, where he himself worked as a handyman, hanging pictures and moving objects to and from storage.

The position came to him on a plate of gold, as they would have said at home, and Tareq became a museum attendant. It was a neat, respectable job, and he was proud that it meant he didn't need to work with his hands: as far as those back home were concerned, this was as good as being a company director. Besides, the role offered plenty of time for quiet contemplation. Over the course of the following months he reduced himself, as requested, to a set of ears and a pair of eyes.

Tareq busied himself with adding and subtracting, comparing his earnings and expenses, brooding over what he wanted to buy, and what he had bought and regretted. He calculated the sum he had left over to send to his parents in Yemen, and thought of the special massage chair that might help ease his father's rheumatism. Would it be possible to ship it over? And if so, how would they manage to squeeze it along the narrow alleyway leading to their home – or, for that matter, through the tiny front door?

Should he go home for the holidays, he wondered? There were rumours that things in Yemen were becoming more unstable – might they become so dangerous that they would shut down flights altogether? Perhaps he should devote his time off to finding a bride instead. His Somali friend Ahmed, a bus driver, had told him about a promising young woman he'd met who was single. She worked at a post office and greeted him ever so politely as she got on the bus every day. If he weren't married himself, Ahmed said, he'd be tempted to ask for her hand.

Tareq didn't get to meet anyone through work. The women at the museum – employees and visitors alike, whether foreigners or Arabs – came from a completely different world. They were the sort of women who walked around on spindly heels that looked like the twigs Tareq used to clean his teeth. He could sooner reach the stars than talk to a woman like that. Life here was expensive, too. Even a sip of water came at a price.

His Egyptian friend bemoaned the fact that the V&A was not more like the antiquities museums in Cairo. If you worked there, he claimed, you could make double your wages by hustling the tourists. Threaten them with grave consequences if they take a photograph, then whisper that you're willing to turn a blind eye should they extend you a handful of cash. Or if you spot someone with a keen interest in mummies, offer to show her some 'special specimens' that are not on public display, then lead her to a back room housing a few bird or dog remains.

Today his train of thought had been abruptly derailed when a woman with familiar features had entered the museum, followed by a television crew. She walked up to one of the paintings on display and contemplated it briefly before turning to the camera. A man handed her a microphone and proceeded to ask her a question in English. She answered in classical Arabic, but a few words slipped out in Yemeni dialect. Tareq inched closer to hear.

'When I was a little girl, there was one mirror in our house. I would gaze into it for hours. My mother tried to wrest me away. She used to say, "If you keep this up, that mirror will swallow you whole!" One day I was helping her bake some bread and I spilled a little salt – she was furious. She slapped me, hard, and said, "On the

Day of Judgement, God will make you pick those grains up, one by one, with your eyelashes!" and it was that threat, that gloating threat, that made hot tears rush to my eyes, and not the slap at all.

'I stared long and hard at those grains through blurry eyes. Slowly my vision cleared and I burst out: "If God is so big and has to take care of the whole universe all the time, will he really be so worried about a few spilled grains of salt?"

'A realisation began to crystallise within me. I began to understand why I kept gazing into the mirror that way. I was asserting my right to look, *really* look: to delve into the world around me and ask questions, even if those questions made people turn away in anger or apathy or fear – questions big and small, about boys and girls, about our life and traditions, about nature and the meaning of it all. Once, when I had been repeatedly shushed, I found myself yelling, not only at my mother, but at everyone, including my youngest sister, who was in the garden playing with one of our goats, "Why are we created with eyes, then? Isn't it so we can see?" And with the greatest urgency I rushed to draw an eye, as if it were a matter of life or death.

'That eye sought to expose what others tried to obscure, what everyone tried to hide from me for fear that I would break the rules, step outside the bounds of the familiar. But the tighter the chokehold on me grew, the more I rebelled by drawing eyes everywhere: on my hands, on my legs, on my clothes and schoolbooks, on the chairs and walls and bedspreads.'

Tareq's heart began to hammer in his chest. He almost cried out, 'I know you! I know who you are! You're Aisha!'

The Englishman broke in with another question. 'Why do you use henna in your paintings? Are oils not available in Yemen?'

The painter smiled. 'Painting materials are available in the capital, Sanaa. But henna is an essential part of my culture and upbringing, of our daily rituals. Plus, I find it has beautiful colours ... and a powerful, evocative smell.'

The attendant's trembling heart could not resist coming closer and closer to the woman from his homeland, to the girl he had once seen squatting in the dirt fifteen years ago. It was said, at the time, that she had lost her mind, mixing henna incessantly and painting eyes, day and night, on anything within reach, even rocks and trees. One neighbour warned the others not to hang their clothes outside to dry, after coming out of her house to find her freshly laundered sheets staring back at her. Others whispered that the girl was possessed: she was not drawing eyes, but cryptic signs.

Tareq had been intrigued by these rumours. He recalled how he had made his way to her house on the outskirts of a neighbouring village. He wanted to lay his eyes on her, and if her beauty appealed to him, he had resolved to ask for her hand and break her free of the black magic. He remembered now how he found her scribbling eyes on pebbles and in the dirt, and when he crept closer, she looked up, straight into his eyes. She smiled and asked, 'Who are you?' In panic, he scrambled backwards and fled. A normal girl would never initiate a conversation with a boy like that! Once at a safe distance, he looked over his shoulder to see her mother dragging her back into the house and raining down blows. When he later heard that she had disappeared – run away, or maybe been killed? – he blamed himself terribly that he hadn't whisked her away that day. But soon, leaving his village for the city, for university and a new life, he began to forget.

She looked younger than him now, tall and willowy, even though they were both in their thirties. The years had not been so kind to him: they had stripped away his hair and puffed up his paunch. How incomprehensibly strange that they should be here now in the land of the English, her mysterious eyes on display in a museum, revered as art, and he responsible for guarding it.

Tareq waited until she had finished her interview, then approached her, hand outstretched. 'I'm from Yemen – from your home town, actually. I just want to say that our pride in you is bigger than this museum. A thousand congratulations.'

She shook his hand, briefly. 'You're so lucky to be living in this oasis of knowledge and beauty,' she said, politely. 'Or do you get tired of seeing the same things every day?'

An image of Tipu's Tiger, sinking its teeth into a British soldier, sprang to mind. The wooden statue with its striped tail was the one piece that had caught his attention since he started working at the museum six years ago, not least because on the tiger's face were inscribed the Arabic words *asad allah*, 'the lion of God'. The tiger once used to produce horrifying mechanical shrieks and moans. More than once he had seen little children squirming out of their parents' grasp to run to it delightedly.

'No, I don't get bored — I move to a different room every day! Anyway, my name is Tareq and I'd be very happy to take you on a special tour of the museum, and maybe show you some of the things that are not on display. My colleague is in charge of the warehouse. Do you live in London? Let me give you my number.'

'No, I live in Aden – I'm just visiting.' He watched her press the digits into her mobile phone.

'Bye, Tareq.' As she smiled and shook his hand, he realised he would never hear from her.

He found himself standing alone in front of her painting. It was bigger than all the others. In the centre of the canvas was an eye the size of the earth. The smell of henna suddenly filled his nostrils.

*Hanoon*, they called it in Yemen: 'she of the tender heart'. A familiar scene from his childhood crept unbidden into his mind: his mother filling a large tub with hot water and henna and submerging herself in it, her skin turning from white to gold.

The eye drew him in, and he basked in the warmth of the Yemeni sun. Its veins were the tremors on a heart monitor, inscriptions in Aisha's secret language. He read: *The eye is the gateway to the soul; the eye is insight; the eye is exploration. The ignorant are blind even if they see; the learned see even if they are blind.*

He understood now that those villagers had been right, in a way: Aisha *was* enchanted, enchanting. As he wandered from one room to another with Aisha's eye, he saw the treasures of the museum anew. Its pupil, crimson, like life-pumping blood, led him through an oasis of knowledge and beauty, to look and explore, to feel and wonder – and to remember.

The antique gilded candelabra were the flickering fireflies that dotted the Yemeni night. The ivory comb was the one his grandmother used to tug through his little sister's tangled hair. A sword of gold echoed the *janbiah* – the curved dagger Yemeni men wore tucked into their belts.

Everything before him – hand-woven rugs and lush textiles, wood inlaid with mother of pearl, pottery engraved with delicate shapes – all this, which was considered part of western heritage, he had seen before in the homes and buildings and mosques of Yemen. Raphael's image of Jesus and the miraculous draught of fish rang distant bells: a parallel legend that told of the answered sea-prayers of a Yemeni sheikh. When he saw a tiny box containing a replica of a skeleton to remind human beings of the day of reckoning; a coloured clay bowl to serve soup to a new mother moments after childbirth; a glass bottle that, if broken, would bury its owner under a hailstorm of disaster – he thought: 'So many countries scattered across the earth. How is it that folklore is almost one?'

Tareq heaved a sigh. An old song bubbled up from deep within, and he let it take him over:

*Oh henna, dear henna, oh drops of morning dew –*
*My sweetheart's eyes are a window that lets the breeze*
*sing through …*

A hand clamped down on his shoulder. He opened his eyes with a start to find his supervisor pulling him to a corner of the room, asking in hushed, harried tones, 'What's going on here?'

'Sorry, I … I don't know what happened … it's like the … I felt for the first time this place – it … it reminded me of home.'

'You still have to keep it together at all times. You know very well how we react when a visitor raises their voice, don't you?'

'Yes. I ask them to stop, and call in security if necessary.'

'All right then. So you know the rules.'

# Babber

ELEANOR THOM

In a phone box on the corner, a man is held captive by a grandfather clock. He rattles the door and glares through the windows into the round, white dial. He is late for work, no time for games, but the clock has an audience and won't lose face. Around the phone box, tourists in flared denims and bright jackets laugh and applaud.

Nearby, the nineteenth-century dildos slalom between the railings. A baby Indian elephant sprays water at a busker while a baboon steals coppers from his violin case. The collection of early surgical implements are pinning tourists' hats to a tree.

The smaller exhibits, the sideshows, only leave their cases once a week, and mostly the crowd plays along, welcoming the distraction while they queue to see the poster pieces, the bigger exhibits that come out every day. The Bodhisattvas, always content, are sunbathing on the steps. Their dazzling moon cheeks and polished bosoms reflect the faces of the visitors, who stand watching with eyes half-shut and hands lifted to shield the glare. At curfew, the Bodhisattvas will slowly ease themselves to their feet and return to their cases.

Diplodocus is surrounded by kids. He pulls at tree branches and sprinkles them with herbivore confetti from his bony jaws. They offer up their Cornettos and half-eaten sandwiches while friends and parents take Polaroids.

The armoury marches out of the museum's main entrance, perfectly in step. Underground passengers jump aside as it parades into the tunnel and the echo doubles the rigid, metallic stamp. They get as far as the ticket office and turn back. A couple arriving on a bus head to the Victoria and Albert Museum. By now they need some tea, and there it is served by the sculptures (a temporary installation, not to be missed).

People come and go all morning and the exhibits have their fun. Usually MISC.100-1975 is out on a Friday, giving rides to babies with dribbly chins. But today, MISC.100-1975 is hiding in the back of a coach from Teesside, and nobody but the driver has noticed. The driver has just come back with his tea in a polystyrene cup, and now he's sitting in the front seat, peeling the wrapper from a Banjo Wafer. This morning he dropped off a church group. Boys and girls on Easter holidays. They're the same as any other kids: sweets, comics and swear words. He knows an exhibit is hiding in the coach because he has seen it in his mirror. He has also heard it shifting about, trying to get comfortable. Hiding is not easy. MISC.100-1975 is not a modern, travel-friendly item that will fold into a corner. To the driver it seems regal, dark and hooded, with huge cobweb wheels and long curling lashes for handles. He angles his mirror to get a better look, not sure what he is looking at. It is decorated with a nest of golden reeds, all twists and spirals. It is an antique. The driver doesn't know how to act around an antique, especially one that is trying to hide. In an hour he will step out for lunch. He'll have his sandwich and he'll put a bet on a good horse. It's the National tomorrow. Maybe the pram will wheel away and bother someone else. He checks his watch as he dunks his biscuit and glances again in the mirror. The thing trembles and stills.

By mid afternoon the weather gets up. Kids make lines outside and their heads are being counted as the rain starts to fall. Exhibits are called back into the museum, a note of urgency in the curators' voices as they do the roll, reading off identity numbers.

There's a rush to the coaches. The boys come first, stripes and checked shirts and smelling of spearmint gum. They call the driver 'mate' as they jump past. Then the girls, long hair in bobbles, all of them clutching bags of toys and pencils from the museum shop. Things for siblings and presents for mothers. A burst of energy sends boys trampling to the back row and the best seats. The adults are still outside and the rest of the kids are clambering onto the coach, choosing where to sit, two by two, more of them climbing in and pushing the ones in front. The rain is hammering. Kids press against the windows and watch the rivulets.

The group leader gets in last. She's already restarted her count, two, four, six, eight … She's not much more than a kid herself. Lovely set of pins. Her hair is wet, plastered to her face. She sidesteps back to the front to tell him they can get going. Rain runs off her cheeks and a drip lands on his hand. He doesn't wipe it away. Nothing is amiss, she tells him, all smiles. He feels like he's been blessed. All souls accounted for.

It's still raining when the coach reaches the motorway. Some of the kids have fallen asleep, and the ones still awake are quiet, chewing on Wrigley's and Opal Fruits or swapping cards. A few of them are singing Jesus songs at the back, but they're keeping it down and the grown-ups don't bother shushing. The driver turns on his fog lights and relaxes into his seat. He's placed his bet and he feels lucky. He puts his foot down. Behind him the kids reach the chorus. More of them join in, singing a song he doesn't know.

Underneath in the darkness of the luggage hold, something startles and moves. It hunkers down near the back where an odd kind of music drifts down through the cracks.

It must be about now, at Exhibition Road, that they realise their Edwardian perambulator has bolted. It shares a case with a doll and a dress, ordinary things depicting daily life, and without the pram there is an empty space, an imbalance.

In an office room they take out the file that belongs to the pram. It hasn't been long in the collection. The new exhibits are always the nervy ones. The file is thin and blue with a white sticker on the front bearing the pram's typed identity number. A curator reads the details, watched by her colleagues, and an assistant clicks a pop-up biro, waiting to take minutes.

'Has someone called the police? Do we know the history?'

The curator reads from the file. 'There's not much to go on,' she says.

'What do we know?'

'Possibly manufactured in Leeds. Found in a house clearance. Tell them to look in back alleys, old housing estates, factory buildings – if they haven't burnt down.'

For a few seconds the minute-taker stops writing and looks up.

'They seem to try and go home, don't they?'

*

There was no pram with the first babber. Prams were pricey. Instead Mrs Green did what her mother had. She carried Our Freddie in her arms or perched him on her hip with a cloth tied around her shoulder. She had liked carrying him, the hurry to the house where she worked in the afternoons and him chattering in her ear about everything they passed.

'Look Mummy, a cart! Mummy, a clip-clop cart. Look, a dog. A dog, Mummy!'

When he grew too heavy to be carried he took the cloth to bed and slept with it. By then it was like an old favoured toy, a soft and fuzzy thing from all the knotting and cuddling they had done with it. He told her it smelt like love. A long time ago, all that.

Freddie is a man by the time they find out they've another babber coming. She and Mr Green laugh that it is the house that has gone and got them another babber. They are in the suburbs now, where the air is healthy, a new place with a proper bathroom, with ventilation bricks in every room. The windows are never stubborn like the ones in their last house. Here you only have to ask and they open themselves. They look out onto a garden with a lawn and beds.

'Put some sweet peas in there,' she tells her husband.

It is a mild summer and the plants do well. They all do well, and the following spring he arrives, a quick labour and not much pain, not compared with the first one. Out comes little Sweet Pea Green.

They've seen the new neighbours, dressed up and taking the air on a Sunday, pushing their young ones around the public gardens. Everything is in bloom, the flowers laid out in patterns and letters spelling out the name of the town. The petals are red, purple and white, with statues at the centre of every bed. The neighbourhood is new and proud of itself, and the fountains sparkle in the sun, toasting their good health. Here you can go out for exercise and not choke to death.

She sees Mr Green stretch a tape across the hallway and wonders what idea he has in his head. And then a few days later he comes home from work with it, pushing it down the road, his big surprise.

'Didn't they laugh at you on the train?'

'Oh, aye,' he chuckles.

There isn't much room in the hallway. They will have to pass it sideways and she will have to hold down her skirts. But this time they have a pram. They will walk out with the new babber all elegant.

Sweet Pea Green spends his first weeks crying and sucking. But soon he sits upright in his pram, lace-bonneted and smiling at everyone. He is strapped in so he can't fall out or clamber down and get his frock mucky, and others walking in the park stop to admire him, newlyweds and old ladies, wrinkly fingers tucking pennies under the quilt and cooing that the lucky someone looks so contented. Mrs Green likes the gentle sway as she pushes the pram in front of her. It bobs like a boat and keeps Sweet Pea sleeping soundly. Even so, she sometimes thinks she would like to carry Sweet Pea, the way she had Freddie, feeling his warm head nestled under her chin. At home, she holds him close, doing the housework slowly with her one free hand. But no one carries their little ones round here. It's all prams. And she's proud of her pram too. So she swallows the idea and keeps it sunk, deep inside her belly.

One day in December she is out doing her shopping. She wants to make a meat pie and she has been to the butcher's and on to the grocer's where she has to go inside for flour. The pram is too wide for the door so she leaves Sweet Pea outside. The pram nestles between the baskets of potatoes and nuts, out of the way of anyone passing by. It rocks the baby gently as she steps away.

There is a queue in the shop. It is busier than usual with Christmas approaching, and a few times she glances over her shoulder to check that Sweet Pea is still sleeping. No sign of upset, so she waits till her turn and buys a bag of flour. She looks forward to the smell of the pie cooking and the whistle as the steam rushes through her little birdie topper. She remembers this thought of the pie later, when she throws away the uncooked meat.

She will remember every second in that shop. The smell of spices, the old woman who waits in front of her, who speaks quietly and has to ask three times for what she wants, and then her turn and the shiny coin she hands over. The walk across the tiled shop floor and out into the cold air. The two steps between her and the waiting pram.

The bag of flour falls from her hands, dusting everything white: her dress, her shoes, the pavement, and the wheels of the empty pram, still rocking. She looks around at first, just nearby, ignoring the rushing in her head. Surely, someone she knows will be there, a neighbour or one of their friends, a child, and they have taken Sweet Pea out of the pram just to cuddle him. He will be right there, perfectly well, and she will have gone and dropped all that flour. But there is no one standing by. Everyone is in a hurry, making their way to a stopped tram-car or struggling through the crowd, laden with bags. Someone passes, pushing a pram. She glances in, but it is not Sweet Pea.

She walks one way, turning behind her again and again. Then she starts to run. She can see people noticing now, heads turning. She falls down and when they pick her up she begs for help. Someone brings a policeman, a young one who doesn't know what to do. She goes up and down the street searching, others with her now, looking into the windows of trams, into shops, halfway up alleyways and back down. Each time she turns she is terrified she has just missed him. She is still looking for that good neighbour, or the child from down the road, or her mother-in-law come to visit. She wants to see them standing there on a corner with the babber, both of them smiling and fine.

Men stop out, Mr Green and Freddie, some of the neighbours from the street, and all of the police making enquiries till late into the night. Mrs Green waits at home, listening, sick, her heart ticking like a clock, willing him home. And then the wretched snow comes down, thick and white as that bag of flour she dropped. In minutes everything is under it and all the shops are dark and closed. She watches the shadows of the men below the street lamps. Men returning to their houses in ones and twos. Only the empty pram comes back, and she slams the door on it. Her husband will find it in the garden later, full to the brim with snow.

Every knock on the door has her hoping at first, but there are no clues, and soon people say they have nothing to go on. They stop looking. She looks herself, every time she is out, but she doesn't go out much. Everywhere there are prams. The babbers all look the same at that age and it is too much when any of them could be hers. She hasn't stepped back in the park once. She wants Mr Green to get the pram sold, but he won't, even once the months have passed, even when he knows his son will be on his feet already.

*Just look at him! Growing up so fast and my goodness, not a teatling any more. Tall like his father.*

Maybe he is still hoping, thinking of later, when the boy and his pals would have taken the pram into the garden and pulled off the wheels for a cart. And perhaps there will be another babber for them yet, he says, though she knows there won't. Still, it's kept.

The last time she sees the pram, her two men have it tied on a rope. They are underneath its breast, hoisting it high into the attic hatch. And it hangs there, an odd, rearranged spider.

*

It's dark when the coach arrives. Kids shake their pals awake and slowly they stand up and gather their things, feeling for jackets, comics, uneaten sweets and dropped cards. They don't talk. Their throats are furry from sleep and the backs of their necks feel itchy from the fuzzy seat covers. They rub their eyes, reach into the black spaces beneath the seats and on the luggage rack, swing bags onto shoulders. A cold draught blows through the coach, and outside fathers wait in cars or mothers stand on the kerb, huddled in coats. The leader goes out first, like Bambi down the steps with her lovely pins. She softly counts out the kids, saying she'll see them on Sunday. God bless.

Soon it is quiet. The engine starts and the coach pulls away, lighter now, gliding round the corner, stopping at the crossing for the kids, past Bambi getting into her Mini, and then away again, straight through the traffic lights, past the shops and the school, over the railway bridge, back home to the depot. The driver hears something now, a tapping, a rolling. He thinks maybe the engine's playing games or maybe there's something loose in the hold.

When the luggage hatch opens the pram crashes out, three wheels off the ground and seesawing left and right. It rights itself though, and it's at the door before the driver can lift a hand. He watches it wheeling away, out into the street light, right bang in the middle of the road. No one is around, only stray dogs and a few men staggering home from the pub. All the other drivers parked up hours ago. He looks to the office where the phone is. The room is dark and shut and the phone is silent on the hook. Already the pram is out of sight so he shakes his head and slams the hatch.

The pram heads for the houses. This is some other town, a place it has never been before. Street after street of small terraces, red brick walls, gardens with bins out front and alleys at the back. There are smoking chimneys, smells from a factory somewhere and dinners left on the stove. A few cars go by, spraying puddles. The pram stops outside a house. Through the window there is a room with orange wallpaper and an old man sitting at a piano. It hesitates and moves on.

The back alleys are safer and darker. Small stones are spat sideways as the pram wheels along. It rolls through dog shit, almost runs aground on a Hopper that a kid has left out. Splashes through mud. Scares cats. Skids on a root but keeps going. The lanes are empty and straight, good for going fast. Dogs bark through gaps in the fences and go after the cats that scram. A group of men block the passage and force the pram to turn around and take another route, and it tears along the alleyways till it finds another stopping place. A woman is taking in her forgotten washing. She wrings the rain from the clothes before slapping them into a tub. The pram turns a corner and goes down another lane. It stops wherever there are signs of life.

At the entrance to one alleyway there is an off-licence. The street is brighter here, and there are one or two people, a little bell tinkling when the shop door opens or closes. The pram's huge wheels cast strange shadows over the pavement, and it inches out. In the middle of the street there is a boy walking alone. They keep their distance. The pram stays a few metres behind, letting the boy set the pace.

When he looks over his shoulder he startles, and the pram stops dead. It waits while the boy studies its cracked leather hood and ancient curves, part insect, part steam engine. The boy's hair blows in the breeze and he chews on his lips, sniffs the cold air. Then he turns and starts walking, and the pram begins to trundle. It catches up and coasts at the boy's side. The boy walks with his hands in his pockets and there is a thin plastic bag looped around his wrist. With each step the bag bumps against his knee. He steals glances at the pram, leaning over to check that it hasn't run off with someone's kiddie inside. When the boy sees that it is an empty pram, he sets his gaze on the wheels and the axles. Old but sound. He throws the bag into the pram and the two move closer. They pass a policeman in the shadows, but he takes no notice. He barely looks out from below the brim of his hat.

The boy and the pram come to a house at the end of a terrace. The front room has thin, pink curtains, drawn shut, and the light from a television flickers behind them. The boy leaves the pram at the gate, takes the bag, and goes up the narrow path to the door.

'There you are! You've been hours.'

The boy swings the bag onto the stairs and turns to go back out. He is nearly at the gate when a woman comes to the door. The pram stays hidden. Only the hood and the handle stick up over the garden wall, and the woman doesn't notice. The boy goes back to her, digs in his pocket and hands the woman some change.

'Were you at Christian Endeavour?'

'No,' he says. 'There was a trip. They went to London.'

The woman seems fine with this. She drops the change in the front of her apron and then with both hands she straightens the boy's jacket.

'Wasn't there one already this year?'

The boy shrugs.

'London, for God's sake,' the woman laughs. 'Tell them to take you to York Minster. I could just about afford that. Don't stay out late, remember? *Doctor Who*'s on.'

'I'll only be a minute.'

She hesitates before bending to kiss his cheek. He's already twisting free of her, turning to go. He takes the pram by the handle now and pushes, round the corner and into the darkness behind the house. There is a gate with a stiff metal bolt, but he coaxes it open and then he turns round and backs into the garden, pulling the pram behind him.

A week passes. Everyone talks about the Grand National. They say it was tremendous. That's the word everyone uses. The boy's grandfather was over to watch with the boy's father, even though neither of them are betting men, and even his mother knows the name of the winning horse. It's all they hear as the race draws to a close and it's a fast name, and it's a good name for a good horse. And it's Red Rum, Red Rum, and it's Red Rum over the line!

The driver goes out on his winnings. Abba's just reached number one and they're playing it on the jukebox. A few girls are dancing but everyone else is talking about the race. They've memorised the commentary, the moment of triumph:

*And he's getting the most tremendous cheer from the crowd! And it's Red Rum, the twelve-year-old Red Rum preceded only by loose horses, being chased by Churchtown Boy. And he's coming up to the line …*

Back at Exhibition Road, the pram's blue file has been marked as AWOL and dropped into a drawer. A meeting has been arranged to discuss the safety of the exhibits. Some of the curators think the objects should stay in their cases. Too many of them are flitting away and never turning up. That or they are found wasting somewhere on a lay-by or in a car-boot sale. They'll turn up completely wrecked, scratched, dismembered, smashed to smithereens.

'It is a pity,' they all agree, and a decision is reached. The assistant clicks his biro, and it is marked in the minutes.

*

It is a fine day, and the sun glints off the four wheels that follow the boy and his grandfather up the hill. The boy wears wellington boots that gulp the air each time he takes a step. He turns every few minutes to check the pram, which is unrecognisable. The great black belly of the thing has been lifted out, and in its place there is something new. It's not grand-looking, just a couple of wooden planks low to the ground, a seat, the brackets and some new bolts, and a steering pivot at the front, a rope attached to it. The boy calls it a go-cart. His grandfather calls it a bogey. But this isn't important. Both have agreed on a name.

When they reach the top of the hill they look out over the town, the cemetery just below them, the railway track, the depots and warehouses, and further away the school and the houses. The boy sits on the grass behind the cart and the old man bends down with his hands on his knees. The boy lifts the seat up and gives the rear wheels a spin. They've been oiled. They're good. His grandfather takes out a small paintbrush and a white pot, and they carefully paint on the name.

'Will it take long to dry?' asks the boy.

'No.'

The grandfather is the only one who watches the maiden voyage, but he feels like a whole crowd watching a race. He can hear that cheering at the final furlong. But not joy, not yet, just something deep down, a long-held desire that can no longer wait. The boy puts his wellies up on the axle, ready to go, and waits for the push.

The old man takes a moment. He looks out over the cemetery and thinks of all the bones beneath the soil, neat bones in wooden boxes in straight rows, flowers in vases on the top. His poor mother is buried there. He takes a breath.

'The air is clean here,' he says.

The boy's nose is running and he wipes it with a sleeve.

'Uhuh.'

The old man places his hand on the back of the seat. He feels the weight of the boy and the cart, and feels the eagerness in the wheels. He watches his grandson pull the rope taut.

'This is cool,' says the boy.

And then the waiting is over. The boy picks up speed and he's away sailing, wheels flickering in a blur and the dust making clouds, the boy whooping with joy as he takes the bumps.

Jumping it clear every time.

*And he's getting the most tremendous cheer from the crowd! They're willing him home now. And it's Red Rum. And he's coming up to the line.*

*And they're willing him home now. And they're willing him home.*

# Black Vodka

DEBORAH LEVY

The first time I met Lisa I knew she was going to help me become a very different sort of man. Knowing this felt like a summer holiday. It made me relax and I am usually quite a tense person. There is something you should know about me. I have a hump on my back, a mound between my shoulder blades. You will notice when I wear a shirt without a jacket that there is more to me than first meets the eye. It's strange how fascinating human beings find both celebrity and deformity in their own species. People sink their eyes into my hump for six seconds longer than protocol allows, and try to work out the difference between them and myself. The boys called me 'Ali' at school because that's what they thought camels were called.

Ali Ali Ali. Ali's got the hump. The word 'playground' does not really provide an accurate sense of the sort of ethnic cleansing that went on behind the gates that were supposed to keep us safe from potential predators. I was instructed in the art of Not Belonging from a very tender age. Deformed. Different. Strange. Go Ho-me Ali, Go Ho-me. In fact I was born in Southend-on-Sea, and so were the boys, but I was exiled to the Arabian Desert and not allowed to smoke with them behind the local cockle sheds.

There is something else you ought to know about me. I write copy for a leading advertising agency. I earn a lot of money and my colleagues reluctantly respect me because they suspect I'm less content than they are. I have made it my professional business to understand that no one respects ruddy-faced happiness.

I first glimpsed Lisa at the presentation launch for the branding and naming of a new vodka. My agency had won the account for the advertising campaign and I was standing on a small raised stage, pointing to a slide of a starry night sky. I adjusted my mic clip and began.

'Black Vodka,' I said, slightly sinisterly, '... "*Vodka Noir*", will appeal to those in need of stylish angst. As Victor Hugo put it so well, "We are alone, bereft and the night falls upon us"; to drink Black Vodka is to be in mourning for our lives.'

I explained that if vodka was mostly associated with the communist countries of the former Eastern bloc, it was well known that the exploration of abstract, subjective and conceptual ideas in these regimes was the ultimate defiance of the individual against the state. Black Vodka had to hitch a nostalgic ride on all of this and be packaged as a dangerous choice for the cultured and discerning.

My colleagues sipped their lattes (the intern had done the Starbucks run) and listened carefully to my angle. When I insisted that Vodka Noir had high cheekbones, a few of the guys laughed uneasily: I am known in the office as the Crippled Poet. And then I noticed someone sitting in the audience – a woman with long brown hair, very blonde at the ends, who was not from the agency. She had her arms folded across her grey cashmere sweater; an open notebook lay on her lap. Now and again she'd pick it up and doodle with her pencil. My sharp eyes (long sight) confirmed that this stranger in our small community was observing me rather clinically.

After my presentation my colleague Richard introduced me to the woman with the notebook. Although he did not say so, I assumed she was his new girlfriend. Richard is known for splashing his footballer's body with a heady cologne, West Indian Limes, every morning. Its effect on me is both arousing and desperately melancholy: I'll never have a body like his. Anyway, it was quite a shock to see him with the woman whose clinical gaze had for some mysterious reason awoken in me the kind of nihilistic lust I was attempting to whip up in my Vodka Noir campaign.

Richard smiled affectionately at me, apparently amused at something he couldn't be bothered to explain.

'Lisa is an archaeologist. I thought she'd be interested in your presentation.'

Her eyes were long-lidded and blue.

'Would you buy Black Vodka, Lisa?'

She told me she would, yes, she would give it a go, and then she screamed because Richard had crept up behind her and his hands were clasping her narrow waist like a handcuff.

As I put away my laptop, I felt an unwelcome blast of bitter anger. I suddenly wanted more than anything else to be a man without a burden on his back. After a presentation we tend to open champagne and instruct the interns to order in snacks. But when I saw a tray of sun-dried tomatoes arranged on tiny pesto-filled pastry cases I wanted to punch them onto the floor. A lifetime spent looking forward to office canapés suddenly seemed unbearable.

I left the office early. I even left without asking my boss what he thought of my presentation. Tom Mines is the Cruel Man of the agency (though he would call his cruelty 'insight') and he suffers from livid eczema on his wrists and hands. He buys jackets with extra-long sleeves – for obvious reasons I am always fascinated by how people conceal their physical suffering. I muttered something about being summoned to an emergency and left quickly before Tom could point out that the emergency was me. But I did not leave before walking straight over to Lisa, aware that Tom Mines had his eye on me, his thin grey fingers twisted around the cuffs of his jacket. What I did next might sound strange: I gave Richard's girlfriend my business card. The surprise she attempted to express with her facial muscles, her raised eyebrows, her mocking lips slightly parted – it really was not that convincing because of what I had seen. When Lisa was doodling in her notebook, she had let it rest open on her lap. From my position on the raised stage, I could see quite clearly that she had drawn a sketch of me on the left-hand page. A picture of a naked, hunchbacked man with every single organ of his body labelled. Underneath her rather too accurate portrait (should I be flattered that she had imagined me naked?) she'd scribbled two words: *Homo sapiens.*

She called me. Lisa actually pressed the digits that connected her voice to mine. I asked her straight away if she'd like to join me for supper that Friday. No she couldn't make Friday. It is usual for people attracted to each other to pretend they have full and busy lives, but I have an incredible facility to wade through human shame with no shoes on. I told her if she couldn't make Friday I was free on Monday, Tuesday, Wednesday and Thursday, and that the weekend looked hopeful too.

We agreed to meet on Wednesday in South Kensington (she said she liked the big sky in that part of town) and I suggested we drink our way through the vast menu of flavoured vodkas at the Polish Club, not far from the Royal Albert Hall. This way we could conduct a bit of field research for my Vodka Noir concept – she said she was more than happy to be my assistant. That night I went to bed and dreamt (again) of Poland. In this recurring dream I am in Warsaw on a train to Southend-on-Sea. There is a soldier in my carriage. He kisses his mother's hand and then he kisses his girlfriend's lips. I am watching him in the old mirror attached to the wall of our carriage and I can see he has a humped back under his khaki uniform. My gaze on this soldier tells me I am looking at him not as a man, but as a specimen. When I wake up there are always tears on my cheeks, transparent as vodka but warm as rain.

There's something about rain that makes me slam the doors of cabs extra hard. I love the rain. It heightens every gesture, injects it with 5 ml of unspecific yearning. On Wednesday night it was raining when the cab dropped me off on Exhibition Road in London's Zone 1. In the distance I could see autumn leaves on the tall trees in Hyde Park. The air was soft and cool. I began to walk up Exhibition Road and knew that where now there are paving stones there were once fields and market gardens. I wanted to lie in one of those fields with Lisa stretched lazily across my lap, and I wanted the schoolboys who told me I was a freak to watch us as we murmured in the London grass. I walked deliberately slowly to the white Georgian town house that is the Polish Club. The building was donated to the Polish resistance during the Second World War and later became a cultural meeting place, a second home to the refugees and exiles who could not return to a Stalin-shaped Poland. As you might guess, I have made it my business to study the deformities of famous and powerful men. Like myself, Stalin was physically misshapen; his face was pitted from the smallpox that he had contracted as a child, one of his arms was longer than the other, his eyes were yellow (people called him 'tiger') and he was short enough in stature to wear platform shoes. No country, or animal, for that matter, would be pleased to be Stalin-shaped, unless he was 'beautiful inside' as morons put it, but he was not: he was angry, hard, paranoid, fatherless – and should have listened to his mother who wanted him to be a priest, which, by the way, is what my mother wanted me to be too.

I have always thought of myself as lost property, someone waiting to be claimed, and always feel grateful to be offered a home for a few hours at the Polish Club. I hung my coat on a wooden hanger, placed it on the clothes rail in the foyer and made my way into the bar, where my booking in the dining room was confirmed by a polite and serene waitress from Lublin. She discreetly invited me to 'perhaps enjoy a drink until my companion arrives'.

Keen to obey her, I ordered pepper vodka. Thirty minutes later I had researched the raspberry, peppermint, honey, caraway, plum and apple vodkas and the sky was darkening outside the window. An elderly woman in a green felt hat sat on the velvet chair next to me, scribbling some sort of mathematical equation on a scrap of paper. She was so lost in thought that I began to worry that somewhere else in the world, another mathematician would pick up on those thoughts and at this very moment, 8.25 p.m., find a strategy to solve the equation before she did. It was possible that while she sat in her chair struggling with the endless zeros that seemed to so perplex her, someone else would be standing on a stage in Brazil or Ljubljana collecting a fat cheque for their contribution to human knowledge. Would I, too, be waiting endlessly for Lisa, who was probably at this moment lying in Richard's arms while he kissed the zero of her mouth?

No I would not. She arrived, late and breathless, and I could see she was genuinely sorry to have kept me waiting. I ordered her three shot glasses of the cherry vodka while she told me the reason she was late was that she had been planning a dig that was soon to take place in Cornwall, but the computer had crashed and she'd lost most of her data.

Sometimes there is nothing that feels as good as living in the present tense. That is where I want to live, in the present, in the here and now for ever; the past of my youth, the there and then was not a good place to be. Is it strange, then, that I am attracted to a woman who is mostly concerned with digging up the past? Lisa and I are sitting in the dining room of the Polish Club on our first date. We arrange the starched linen napkins over our laps and discuss the oily black eggs, the caviar that comes from the beluga, osetra and sevruga varieties of sturgeon. The waitress from Lublin takes our order and Lisa, naturally, wants to know a little bit more about me.

'So where do you live?' My anthropologist asks me this as if I am an exotic find that she is required to label in black Indian ink.

I tell her I own a three-bedroomed flat with a west-facing balcony in an exceptional Victorian double-fronted villa in Notting Hill Gate. I want to bore her. Better slowly to prove more interesting than I first appear. 'It's a pretty good conversion and I have access to a communal wine cellar.'

Lisa looks bored.

She plays with the ends of her hair. She shuts her eyes and then opens them. She fiddles with her mobile, which she has placed on the table. I don't own a mobile as a matter of principle. Mobiles are the modern umbilicus – something adults need to hang on to in order to convince themselves they are not bereft and alone in the world.

Lisa shuffles her shoes, which are red and suede. She eats a hearty portion of duck with apple sauce and discovers I like delicate dumplings stuffed with mushroom because I am a vegetarian. When she stabs her fork into the meat it oozes pale red blood, which she mops up with a piece of white bread; little delicate dabs of the wrist as she brings the blood and bread up to her mouth. She eats with appetite and enjoyment. That she is a carnivore pleases me.

After a while she orders a slice of cheesecake and asks me if I was born a hunchback.

'Yes.'

'Sometimes it's difficult to tell.'

'What do you mean?'

'Well, some people have bad posture.'

'Oh.'

Lisa licks her fingers. Apparently it's an excellent cheesecake; I am pleased she is pleased. The waitress offers us a glass of liqueur from a bottle that has 'a whole Italian pear' lurking inside it. The pear is peeled. It is a naked pear. We accept, and I say to Lisa, 'We should get that pear out of the bottle and make a sorbet with it' – as if that is something I do all the time. In fact I have never made sorbet. She likes that. It is as if the invitation to wedge the pear out of the bottle is like freeing a genie. She becomes more animated and talks about her job. Apparently what most interests her is the human form. When she finds human remains on a dig – bones, for example – they have to be stored in a methodical way. Heavy bones, the long bones, are packed at the bottom of a box, while lighter bones such as vertebrae are packed at the top.

'Archaeology is an approach to uncovering the past,' she tells me, sipping her liqueur, which strangely does not taste of pear.

'So when you go on a dig you record and interpret the physical remains of the past, is that right?'

'Sort of. I like to know how people used to live and what their habits were.'

'You dig up their beliefs and culture.'

'Well, you can't dig up a belief,' she says. 'But the material culture, the objects and artefacts that people leave behind, will give me clues to their beliefs.'

'I see. You know why I like you, Lisa?'

'Why do you like me?'

'Because I think you see me as an archaeological site.'

'I am a bit of an explorer,' she says. I'd like to see the bone that protrudes in your thoracic spine.'

At that moment I drop the silver fork from my right hand. It falls noiselessly to the carpet and bounces before it falls again. I bend down to pick it up, and because I am nervous and have downed too many vodkas, I start to go on an archaeological dig of my own. In my mind I lift up the faded rose-pink carpet of the Polish Hearth Club in South Kensington and find underneath it a forest full of wild mushrooms and swooping bats that live upside down. This is a Polish forest covered in new snow in the murderous twentieth century. At the same time, in the twenty-first, I can see the feet of customers eating herrings with sour cream two metres away from my own table. Their shoes are made from suede and leather. Around them a grey wolf prowls, its ears alert to the sound of spoons stirring chocolate-dusted cappuccinos. When the wolf starts to dig up an unnamed grave that has just been filled with soil, I'm frightened by the dark forest in my mind, so I pick up the fork and nod at Lisa, who has been gazing at the lump on my back as if staring through the lens of a microscope.

The rain tonight is horizontal. It makes me feel reckless. I want to give in to its force. As we walk onto Exhibition Road I slip my arm around Lisa's shoulders and she does not grimace. Her hair is soaking wet and so are her red suede shoes.

'I am going home,' she tells me. She hails a vacant taxi on the other side of the road, and all the time the warm rain falls upon us like the tears in my dream. Her voice is gentle. Rain does that to voices. It makes them intimate and suggestive. While the taxi does a U-turn she stands behind me and presses her hands into my hump as if she is listening to it breathe. And then she takes her forefinger and traces around it, getting an exact sense of its shape. It's the kind of thing cops do to a corpse with a piece of chalk. Now Lisa bends down and opens the door of the taxi. As she slides her long legs into the back seat, she shouts her destination to the driver. 'Tower Bridge.'

He nods and adjusts the meter.

When she smiles I can see her sharp white teeth.

'Look, you know that Richard is my boyfriend – but why don't you come home with me for a coffee?'

I don't need any persuading. I jump in beside her and slam the door extra hard. As the cab pulls out, Lisa leans forwards and starts to kiss me. Is she curious to find out if her sketch of *Homo sapiens* was an accurate representation of my body?

The meter is going berserk like my heartbeat while the moon drifts over the Natural History Museum. Somewhere inside it, pressed under glass, are twelve ghost moths (*Hepialus humuli*), of earliest evolutionary lineage. These ghosts once flew in pastures, dropped their eggs to the ground and slept through the day. There is so much of life to record and classify it's hard to know what kind of language to find for it, so I will start exactly where I am now. Life is beautiful! Vodka is black! Pears are naked! Rain is horizontal! Moths are ghosts! I was born in the Arabian Desert! Only some of this is true, but you should know that this does not scare me nearly as much as the promise of love.

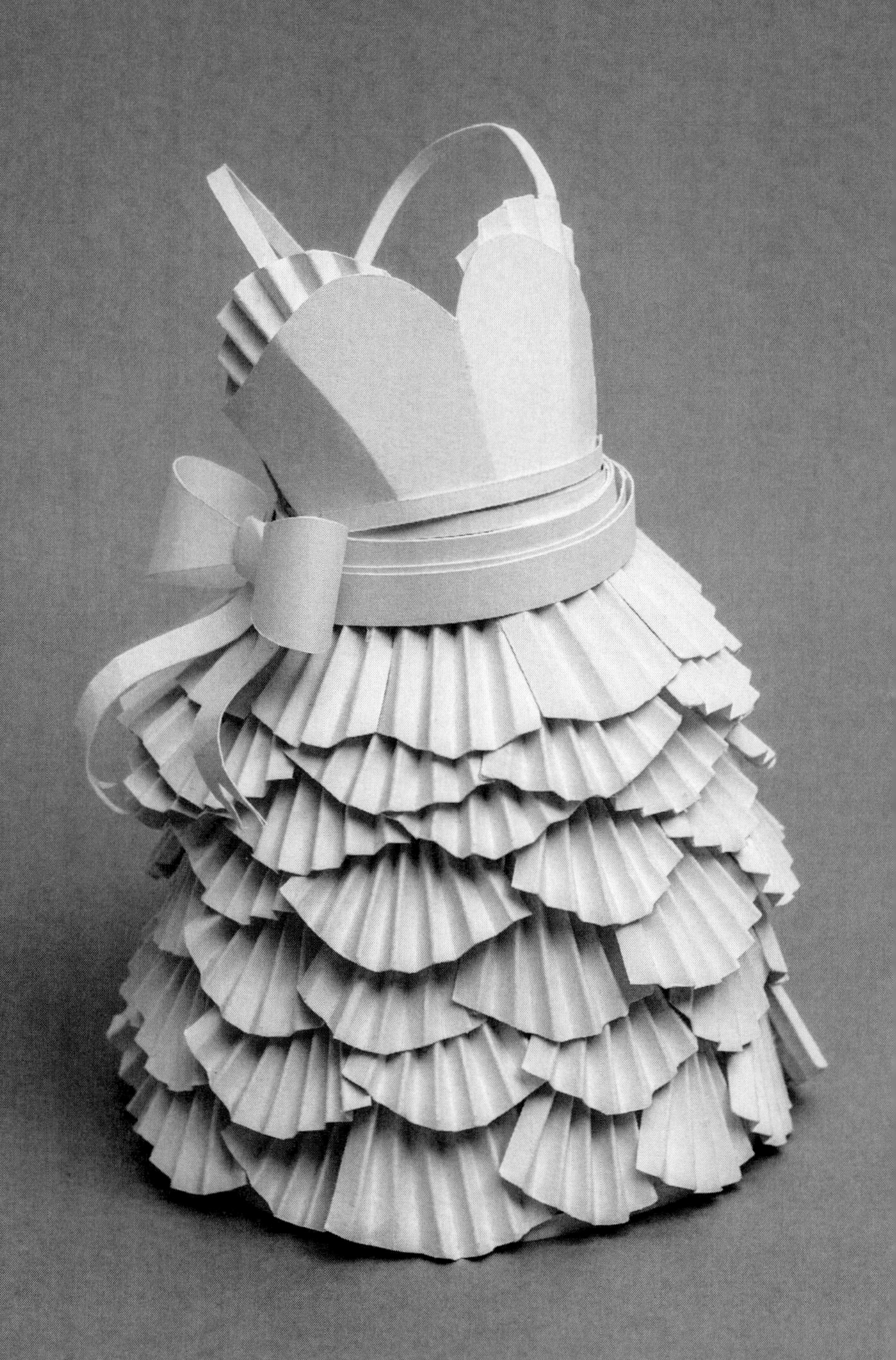

# Message in a (Klein) Bottle

RUSSELL HOBAN

*To the memory of Marcia Wilson*

She was beautiful like a woman in a dream whose face vanishes as you wake up. Words from Rilke came to mind: 'For Beauty is nothing but the Beginning of Terror ...'

She stood before me in the Science Museum. Behind her was a display case full of Klein bottles. Her eyes were green, her long coppery hair beckoned with its gleams and there was a wildness about her; almost I seemed to hear pan pipes and the rhythmic stamping of the goat-legged god.

I was at the Klein-bottle exhibit because it's one of my contemplation points; I come here every so often to think about Infinity and that sort of thing. I could think about Infinity looking at the stars but the scale is more human here and there are more chances of meeting someone interesting. Another of my contemplation points is Van Hoogstraten's *Peepshow* in Room 18 at the National Gallery. In the peepshow is a little black-and-white dog whom I call Hendryk. The peepshow is a box of tricks in which the viewer is fooled into seeing things as they are not by the use of apparent perspectives that are false. Hendryk and I often discuss the Illusion of Reality and the Reality of Illusion. I always come away from our talks refreshed, after which I go down into Trafalgar Square, consult Landseer's lions and exchange a few words with Admiral Nelson. But I digress.

The green-eyed beauty looked me over as if she were buying a horse. When she spoke her voice was as clear as a mezzo-soprano bell. 'You're pretty old,' she said.

'What else is new?' I neighed.

Her green eyes flickered. 'Want to be young again?'

My youth had not been a happy time. 'I'll have to think about that,' I said.

With her eyes on my face she did a sort of shimmy that began at her shoulders and passed like the travelling impulse of an ocean wave down the length of her body to her feet.

'OK,' I said. 'What do I have to do?'

She eyed me critically. 'How daring are you?'

'More than some, less than others – it depends on the situation.'

'How are you with going into something where you don't know how or even if you'll come out of it?'

'Why would I do that?'

Fixing me with a promissory smile she did her ocean-wave shimmy once more.

Outside in Exhibition Road the sun was shining, there were people and coaches and ice-cream vans. She stood there looking at me with her beauty ticking over like something with twin carburettors.

‘Vroom vroom,’ I said quietly. ‘I’m your man.’ We all have to go some time, I was thinking, so it might as well be in a good cause.

‘Do you love me?’ she said.

‘Yes,’ I said, ‘I love you.’

‘I don’t mean like an old man’s one-night fantasy,’ she said. ‘I mean, like a wild ocean under a grey dawn; I mean, like an albatross soaring in high sunlight. Do you love me like that?’

‘Yes,’ I said, ‘I love you like that.’

‘What about spaces?’

‘What kind of spaces?’ There was a shoulder bag on the floor beside her; she sat on her heels by it, her short skirt offering a flash of legs, and took out a complex Klein bottle identical to number 15 in the display. The card in the exhibit said:

> *These Klein bottles were made for the Museum by Alan Bennett during 1996. Bennett was interested in the relation between the Klein bottle and the Möbius strip, a one-sided surface featured in case N17 etc.*

*Encyclopaedia Britannica* defines the Klein bottle thus:

> *Topological space, named for the German mathematician Felix Klein. The surface is not constructible in three-dimensional Euclidean space but has interesting properties, such as being one-sided, like the Möbius strip …*

‘This is Bennett’s fifteenth variation on the theme,’ she said. The thing was suggestive, in miniature, of a wind instrument for a

Martian marching band. 'It passes through itself five times,' she said, 'and you know what else?'

'Not yet.'

'It's an itinerary.'

Suddenly I wanted to get away from her, shimmy, legs and all.

Seeing me poised for flight, she grabbed me with her green eyes and said, 'What are you afraid of?'

'If that's the itinerary,' I said, 'I'm not taking the trip.'

'And you said you loved me!'

'I do, but I have no intention of passing through myself five times or whatever. My mama didn't raise no fools.'

She switched off her beauty and sulked.

'It's no use sulking,' I said.

'I'm not sulking – look again.'

I looked. She had switched on Mute Appeal. 'OK,' I said, 'speak your Mute Appeal.'

'I didn't choose the itinerary,' she murmured with Touching Vulnerability. 'Passing through myself five times with you is not my idea of a whole lot of fun: it's my punishment.'

'Who's punishing you?' I said.

'My mother.'

'Your mother! Where?'

'Where what?'

'Where'd she lay this on you?'

'Here. Where else? This is where we live, OK? We're inhabitants.'

'You eat here, sleep here, live here round the clock?'

'Yes. What's so strange about that?'

'Nothing, I guess. Are you able to go out?'

'Sure – we're not prisoners, we go wherever we like.'

'How'd this come about?'

'Do you think things have souls?'

'What kind of things are we talking about?'

'The *Rokeby Venus* in the National Gallery, for example?'

'Definitely.'

'The *Columbine* locomotive here in this museum?'

'Yes.'

'Well, souls pull other souls. Say the *Columbine* or James Watts's steam engine pulls a visitor who comes back again and again and after a while they don't go away any more – that's how people become inhabitants.'

'Are there inhabitants in other museums?'

'Not only museums: everywhere. You front people are just what's in front of us back people.'

'Is that what I am, a front person?'

She regarded me thoughtfully. 'For now.'

'And later?'

'That remains to be seen. Let's talk about something else.'

'All right. Can you tell me why you're being punished?'

'It's a long story.'

'I've got time to listen, I'm self-employed.'

'What's your name?'

'Walter. What's yours?'

'Ondine.'

'Ondine! Are you a water nymph?'

'If I had a fiver for every time I've been asked that I'd be a wealthy woman.'

'Sorry. But why *are* you being punished?'

'Mum and I don't see eye to eye on what you might call the Big Picture. And she's got the power to punish me, so I get punished.'

'Tell me more about what you and your mother disagree on.'

'This is not the time for that. Let's get this trip over with.'

'Yes, but how? We'd have to be the size of a birdshot pellet to get through that tubing. How're we going to manage that?'

She showed me what looked like a black jelly bean.

'What's that?' I said.

'I don't know. Something ethnic. I got it from one of the inhabs at Natural History. Although we can't actually get small enough for the trip we can *experience* it with this.'

'Will I come out the same as I go in?'

'Everybody changes from moment to moment: that's life.'

'That's an evasive answer, Ondine.'

'What're you, Walter, a certainty freak? I'm doing the trip with you; we're in this together. What more do you want?'

'A little more daring than I've got, actually.'

'Everybody wants a little more, sweetheart: the three hundred Spartans at Thermopylae would have liked a few hundred more; Custer would have been delighted with four or five more regiments at the Little Big Horn; General Gordon could have used a little more backup at Khartoum. Heroes just grit their teeth and get on with the job.'

'And they tend to die early.'

'You looking for immortality?'

'Maybe I'm just not a hero.'

'Better hero up fast then: this is no time to show the white feather, OK? Let's do this thing already.'

'We've been getting some curious glances from passers-by. Are we going to do it out here where everybody can see us?'

'No.' She led the way back inside to a dark little oubliette with nothing in it but some jumbled stacks of *Nature* on the floor. She set the Klein bottle down, showed me her jelly bean and said, 'Ready?'

'Do we hold hands or what?'

'If you like. Kiss me for luck and we're off.'

'You scared?'

'Of course I'm scared – I don't know any more than you do about what's going to happen and it *is*, after all, a punishment.'

'Right. Remind me, why am I in this with you?'

'Because you love me. You said you did. You do, don't you?'

'Of course I do … hang on.'

'What?'

'You've never said you love *me*.'

'I know.'

'Do you?'

'I've never loved anyone and I don't know if I'm capable of it.'

'Why is that?'

'I don't know. Half the time I'm not even sure that I exist.'

'But you want me to love you, and you want it with wild oceans and soaring albatrosses and all the trimmings.'

'Please don't mock me, Walter – in practical matters I function pretty well but emotionally I'm a mess. I want you to stick with me, if that means anything to you. Does it?'

'Yes, it does.'

'*Will* you stick with me?'

'Yes, I will.'

'Because … ?'

'Because I love you.'

'Can you say more? I'm sorry to be greedy, but I don't know how to take in whatever this is between us. Do you and I belong together? We don't look like a well-matched couple.'

'But you said you wanted me to stick with you.'

'Yes, I did but I don't entirely understand any of what's

happening.'

'Ondine, at my age I've learned to be true to my own craziness. I fell in love with you irrationally and I'm content to go where it takes me. How much craziness is there in you?'

She looked at me in silence for a moment, then, 'Let's get this trip over with,' she said quietly.

I held her close and kissed her. I could feel her ribs through her blouse. Her self-assurance seemed gone and I wondered if I could protect her. Then we both put into our mouths what we hoped were not one-way tickets.

Oh! How to describe the indescribable? Nausea, dizziness, violent stomach pains. Holding tight to Ondine's hand I kept my eyes shut until the world stopped spinning. Eventually a stillness arrived and I opened my eyes to see number 15, huge and frightening, gaping at us.

We approached the opening that seemed the obvious point of entry and we paused to consider how to negotiate the glittering glass coils curving above us. I had been expecting us to be sucked in with a whoosh but apparently it wasn't going to be that simple.

'We're going to have to run all the way,' said Ondine, looking worried. 'You can see by the way the tubing curves round that we'll be upside down for part of each passage, so we've got to develop enough speed to carry us around. Can you do it?' The way she looked at me sadly and hopefully went straight to my heart.

'I'll do my best,' I said, 'and if it kills me that'll wipe the slate clean.'

Ondine shook her head: 'Don't say that, Walter. Try in your mind to see yourself doing it. Please, if you love me, don't leave me here alone.'

'I'll never leave you alone, sweetheart.' I took her hand. 'Let's roll.'

We rolled. Upside-down running? Easy-peasy. The black jelly bean must have had a turbo effect: I was light, I was speedy, I could have danced all night. My hearing had all the colours of the spectrum; my seeing was like a Bach fugue of endless contrapunti. I caught Ondine's eye and we nodded to each other. In we zipped, up, up and over and around that glittering coil and out into …

O, the clarity of it! As far as the eye could see, the eternal blue of childhood's summer sky. And we were naked children paddling in the warm sea that lapped about our legs and hissed on the sand that slid back under our toes. And the sadness, the sadness of childhood that knows not the chill of eternity and the nothingness of no return! We hugged each other and wept and were in the second coil, centuries older but children still.

With each coil the sadness became more intense, heavier, flattening our minds into wordlessness. I remember weeping and grunting as I ran on all fours and I suppose we must have done the whole thing because we were back in the little empty room with the *Nature* magazines, lying exhausted with Ondine's head resting in the crook of my arm as I fell asleep.

I woke up with my arm in the same position but Ondine was gone. In my sudden bereftness I saw that she had become for me that tree on a hillside that I must have in my daily vision. For a few moments I sat motionless while the metaphor visualised itself. I saw the early sunlight on the leaves that stirred and whispered in the summer breeze. The tree was a birch, slender and girlish.

Then I shook myself and lurched out of the little dark room and stumbled to the Klein-bottle exhibit, hoping against hope. She wasn't there. Desperately I hurried to the exit and burst into Exhibition Road where ZONK! The sunlight hit me like a ton of dustbins. Full ones. Oh the coaches, the ice-cream vans, the thin blue sky with so much mileage on it!

I sat down on a bench gasping and wondering what to do next. A black motorcycle puttered into view, a Royal Enfield. A crazy-looking old woman in leathers but no helmet dismounted, her white hair in a ratty ponytail. She sat down beside me and laughed in my face. Bad breath. 'I'm her mum,' she said.

'Whose?'

'You know.' Cackle, cackle. 'I'm her mum but I'll never be your mum-in-law, old lover boy.'

'I wasn't thinking of marriage.'

'Oh no, of course not – you're the free-love type. Well, sonny, there ain't no free lunches and there ain't no free love. You loved *her*, oh yes and very poetically I'm sure, but did she ever say she loved *you*?'

'That isn't something I want to go into with you.'

'Hoity toity! You don't because look at you: why would a juicy young beauty like her go for a dried-up old thing like you?'

'You can mock if you like,' I said, 'but I'm the one she went through number 15 with, I wasn't too dried up for that.'

'You don't look all that daring, if you'll pardon my frankness. How did she get you to do it?'

'I couldn't resist her Touching Vulnerability.'

'I'm deeply moved. What'd she do, shimmy for you?'

'What she did is none of your business.'

'That's where you're wrong, mister. I'm boss here and *everything* is my business, especially my daughter. And by the way, her shimmy cheques bounce.'

'Why were you punishing her?'

'Because she needed it, that's why: she won't do as she's told, she's got all kinds of crazy ideas, and half the time I can't even find her when I want her – and moody, my God! The other day she was all scrunched up in the cab of the *Columbine* with headphones and a little newfangled machine and she was crying. I looked at the CD box and she was listening to *La Trabbiada*.'

'*La Traviata*. I cry at that one too.'

'And the cast! Foreigners every one.'

'Isn't Ondine old enough to be under her own authority?'

'Not while I'm in charge here, and I have no intention of retiring.'

'How'd you get to be her mother?'

'I ran into this handsome inhab down the road and the rest is Natural History.'

'That would've been about twenty years ago?'

'You're trying to guess my age; I look older than I am. I was never pretty but I've got big charisma.'

'Yes, quite. I'd love to stay and chat but I must find Ondine.'

'That'll take you a good long while and she's never going to be your sweetie-pie – don't kid yourself that you're the only thing on her mind: she has projects, she has duties.'

'Like what?'

'Never mind, you don't need to know. Anyhow, she's not the right sort for you. Why do you keep running after her?'

'She may not be the *right* sort but she's *my* sort and I love her, OK? See you.'

I left with the sound of her cackling in my ears and I searched high and low, from Veterinary History on the fifth floor down to the restaurant in the basement, not neglecting anything in between, such as James Watt's steam engine and the *Columbine* where I even looked for her in the cab. After a long time and a lot of legwork I had to admit that sheer plod was not getting me any closer to Ondine.

In the past that sort of non-result might have constituted a severe setback but I was no longer disposed to accept failure meekly and I was beginning to know my way around. Without any further waste of time I went to the Museum of Natural History to find myself a purveyor of ethnic pharmaceuticals. Accordingly I took up a station by T. Rex and stood there fanning myself with a twenty-pound note. I was not inconspicuous, and among those who showed interest were a couple of breezy young women who wanted to know if I was looking for company. I thanked them, explained that I was spoken for, and stopped fanning.

Squadrons of children accompanied by teachers appeared and disappeared, time passed and after a while a Gypsy-looking young man approached me and said, 'What?'

I told him what I wanted. 'Twenty more,' he said. 'You got something she touch?'

I pointed to my mouth. 'She kissed me.'

He said, 'You wait, I bring Granny.'

T. Rex and I yawned together. Children came and went, and in the fullness of time Gypsy and Granny appeared. Granny was a little old woman all in black, with a face like a winter apple, jet-black hair in a single plait down her back, golden hoop earrings, and several gold rings on her fingers. She looked at me long and searchingly, then said something in Romany. Her grandson, who called himself, generically, 'Zingarello', translated: 'This woman, how much you love? Little? Big?'

'Big.'

'Till next month? Next year?'

'For always.'

More Romany from Granny.

'Say woman name three times,' said Zingarello.

'Ondine, Ondine, Ondine.'

Pause.

'Ben down, Granny mus kiss.'

I was surprised by the softness of Granny's lips and the sweetness of her breath. 'Tomorrow,' said Zingarello, 'you come, pick up medicine.'

Where to spend the night? I have a house but the idea of sleeping in that stale and empty space did not appeal to me, so I went to Knightsbridge and bought a sleeping bag, toothbrush and toothpaste at Harrods; then I returned to the Science Museum and the little dark and empty room where Ondine and I had begun our trip. I laid out the sleeping bag with a little stack of *Nature* for a pillow; then I had a meal at the restaurant, visited the lavatory and retired in the late afternoon for the night.

Next morning I was back at the museum as soon as it opened. T. Rex and I waited impatiently for Granny and Zingarello and after what seemed a very long time they turned up. I bowed to Granny, she nodded and smiled and gave me something very small tied up in a black silk kerchief. Then she sang to me wordlessly in a faraway wavering voice that rose and fell, swaying like the trees of childhood memory. After about a minute she stopped abruptly, kissed me and hugged me, then pointed to my little parcel and said something to her grandson.

'When swallow this,' he translated, 'you are sitting comfortable, yes?'

'Yes, indeed,' I said, and so we parted. I understood the wordless song perfectly, and full of hope I hurried back to my hideout in the Science Museum, where I seated myself comfortably and unwrapped my tiny parcel. Printed in red on the black silk kerchief was a sheela-na-gig, the schematic female figure opening with both hands her genitalia. This figure, which was not at all erotic, is reckoned by those in the know to have an apotropaic function. Reflecting on this I took out of the kerchief what looked like a red Smartie.

'Here goes,' I announced to the dark and silent room, and put it into my mouth.

Oh, but it was bitter! And such a wave of eidetic multiplicity swept over me that I had to shut my eyes against the swarming tiny Ondines that filled them: Ondine at the V&A, the Royal Festival Hall, the Serpentine, London Eye, Harrods – here, there and everywhere, like a dyslexic sat-nav, and I had no owner's manual nor any idea how long the Smartie effect might last. With practice I learned how to use my eyes like bifocals looking for the most recent Ondine, which showed itself as the most vivid one.

I don't know how long this went on: I slept at the museum, showered at home, and ate wherever I was when I got hungry. Eventually I found myself in Trafalgar Square on a warm summer evening, an elegiac and Duino evening, an evening redolent of youth and hope and regret. The street lamps were lit against a sky still light, a stage effect that almost makes me cry. On the south side of the Square golden windows glowed in the redness of double-decker sightseeing buses; the bronze merpeople gleamed in the spray of the fountains where the mallards swam in domestic tranquillity; boys reclined on the docile Landseer lions while high above them in the fading light Nelson brooded on his column, remembering Emma and Mediterranean twilights long gone. There were not many pigeons and the people coming from the National Gallery down into the Square scattered in patterned groups as in the opening scene of an opera. And there was Ondine standing in front of me.
'I didn't mean to worry you,' she said, 'but I needed to be alone for a while, I needed to think about things.'

'Did it help?'

'Not much.' She drew her hand across her brow. 'What am I going to do with you?'

'What is it that you do?'

'What do you mean?'

'I mean, when you're out of my sight, which is most of the time, how do you fill your days?'

She was watching me thoughtfully.

'What?' I said.

'I'm wondering how much to tell you.'

'Tell me everything.'

'Why?'

'This thing between you and me, it isn't just a random happening – there's some kind of purpose in it.'

'What kind of purpose?' She was listening with interest.

'I don't know. Maybe we're a demonstration of something.'

'What?'

I walked slowly down my brain's main highway, doing it *langsam, misterioso.* Presently a billboard appeared: 'CRAZINESS', it said, 'IS THE ROCK ON WHICH THE HOUSE OF SANITY IS BUILT.'

'What's that supposed to mean?' said Ondine.

'I'm not sure, I'm just a pilgrim on this road.'

'Man, you really are weird, you know that?'

'Yes, and getting weirder by the minute.'

Ondine laughed and threw up her hands. 'I give up,' she said. 'I'm yours. Take me!'

A certain amount of hugging and kissing ensued. When we had caught our breath she said, 'Now that I'm yours ...'

'Now that I'm yours'! Were sweeter words ever uttered by a sweeter woman? *My* woman, my Ondine!

'Yes, darling,' I said after a few more kisses, 'go on.'

'Now that I'm yours I want to tell you everything.'

'And I want to hear everything. Go ahead, sweetheart, I'm listening.'

'First of all, I'm not what you think I am.'

'What are you?'

'I'm an idealist.'

'I'm sorry to hear that.'

'Does that put you off me?'

'It certainly makes me see you in a new light.'

'Worse than that, I'm an organiser.'

'What are you organising?'

'The back people. If I can get us back people to present a united front I think we can turn this whole thing around.'

'By "this whole thing" you mean … ?'

'The world situation: political, financial, social, ecological – the whole sorry mess.'

'And the back people are going to turn this around?'

'Yes, we'll do it when we take over from the front people.'

'Then the back people will be the front people, right?'

'Right.'

'Darling, I don't like to disillusion you but I have to tell you that Frontness corrupts, and Absolute Frontness corrupts absolutely.' Ondine smiled (indulgently? *Condescendingly*?). 'That's how it's been up to now but we won't make the same mistakes the fronters before us made. Are you with us?'

'Whither thou goest I will follow, although I may weep from time to time amid the alien corn.'

'You're a writer, yes?'

'Art historian.'

'Well, we'll be making history. Will you help me with our

manifesto?'

'Of course. I take it this is to do with the Big Picture that you and your mum don't see eye to eye on?'

'In more ways than one. Her ambition is to buy a gambling casino and our trip was my punishment for refusing to help her raise money for it.'

'How were you meant to do that?'

Ondine made a wry face. 'Escort work and light lifting.'

'Your own mother? What's light lifting?'

'Wallets, watches, jewellery, whatever can be fenced or pawned.'

'Good heavens! I'm going to take you away from all this.'

'The sooner the better. Where to?'

'I have a house in Kensington with a you-shaped emptiness for you to fill up.'

'Whither thou goest I will follow,' she said with a kiss, and thither we repaired, to celebrate with champagne and salt-beef sandwiches.

Ondine and I settled down to a life of domestic bliss and political revisionism and Mum withdrew completely from the Big Picture, her illegal activities forcing her to leave town one jump ahead of the Law.

So there we are: our trip with all those passages through ourselves brought us to a pretty good place in what is not the end but a new beginning. Mum is now my absentee mum-in-law and Ondine's shimmy-cheque did not bounce. My message to the world is this: when in doubt, be true to your own craziness. If you have nothing better to do.

# About the Authors

## KAMILA SHAMSIE

Kamila Shamsie is the prize-winning author of five novels, including *Burnt Shadows*, which was shortlisted for the Orange Prize for Fiction, and has been translated into over twenty languages. She has also written a work of non-fiction, *Offence: The Muslim Case*. A trustee of Free Word and English PEN, she grew up in Karachi and now lives in London.

## ALI SMITH

Ali Smith is a writer of novels, short stories, plays and criticism. Her novel *The Accidental* won the Whitbread Novel Award in 2005 and was shortlisted for both the Man Booker Prize and the Orange Prize for Fiction. Her most recent novel is *There But For The*, published by Hamish Hamilton. She lives in Cambridge.

## CLARE WIGFALL

Clare Wigfall was born in London in 1976. Her debut collection of short stories, *The Loudest Sound and Nothing*, was published by Faber and Faber in 2007 to great critical acclaim. In 2008 she won the internationally renowned BBC National Short Story Award for 'The Numbers', the opening story from the collection, and was nominated by William Trevor for the E.M. Forster Award. She currently lives in Berlin.

## IAIN SINCLAIR

Iain Sinclair was born in 1943 in Cardiff and now lives in Hackney, East London. The psychogeography of London is a central theme in his work. He is the author of many books including *Lud Heat*, *Scarlet Tracings*, *Downriver* (winner of the James Tait Black Memorial Prize and the Encore Award), *Landor's Tower*, *London Orbital* and *Hackney, That Rose-Red Empire*, shortlisted for the 2010 Ondaatje Prize. He is also the editor of *London: City of Disappearances.*

## ABDULRAZAK GURNAH

Abdulrazak Gurnah was born in 1948 in Zanzibar. He came to Britain as a student in 1967 and now teaches literature at the University of Kent. He is the author of seven novels, which include *Paradise* (shortlisted for both the Booker and the Whitbread Prizes), *By the Sea* (longlisted for the Booker Prize and awarded the RFI Témoin du Monde Prize) and *Desertion* (shortlisted for the Commonwealth Prize). His most recent novel is *The Last Gift*, published by Bloomsbury in May 2011.

## HANAN AL-SHAYKH

Hanan al-Shaykh was born in Lebanon and grew up in Beirut. She was educated in Cairo and wrote her first novel there when she was nineteen before returning to Beirut to work as a journalist for *Al-Nahar* newspaper and *Al Hasna* magazine. In 1975 she left Beirut because of the civil war, and since 1984 she has lived in London. Her work has been translated into more than thirty languages and is now published around the world. Six of her novels have been translated into English – her novel *Only in London* was shortlisted for the Independent Foreign Fiction Prize – and she is also the author of a memoir, *The Locust and the Bird*. Her adaptation of the classic Arabic tales *One Thousand and One Nights* was written to coincide with the 2011 world tour of a musical and theatrical production directed by Tim Supple.

WIAM EL-TAMAMI is a writer and translator. Her work has appeared in *Granta*, *Banipal* and *Alif*, among others. In 2011 she was awarded the Harvill Secker Young Translators' Prize. She has lived in Egypt, Kuwait, England and Vietnam, and is currently based in Cairo.

## ELEANOR THOM

Eleanor Thom was born in London in 1979. She won the New Writing Ventures Award in 2006 with a chapter of *The Tin-Kin*, her debut novel, which was based on photos, artefacts and memories of Eleanor's mother's Travelling family. It was awarded The Saltire Society First Book of the Year Award. Eleanor was selected by the *Guardian* as one of the twelve best new novelists of 2011. She lives in Ayr with her husband and son.

## DEBORAH LEVY

Deborah Levy writes fiction, plays and poetry. Her work has been staged by the Royal Shakespeare Company. Her highly acclaimed novel, *Swimming Home*, serialised on BBC Radio 4, is published by And Other Stories. Deborah was Writing Fellow at the Royal College of Art and lives in London.

## RUSSELL HOBAN

Russell Hoban was born in Pennsylvania but was a resident of London for more than thirty years. He was the author of many extraordinary novels including *Turtle Diary*, *Amaryllis Night and Day*, *The Bat Tattoo*, *Her Name Was Lola*, *Come Dance with Me*, *Linger Awhile*, *My Tango with Barbara Strozzi* and, most famous of all, the modern classic *Riddley Walker* (described by Anthony Burgess as 'what literature is meant to be'). He wrote some classic books for children including the *Frances* books and *The Mouse and his Child*. He died in December 2011 at the age of eighty-six, survived by his wife and children.

# About the Editor

Mary Morris began her editorial career at Bloomsbury Publishing in 2003. She went on to manage the general list at Gerald Duckworth, publishing literary fiction, history, biography, popular science and travel books. She has since worked as Senior Development Editor at the British Museum Press and is now a fiction editor at Faber and Faber. She co-runs the Faber Social, a monthly literary night in London, and is part of the books team at Port Eliot Festival.

# Finding my Rainbow

Yvonne Junor

First published by Busybird Publishing 2023



**ISBN:**
Paperback: 978-0-646-87810-2
Ebook: 978-0-6458622-0-1



**Cover Image:** Adobe Stock

**Cover design:** Busybird Publishing

**Layout and typesetting**: Busybird Publishing

Busybird Publishing
2/118 Para Road
Montmorency, Victoria
Australia 3094
www.busybird.com.au

# Dedication

*This book is dedicated to the memories of my husband, Grant Lamont; my parents, Clive and Christine Junor; and my sister Joy French (nee Junor) Though you are all gone, you are all forever loved and never forgotten.*

*To my daughters Elisha and Jacinta, I love you dearly and am so proud of you.*

*To my family, friends, doctors and counsellors who have shared my journey, thank you.*

*Lastly, a special thanks to my editor Annie Collins, whose skill and guidance has made all the difference to this book.*

# Contents

# Introduction

I've always been a nurturer, taking an interest in all aspects of health. My leanings towards working in the nutrition, healing and creativity industries are testament to that. As a child of the sixties, I enjoyed being physically active, appreciating the benefits of exercise and fresh air for my health. We rode our bikes, climbed trees, played in the parks and local quarry, and made mud pies in the unmade road.

The only painful and difficult part of my childhood was a diagnosis of cholesteatoma – a condition Oscar Wilde is believed to have suffered from. He purportedly died of meningitis brought on by this condition.

For me, it took the form of a growth in my left ear, causing a middle-ear infection, which destroyed my mastoid bone and left me with hearing loss. This led to several operations, including inserting tubes in my ear drum, a skin graft and removal of tonsils and adenoids –the favoured medical treatment at the time.

Understandably, my parents were anxious, and my sister Anne said she could remember our mum busying herself with housework on the days of the operations to try to take her mind off worrying. Personally, I dreaded the doctor visits – the treatment was painful. But it also had a mental and emotional impact on me. The primary school I attended had a swimming pool, and since I wasn't allowed to get my ear wet, I had to sit on the sidelines, isolated and miserable.

As I grew older, I developed my love of nurturing by undertaking qualifications in food, the arts and aged care, and by travelling to expand my cultural awareness. What I wasn't prepared for was the impact that mental health issues, both inside and outside my home, would have on my personal development, nor the path of learning and growth it would lead me on.

Like a lot of young women of the time, in my twenties, I yearned to be married with children, thinking this would fulfil the most important part of my life. And it did for a time, albeit arriving later than I expected. It was a dream come true, but as with all dreams, not everything was as fairytale perfect as I imagined it would be – darkness lingered in the corners, waiting to play its role.

The man I married had intense emotional needs and a dependant personality. Of course, I wasn't conscious of this in the early stages of our relationship – it only became apparent when his mental health issues worsened. What played out led to my own nervous breakdown in direct response to his deterioration. A double whammy. Now, in my role of nurturer, not only did I have to look after him, but somehow, I had to find a way to heal us both within our crumbling relationship.

My pursuit for healing went into overdrive, but ultimately, it wasn't to be, and the worst imaginable outcome sent me and my children spiralling into despair. Although I believe my husband and I were destined to be together – in the grand scheme of things, there were spiritual lessons each of us were to learn in our time together – he did not heal on this physical plane and, instead, chose to take his own life.

My story is one of tragedy and triumph, of enlightenment as to why humans feel compelled to act in certain ways, why we push in directions that are detrimental to our own wellbeing and perhaps that of others. Why our journeys lead us on paths unknown, yet seemingly destined. But ultimately, it's a story of healing. From being at my lowest point in life, facing debilitating adversity and fighting to rise above it all.

Writing this book has been a lifelong dream. I feel excited, nervous and happy to have achieved this project. It is my wish that it provides a message of hope, faith that there are always ways to heal from the traumas we are dealt in life.

# The Shed

## January 2010

Monday morning, I woke at seven o'clock to the sound of bird song outside my bedroom window and a blue-sky dawn streaked with orange. The children must have been still fast asleep. My husband, Grant, was due to return to work this day, and I turned to look at him. We'd argued the previous night and gone to bed angry – him saying no one was helping him with his anxiety, depression, huge mood swings and suicidal thoughts. Me, exhausted, at the end of my rope.

His side of the bed was empty, the doona pulled back, sheets cold to the touch. Sometimes this was the case with his insomnia. Often, he would fall asleep on the couch and not come to bed at all.

Instantly hyper-alert, I got up to search the house. There was no sign of him inside, so I headed out the back. Heart wrenching, I walked towards the garden shed and tugged at the door. Locked. I went back inside to get the keys, but they wouldn't open it. Bending to look through a crack, I spotted his back – his body, still clad in pyjamas, lying on the dirt floor.

It was one of those bizarre experiences when what I was seeing, my mind couldn't fathom or process. My stomach twisted in confusion and disbelief. Yet, without a shadow of doubt, I knew he was gone.

# First Date

## 1990

I met Grant when I joined an introduction agency. I'd decided I needed to expand my horizons if I was going to meet a suitable partner. This was before on-line dating sites were commonplace. I'd only had a couple of dates before I was introduced to Grant.

We met for dinner at Zagames – a local hotel restaurant – and my first impression of him was that he was highly intelligent, shy and introverted, but had a quick wit and dry sense of humour. He had recently been seconded to work in Canada and was recalling his experiences of living through their freezing winter. Just prior to that he had worked in Antarctica for sixteen months. I was impressed with the conditions he'd endured. Working in situations like those, you'd need strength, determination and resilience.

'How did you cope with the extreme cold?' I enquired.

'We had the proper thermal clothing and protection needed.'

'Gosh, that is amazing. I don't think I would've survived.'

At nearly six feet (185 cm), he had hazel eyes and brown hair. Quite handsome. An engineer with Telstra, maths and science were his forte – the opposite to my creative soul.

He'd obviously been well educated, coming from a background of Melbourne Boys High School – a private school equivalent in the public system – whereas I'd attended public schools. First, Heidelberg Primary, where we had still used blackboards and chalk and were expected to drink milk that had sat in the sun for hours, then Banyule High School where my report cards showed my favourite subject as art and that maths was not my strong point.

It was what my father could afford at the time. Unbeknownst to Dad, I'd once overheard him telling a fellow parishioner how much he wished he could have sent his children to private schools. I had mixed feelings about his comments. Obviously, he desired that for us and felt regretful. Yet, I myself had no such regrets. In my mind, a private school wouldn't have given me any advantage in life, and I felt confident forging my pathway within the education I had within the public school system.

Grant pursued adventurous activities such as parachuting, parasailing, scuba-diving and cave diving. He also gained a restricted pilot's licence. He enjoyed camping and outdoor activities such as fishing, crayfishing and water skiing.

I admired his passion for life, his penchant for living on the edge. It made him seem a little dangerous. On reflection, I believe it was his personality and mental state that contributed to his pursuing adventurous, sometimes dangerous, activities. But back then, I didn't know he possessed the need for an element of mental challenge, even recklessness, and that life on a daily basis would become an incredible challenge for him. Perhaps taking it to the absolute edge was okay with him, since he was in such a fragile state. Perhaps, unconsciously, he considered it fine, even if the consequences were dire.

There, over dinner, I shared the high points of my life's journey so far: my training in cooking, work in retail, creative pursuits, recreational pursuits – jogging and bike riding – and my love of travel.

'One of the most adventurous pursuits I have ever done was a five-hundred-kilometre bike ride on the east coast of Tasmania. It was the fittest I'd been.'

In some respects we were polar opposites. Him: logical, analytical, orderly, strong in maths and science – left brained. Me: creative, emotional and intuitive – right brained. I tend to be innovative in my thinking, with a need to express myself freely and a desire to help others. But somehow, we clicked while sharing travel stories and the enjoyment of good food. Perhaps from his perspective, I was a nurturing, caring person with a dash of adventure.

The conversation flowed, and we agreed to meet again. As I left Grant, I felt a surge of happiness and joy that, *yes*, I had found the one.

Grant's taste for adventure had led him to spend sixteen months in Antarctica as a scientist studying the ionosphere. He'd completed scientific work in some of the harshest conditions in the world. Dealing with gale-force winds, freezing temperatures and crevasses, he'd had a tough and challenging career. Danger would have been ever present, living in such conditions.

The isolation presented its own unique challenges, particularly if a medical emergency happened – a plane was the only way to rescue someone. 'I once went outside by myself and slipped on ice,' he said. 'Fell on my back. Luckily, I wasn't hurt to badly and was able to get back inside.'

I pictured him lying there, unable to move. He could have frozen to death.

'There was only one doctor among the twenty staff. When I landed back in Tasmania coming back it was strange being back in civilisation again.'

At times, they would go on expeditions to designated stations. 'The temperatures were so freezing, we'd wake up with ice formations above our mouths.' He showed me beautiful photos he'd taken of rookeries with thousands of penguins, rock and ice formations, the sun glistening on the snow. 'The smell of the rookeries was overwhelming, and the chirping sounds of thousands of penguins too: Emperor, Adelie, Gentoo, Chinstrap, Macaroni and Rockhopper.'

Grant also explained how important the chef's role was – good food was essential to keep the morale up, given the extreme cold, isolation, physical demands of living in such a harsh environment.

Coming from a cooking background, this made perfect sense to me. Food can represent so many things to the individual. Apart from physical sustenance, it arouses our senses of taste, smell and sight. We associate food with social and cultural experiences, celebrating all of life's journey.

I could only imagine the logistics for food planning, with supplies being either flown or shipped in, and a twenty-four-hour roster to ensure the generators were maintained. Obviously, anything threatening the power would be disastrous

# My Twenties

## 1970 – 1988

### Love of cooking

I have always enjoyed cooking and love experimenting with recipes. This may have stemmed from my childhood where I was fussy about food, to the point that my mother would cringe with embarrassment if she was on canteen duty and I insisted on her making a particular order. I would want half a cheese and tomato sandwich and a chocolate roll. (not a whole one).Even today, both my daughters would describe me as finicky about food. It needs to be appetising, stimulating and inspiring.

But back in those days, flavours were simple and bland. Bottling fruit and making jam was popular – peaches, apricots and plums were carefully prepared and cooked in Fowlers kits. Sunday lamb roasts with mashed potato were typical. So much so that I tend to avoid it now.

Perhaps, deep down, my tastes were more sophisticated than the culinary options of the times. I think this motivated me to experiment with different foods and, ultimately, train and work in the field. I enjoy so many aspects of food: taste, aroma, visual stimulation, social interaction, cultural differences and traditions, and growing my own vegetables, fruit and herbs.

Growing up, I was blessed to have a neighbour, Grace, who was a superb cook. I still recall watching her form and steam pork dim sims, a delicacy of her Chinese heritage. They were the most delicious I have ever eaten. Grace's recipes and techniques had a significant impact on my views about food, expanding my knowledge and palate.

Australian food culture in the sixties and seventies was so limited compared to today. Takeaway, a rarity in our family, was limited to fish and chips, Chinese or Italian. When I was eight years old our family went to a wedding reception that was vegan – something barely heard of in those days. The main course was nutmeat. I only managed to swallow one mouthful, leaving the rest on my plate. It tasted awful, and I complained loudly. My sister Joy swiftly kicked me in my shin to quieten me.

I take pleasure in relating this to my daughters – one who is vegan and the other vegetarian. How lucky they are to have so many options these days.

## Studying home economics

At the age of seventeen, I was faced with a decision – what direction should my career take? As I my interests leaned towards food, I applied to study home economics. Unsure though, I pondered the option of deferring for the year, perhaps travelling. But at seventeen, I didn't have the confidence to make that decision, so I pushed those thoughts aside.

By the end of the first year, I'd found the course too demanding and ended up leaving. On reflection, I sometimes wish I had taken that year off. Maybe it would have given me a clearer perspective on where I was heading.

## Cooking apprenticeship

In 1980, I was offered a cooking apprenticeship at an elderly citizens residence. As I was still contemplating my future in terms of study, work and life direction, I decided to continue pursuing a career in food.

The menu was quite traditional: roasts, stews, fish and chips, apple pies and scones. The most challenging dish was tripe – the lining of sheep, pig or cattle stomachs – which literally took the lining off the pot. The smell made me nauseous, yet the residents loved it.

## Malaysia and Singapore

In 1981, I took my first overseas trip to Malaysia and Singapore – such a contrast to Australia. At twenty years of age, and accompanied by a girlfriend, I was keen to experience other cultures, food and religions. I still remember the excitement as we flew into Kuala Lumpur – the lights of the city, surreal and thrilling. As I stepped off the plane, the heat and humidity, combined with the smell of jasmine, was overwhelming, but I loved it.

Having grown up closeted by a strict religious family, I wanted to fully experience this new culture – the delicious aromas of food, the colourful chaos of city markets, a humbling visit to a Buddhist temple with its wafting incense and monks deep in prayer.

Our first stop was the Hilton Hotel – a highlight for me, since I hadn't stayed in a hotel before. Exploring the city, I was struck by the contrast in wealth and poverty. The tour took us to a rubber tree plantation in the countryside, and I really enjoyed visiting a batik factory with row upon row of beautiful fabrics. However, it was confronting to be up close with so many venomous snakes at a snake temple in Penang, where the air was heavy with incense – reputed to keep the snakes calm.

Singapore was a bustling city – a shopper's heaven in the eighties – yet, due to the government's policies, its streets were impeccably clean. I did all the typical tourist attractions: visiting the National Orchid Garden, sipping a gin-sling at the famous Raffles Singapore and enjoyed delicious satays from street stalls. Visiting Changi Prison was a sombre experience, as I reflected on its macabre past as a prisoner of war facility during World War II.

On my last day, Thaipusam – an Indian festival – was in full swing. Here, in the heat and humidity, entranced devotees fearlessly pierced their faces and bodies, then carried or dragged heavy sleds attached to their bodies with hooks and skewers. I wondered at their ability to endure the pain of these feats.

My first overseas trip was everything I'd hoped for. It opened my mind, widened my horizons and ignited my desire for future travel.

## Box Hill Hospital

Back at the elderly citizens residence, it became apparent they did not want to continue to my apprenticeship. In hindsight, I was far too young to be in an aged-care workplace surrounded by predominately mature men – as was common of cooks at the time. So I changed to Box Hill Hospital to finish my apprenticeship.

A lot of the cooks were from post-war Europe with English their second language. Again, most of the cooks were men, so there was a sense of camaraderie among the few women, as some of the men could be crude and sexist in their attitudes. The man in charge of the pastry section had very poor personal hygiene, spoke very little English and jealously guarded his section. It was appalling to watch his deficiency in food hygiene, but if anyone tried to challenge him, he yelled obscenities, then continued on his merry way. He had unkempt hair, a strong body odour and always a dirty uniform. Unfortunately, the catering manager was gutless, so didn't tackle the issues.

It was heavy, physical work. Being younger then, I coped with it; however, the heat of the ovens in summer left me lightheaded, flushed, sweaty and weak, and in winter, the freezer room left me shivering. The food I cooked was typical of hospital fare. Friday was fish and chips day. The oil from the fryers seemed to permeate our clothes, hair and skin, and by the end of the day, we stunk of oily fish and chips. I still remember peeling a bucket of onions and crying my way through it, my eyes burning from the sulphuric acid. By the end of the apprenticeship, I'd had enough. The food lacked inspiration, the work was boring and physically challenging, and the hours not conducive to a good social life. I couldn't see this as my future.

It was at this time I met Louise, a student dietician. The first thing that struck me about her was her intelligent, sparkly green eyes and vivacious personality. Her free spirit transcended the dreariness and monotony of this workplace. An individual, who spoke her mind, Louise was confident and assertive, not one to suffer fools. Working in the catering/dietetics section of the hospital was quite hierarchical, and I think both of us struggled within that – probably why we hit it off immediately. That and her comment that she was planning a skiing trip to France.

'Wow, that sounds exciting,' I said. 'I'd love to go there myself one day.'

Louise was completing her course as a mature age student. This idea inspired me to change my career and go back to full-time study later.

Over the years, we forged a wonderful friendship, established over a love of good food and wine, similar outlooks on life, a shared sense of humour, unconditional support and kindred spirits. Today, our friendship is stronger than ever.

## Cooking apprenticeship

The year after my home economics course, I began my training at the William Angliss college, another institution of mostly males – I certainly don't recall any female teachers. I learnt all the skills of French cooking, including specialities such as butchery, entrees, ice carving, margarine modelling, sauces, main courses and patisserie. I was proud when I was selected to enter a cooking competition. There were ten participants, we were given two hours to cook a three-course menu. The tension was high, and the heat was on literally as we sweated over a hot stove! I also won a prize for creating a dessert that I called Brandy Alexander Surprise – a white chocolate mousse flavoured with brandy and crème de cacao, topped with a strawberry dipped in chocolate. Delicious!

At one stage, I did some agency cooking. One job was at a hotel in outer Melbourne. I was horrified to find meat covered in slime. It was a terrible dilemma: how could I serve this to people? How could a hotel allow this? I had nightmares of being responsible for a food poisoning outbreak. Another awful job was at a rooftop restaurant in Carlton. It was a hot summer in the midday heat, and I was in charge of the barbeque. In full chef uniform with no shade, sweat pouring off me, I thought I was going to faint.

Yet, my love of food and its changing culture remained. The last forty years has seen such a fundamental shift in how we view and enjoy food, but still, staple favourites such as chicken schnitzel with chips and salad, spaghetti, fish and chips, pizza and Chiko Rolls are just as popular today.

Back in my youth, foods seemed richer and heavier – steaks with sauces; buttery, garlicky crumbed Chicken Kiev; pastry covered Beef Wellington. And desserts too – creamy chocolate mousse, crème caramel, fried apple fritters. Chinese food was the most common Asian food, including favourites such as sweet and sour pork, spring rolls and fried rice.

Now, our multi-cultural broadening as a population has influenced our eating habits, and we're spoilt for choice with restaurants and food stores that cater for South-East Asia cuisines from Thailand, Vietnam, Laos and of course China. Melbourne also has a high population of Greek and Italian people who have introduced us to the health benefits of the Mediterranean diet with its higher proportion of olive oil, legumes, nuts, unrefined cereals, fresh fruit and vegetables, with a moderate proportion of fish, cheeses, yoghurt, wine, but a lower consumption of meat products.

Food encompasses all our senses, the sight enhances our appetite, aroma stimulates our sense of smell, adding to the delight of the taste of the food. Of course, so many of our memories are intertwined with food: birthdays, weddings and Christmas. And scientific knowledge about our gut and microbiome has given us greater insight about the impact of food and nutrition on our health.

Lifestyle and cooking shows have also had great impact on the diversity of our food culture. Very recently, Covid has highlighted people's enjoyment of home style cooking.

We have many cooking/lifestyle shows such as MasterChef and My Kitchen Rules. I think the success of these shows taps into the psychology of food and cooking, it is a means by which we express our love and care for people. I think given the restriction and impact of Covid on us, food perhaps is one factor that gives us comfort and reassurance during uncertain times.

Living in Melbourne we are so blessed to have such a wide variety food resources, cafes, restaurants and cultures. I think we have one of the best in the world. Every time I travel overseas, I come back and appreciate how good we have it in Melbourne.

## New Zealand

Another trip I did was to New Zealand, a stunning country full of natural beauty and, of course, lots of sheep! After a visit to a friend Jenny in Auckland, I did a bus tour to Dunedin. A couple of my favourite memories from that trip were the bubbling mud pools oozing sulphurous steam in Rotorua, and the luxurious feeling of floating in the hot pools, so hot to the point they were almost uncomfortable. Milford Sound was a spectacular sight by boat ride. Reminiscent of Norway, waterfalls cascaded off the sides of the fjord. The experience was topped off with a dinner of champagne and crayfish.

## Change in study

By 1984, I'd completed my cooking apprenticeship of four years, and it was time to review my life's direction. One thing was clear – I didn't want to pursue a career in cooking; the low wages and status, physical demands and boredom it presented weren't appealing.

Instead, in 1985, I returned to full-time study, commencing a Bachelor of Arts, Recreation. My father couldn't understand why I would leave a secure job. I understood his point of view; his generation was one of missed opportunities – he'd started accounting studies at night school but developed spondylitis, which prevented him from completing it. But I was keen to better myself and my opportunities in life. I think seeing the lack of opportunities in my parents' lives spurred me on.

I enjoyed the challenge and mental stimulation of my studies, meeting new friends, pursuing new interests and expanding my horizons. Even though it was the right choice for me, it was a sacrifice in terms of other options for my life, restricting me financially and delaying the independence of moving out from home.

Unfortunately, the strongly held belief of the eighties that society was heading towards a focus on leisure, did not turn out to be the case, and I found myself struggling to find employment in my field of study.

## Working in retail

By the end of 1987, despite my efforts to get a job in my field of study, I was unsuccessful. My career of choice would have been to work in an arts or community/neighbourhood centre, but once again, I had to pivot my career by applying for a casual Christmas retail position at Myer Northland.

My first position was on the fragrance counter and wrap bar for Christmas presents. I loved that job with its customer interactions, and it was fun to try out all the different fragrances, including the men's. It gave me an appreciation of all the elements that go into a perfume – was it floral, woody, spicy or citrus? It was lovely going home smelling of expensive fragrances.

Next, I was fortunate to gain a position in the personnel department – a time when typewriters were still standard equipment and computers were a novelty. Unfortunately, the personnel manager was mentally and emotionally abusive, yelling and belittling us for the slightest reason. Her angry outbursts had me feeling constantly on edge. This was one of my first encounters of directly dealing with someone who had mental health issues.

Though it was challenging dealing with her abuse on a daily basis, and I worried about the impact on my own mental health, the job was important to me. The range of experience I gained while working at Myer was wonderful – everything from marketing, switchboard and administration. They were fantastic at training their staff, and I took every opportunity that came my way. So, there was no way I was going to leave on this particular manager's account. Thankfully, complaints were made by staff to upper-level management, and she was demoted and sent to another store.

## New Caledonia

In 1988, I took a trip by myself to New Caledonia, staying, as was fashionable at the time, at Club Med. Things didn't get off to a good start when I developed asthma and a chest infection. Vulnerable and too exhausted to ask for assistance, I lay in a chair by the pool, not noticing the sun. Yes, I ended up sunburnt as well.

Eventually, I recovered and met three fellow Australians. I was single at the time, lonely and unsettled, wanting to find a life partner, so it was lovely to have some male company. We enjoyed bus trips into Noumea – the archipelago's capital – shopping for souvenirs, fragrances, make up and clothes. As New Caledonia is a territory of France, most locals spoke French.

One occasion, I took a catamaran trip out to an island. I was lovely cooling off in the shallow water until a sea snake swam up close to me. We danced the night away in the disco, light and carefree, and one night, as I returned to my room, I was blessed with the reflection of the moon on the water and the stars shining brightly. Absolute magic!

Then I met Grant.

# Marriage

## 1991

### Fiji

We had been dating for six months when we decided to have our first holiday together. It was a significant stage in the development of our relationship, one of those make-or-break times, and I was a little apprehensive.

We chose Fiji, staying on the Coral Coast and Treasure Island. We both relaxed, enjoying the sunshine, swimming, and snorkelling. It was *bula* greetings to everyone, everywhere, and everything happened on 'Fijian time' – an easy pace. The trip had its challenges – I got a urinary tract infection and Grant suffered a bad case of sunburn.

We all react differently in times of illness. For me, my infection left me in pain and less inclined to be intimate, while the discomfort of Grant's sunburn made him irritable and less conversant. It was a time of learning for both of us, and in hindsight, I did think it was a bit odd that he was so withdrawn at times.

Nevertheless, we enjoyed the tropical fruits and the laid-back attitude of the Fijians. A steam train ride showed us the mangrove swamps and sugar cane plantations. Treasure Island was a paradise of white sands, sparkling blue waters and colourful coral. Stingrays glided past us along with angel fish and octopi. So many different fish. Truly one of the most beautiful places I have ever snorkelled in. I have yet to see anything surpass its beauty.

## Proposal

By 1992, we'd been together a year, and I felt it was time to establish if our relationship was serious enough for a commitment of marriage and children. Up to this stage, Grant hadn't indicated his thoughts on our future. Being thirty, I was keen to start a family and not hang around in a relationship if we didn't have the same goals. So, I gave him an ultimatum, asking him what he felt about our relationship. Did he love me? Was he wanting marriage and children? It took him by surprise, and he didn't how to respond. As he was unable to give me an answer, I told him I was breaking up with him. There were a lot of tears. Shell-shocked, Grant said very little. With a heavy heart, I packed my bags, left the house and drove home to my parents.

When I shared the news with my mum, she was stunned and saddened to hear my news, but understanding and accepting of my decision. Though heartbroken, I was quite firm about the break-up. If Grant wasn't going to make a life with me, I would seek a relationship elsewhere, so it was up to him if he wanted to get back together, I didn't specify a time frame, the ball was in his court.

Shortly after, he changed his mind, and we became engaged.

I've been asked if, in hindsight, it was the right decision to marry, given what happened later. I still, to this day, feel it was the right decision. I have no regrets at all. For whatever reason, Grant and I were drawn to each other and shared a love and life together, even with the issues that arose within the marriage and its tragic ending. I don't believe I coerced him into marrying against his better judgement. If anything, having myself and the girls quite likely extended his life. Despite all, Grant loved the girls and me. He worked hard to provide for us. In the scheme of things, it was our destiny.

~

We bought a house in Glen Iris – a 1921 weatherboard Californian bungalow, partly renovated with a lot of potential for improvement. The next few months were busy with wedding plans, setting up the home and establishing the garden.

On the 11th of April 1992, I woke to a beautiful warm, still and sunny day, full of anticipation for starting a new major chapter of my life. I was a traditional bride with a full-length dress and veil. Mum was a talented seamstress and milliner and would have like to have made my wedding dress but felt it was too big a task at her age; however, she made the bridesmaid dresses for both my sisters. She had always made our clothes and was proud when someone from the church commented 'the Junor girls were the best dressed girls'.

My sister Joy made the flower girl dresses and a family member made my dress – full-skirted with lace, fluffy tulle and puffy sleeves. It was tricky stepping into the carriage with its beautiful white horses, but a unique and exhilarating way to arrive at the church, hearing the clip clop of the horses' hooves. Truly a princess moment. My sisters, nieces and nephews were part of the bridal party.

Dad walked me down the aisle. It was a proud day for him as he had fought so hard to retain the church's original status – in 1977, the Uniting Church was formed from the Congregational, Methodist and Presbyterian churches. By collecting enough signatures, my father's petition enabled the Heidelberg Presbyterian Church to continue, rather than being merged into the Uniting Church. It was a bit of a David and Goliath battle, but to my father's credit, he achieved this.

A lot of our family life centred around this church, our Sundays taken up by services and Sunday school, then a traditional Sunday roast. Dad taught the Sunday school, and being a lay preacher, loved to preach his sermons. My parents had lived in Heidelberg for years, Dad having bought a block of land there in his younger days, where he built a home for him and Mum.

In this building, held so dear by my family, Grant and I exchanged vows in a beautiful ceremony. Our wedding photos were taken in the local Warringal Park with the autumn colours creating a stunning backdrop. It meant a lot to me to have our photos taken there, since I had many happy memories of these parklands, both as a child and adult – school excursions, jogging, bike riding or enjoying it with family and friends. Our wedding reception was in an Edwardian-style house, old-world, intimate.

## Honeymoon

Our two-week honeymoon was in Vanuatu. But to our horror, the hotel we'd booked for the first week was full of mould due to a hurricane. The mould was everywhere, even on the pillows. Despite our protests, there was nothing we could do as we had paid in full.

Fortunately, we had booked a different place for the second week, so we just stayed out the hotel as much as possible. We visited a traditional village, experiencing their culture – food, dancing and, of course, the kava ceremony. Participating in their lives felt like going back in time. The village had several rudimentary huts – some for sleeping, others with a fireplace for cooking. I was struck by the contrast between these village people and our lives back home. Despite living in such impoverished conditions, they appeared to be happy and content. Perhaps we can all learn something from their attitude to life.

Grant had a strong risk-taking and adventure-seeking element to his personality, so when he saw the trip to Mount Yasur, an active volcano on Tanna Island, he was immediately interested. I was less of a risk taker than Grant, not as adventurous, yet I felt this was an adventure not to be missed, one of those once-in-a-lifetime experiences.

With Grant excited and me apprehensive, we travelled to the remote Tanna Island. I sat in the six-seater aircraft on our way to White Grass Airport, wondering if the plane went down or the volcano erupted who would know? It was one of those life choices we made – we weighed up the risks and fears and decided to take the plunge.

Mount Yasur is one of the world's most accessible active volcanoes. It's believed to have been erupting for eight hundred years, sometimes several times an hour. Captain James Cook visited the island in 1774. About 20,000 visitors pass through the airport a year, primarily to visit the volcano.

The trip to the volcano itself was a bumpy, ninety-minute journey from our hotel on Tanna's north-west coast. The four-wheel drive took us across the island and through a mountainous region known as Middle Bush. We had a short break in our drive with the opportunity to see Mt Yasur in the distance. It was a spectacular sight, wafts of ash cloud rising above the crater.

'Grant, can you feel the rumbling?' It felt like thunder under our feet.

'Yes. I can hear it too,' he replied, excited.

'Does it feel eerie to you?'

'Quite strange, quite primal.'

Both of us were entranced, captivated, almost in its spell. Yet also aware of potential danger and how far away we were from our lives back home.

Before we ascended the mountain, we attended a kava ceremony where the chief of the village was asked permission to climb the volcano. He replied in Bislama, the national language of Vanuatu, that it was okay to climb. I found it somewhat comforting, from a spiritual perspective, that the villagers have such a strong connection with the mountain. They believe they can talk to the mountain.

On this day, the volcano had been given a level two rating, which was ideal. Any higher, the climb wouldn't be permitted. Any lower, we would have missed the fireworks. No show.

Our visit coincided with sunset when the molten lava glowed ever brighter against the darkening skies. The volcano was spectacular, measuring 361 metres high and 400 metres wide. Quite overwhelming. We got within nearly two metres of the crater, and it felt like standing on a precipice, both of us were entranced by this spectacular show of mother nature.

'Can you smell the sulphur?' I asked Grant.

'It stinks, and I can feel the heat too,' he replied.

Time seemed to stand still, mesmerising us. I focused on taking photos, my senses overwhelmed by the vibrant colours of the lava, the strong sulphur stench, the radiant heat and the excitement we shared as a newly married couple.

Ash-laden clouds mushroomed in the sky. Regular explosions erupted from deep within the bowels of the mountain. Chunks of molten lava spewed towards the heavens. It gurgled, it growled, it spat, it hissed and was absolutely spectacular. The experience was an exhilarating dichotomy of danger and magnetic attraction.

It was hard to leave the mesmerising scene – one of the most outstanding experiences of my life. However, one was mindful of the gods and not to tempt fate. As we sat in the car, returning to our accommodation, we held hands, saying very little as we reflected on the spectacle of nature we had just experienced.

Looking back, perhaps a parallel can be drawn here regarding the early days of marriage – the initial exciting attraction to someone, inherent with risk. We put our hearts on the line, leaving ourselves open and vulnerable.

## Renovations

Back home, Grant and I settled into married life. Given the age of our house, it was ripe for renovation, and we tackled it with enthusiasm. One of our first projects was the kitchen, which was seventies style with a brown and orange theme. It had wood panelling, vinyl flooring and a brick fireplace originally used for cooking. The pantry was 1920s style. What a difference it made to have a new kitchen with an island benchtop, new pantry, dishwasher, oven and cooktops. Decorated in cream, it was bright and wonderful.

Bedroom storage was limited, not functional, so we installed wardrobes. Grant was a talented, practical handyman with the ability to turn his hand to any skill required for the renovations. He had the ability to teach himself anything he didn't know. He painted and wallpapered, renovated the laundry, paved the garden, built sheds and installed an attic stairway and room. And he was an absolute genius when it came to computers. With my creative side, I focused on making cushions, curtains and decorating the home. And with my love of gardening, I took joy in creating beautiful flower beds and planting herbs, vegetables and fruit trees.

At this point, I had left Myer and was working at Kmart head office. Grant held a demanding role as a project manager with Telstra, one he performed well with his perfectionist, neat nature and meticulous attention to detail. This side of his personality, while an asset in his professional life, had drawbacks in our relationship.

When two people begin their lives together, it's a critical stage in the relationship – learning about each other, negotiating key elements of personalities. My level of order and tidiness was less than Grant's, so that was a ready source of conflict. But the more challenging problem was his obsessiveness. If he was focused on a particular project, it was sometimes difficult to distract him from it.

There would be many times in our marriage when this would have a profound impact, like when Grant was installing the attic ladder, and our daughter Jacinta and I were sick with chicken pox. We were very unwell with flu-like symptoms, but I was cooking dinner and tending to the girls, who were aged two and three at the time. Exhausted, I stood at the bottom of the attic ladder, pleading with Grant to stop his work and help me. But he was totally focused on the job, oblivious to my needs and feelings of desperation and abandonment.

Other times, he would be working on his computer, lost in his own world, and yet again, I would have to manage everything – the girls, housework, pets – all the while feeling resentful that I was carrying most of the domestic load even though we both had jobs. It never occurred to him to help with cooking or even just washing the dishes. So as time went on, it became a source of conflict within our marriage.

## Murray River

In July 1994, we had a holiday in Echuca. Our plan was to hire a houseboat and enjoy the sights of the 'Mighty Murray'. We found a motel and enjoyed our first night away. At sixty-thirty in the morning, I woke alarmed to find Grant not in bed. Questions raced through my mind. Where was he? Was he safe? Should I call the police?

As I sat petrified, feeling abandoned and far from home, he walked through the door.

'Grant! Where have you been?'

'Just driving,' he said, voice flat, shoulders hunched, eyes glazed – a sad air about his whole demeanour.

'I was worried sick about you. I didn't know what happened, if you were okay.'

He grunted and got into bed, where he slept for a couple of hours. When he woke, things were awkward. This dramatic event hung between us, neither of us knowing how to broach it.

What I can now presume is he experienced an extreme low in his mood disorder, but I didn't have the life experience or knowledge to understand this. Back in the nineties, mental health issues weren't acknowledged as they are today. So, I pushed my concerns aside, and we continued with our holiday.

We hired a houseboat, got all our food supplies and began our adventure on the Murray River. The boat was enormous and the kitchen well equipped, so we enjoyed fine dining. It's interesting that, when we were on holidays, Grant took a far greater role in food preparation and cooking than compared to home. Somehow, he seemed to enjoy it. I loved that we could enjoy the rituals of cooking and enjoy a glass of fine wine at the end of a day.

Steering the boat was challenging but fun. One time, Grant stood on the bank while I tried to get the boat to head in a certain direction. It was like what I imagine driving a heavy truck would be.

As I tried desperately to co-ordinate the boat's movement, all the while negotiating a low water level, the current and exposed tree roots, Grant signalled with his arms. Times like these tested our relationship, but though I was feeling out of my comfort zone, Grant kept his cool and patiently directed me out of the predicament.

We chugged along the river, relaxed in each other's company, observing the beauty of nature, the smell of the lemon eucalypts and the abundant wildlife. Magpies sung, cockatoos screeched and kangaroos grazed. At night, we set up a campfire on the bank – there's nothing like finishing the day, sitting around a crackling fire. Warmed by the fire, we sipped our wine and reflected on the highlights of the day, the birds and animals we observed, the beauty of the bush. Mornings, we woke to mist swirling over the river. Magical. I loved the pace of the houseboat; it forced us to slow down, chill out and enjoy nature. After a week on the houseboat, we returned to Echuca. Navigating the Murray had been a challenge but lots of fun. A bonding experience for both of us.

## Finances

Prior to meeting Grant, I'd purchased a two-bedroom flat in Thornbury. I was proud of my achievement – even though I'd been on a low salary and it was at the peak of the eighties with seventeen per cent interest rates, I'd managed to achieve this at age twenty-eight.

Though Grant was cautious about starting a family, he deferred to me as to when we should start trying. Since I was thirty-one and he was thirty-three when we married, I was keen to not leave it too long, fertility being an unknown factor until we started the process.

Grant had a mortgage for our home, and I still had a mortgage on my flat. So, in preparation for living on one salary, I would need to sell – as it turned out, an agonising process. The economy and market had dropped like a bombshell. It took three real estate agents, two auctions and two and half years. Ultimately, I was forced to sell for less than I had bought it for. I was devastated by this loss; I'd worked so hard to achieve this goal. Being independent by nature, I was depressed to have lost so much of my investment, particularly when I was contemplating motherhood and needed it most.

# Children

## 1995

### First pregnancy

In December 1995, after two months of trying, I became pregnant. It was wonderful to achieve the goal of motherhood. Grant was excited but apprehensive. I suffered morning sickness for weeks, which fortunately settled down by the second trimester. During the winter months, the hormones kept me warm, so I was able to wear much lighter clothing.

The pregnancy progressed well, right up until July when I had this dream about having an illness beginning with the letter 'p'. In the morning, I woke up bleeding. Alarmed, I rang the hospital straight away. After being examined, I was told I had *placenta praevia* – a condition where the placenta covers the cervix. Bed rest was the only treatment, requiring me to leave my job earlier than anticipated. Letting go of that financial independence scared me. It was a big adjustment for Grant too; he was now the sole breadwinner.

But also, the pregnancy took my focus off him.

## Dad's death

A few months later, at the age seventy-nine, my father suffered a stroke and had to go into full-time residential care. I was heartbroken to see him decline, but he was stoic and never complained. He suffered a second and, ultimately, a third stroke, which took his life on 16 April 1996, before Elisha was born.

Still, I was pleased to have been able to share the good news of my pregnancy with him. And after his death, while I was still pregnant, I had another dream. This time I saw Elisha and Dad playing together. It gave me comfort that they were connected in spirit.

My father's nickname for me was 'Tootsie'. Our relationship wasn't a strong one, but I knew he loved me and that he was proud of my achievements, my cooking and recreation qualifications, getting married in the church he had campaigned to keep. He wasn't the type of father I could discuss life issues with – my mum was the go-to person for that. Perhaps the most challenging aspect about his passing was the relationship I so wished we could have had.

We buried Dad in the Eltham cemetery – a beautiful natural setting with a creek running through it and ducks waddling around. It was a peaceful and tranquil place, perfect for contemplation and reflection. It still is.

## A difficult pregnancy

I was admitted to Cabrini hospital two weeks prior to the birth, in case of any unexpected haemorrhaging. This was a special time of nesting with friends and family visiting. I enjoyed reading and being spoiled with delicious food – while not being sick. But this was all overshadowed by Grant's rising stress.

The imminent birth of our child was a significant challenge for him. He had a dependant personality and felt insecure at the prospect of a baby depriving him of my attention. He announced he was buying a bed for the extra bedroom so he could still get his sleep.

I was devastated. It was as if he'd pulled a rug out from under me. Right at this critical time of pregnancy and health complications, I needed him most. But he was leaving me feeling unsupported, abandoned and insecure.

I probably shouldn't have been completely surprised. I was well aware of his dependency and rigidity, his minimal support around the home. Still, it didn't soften the blow. This wasn't how it was meant to be when you're having a child.

At 6:42 pm on 14 August 1996, our daughter Elisha Celeste Junor Lamont was born by caesarean section. Upon waking from the general anaesthetic, I found Grant beside me. He wheeled me to Elisha's humidicrib, so happy and proud of our daughter. I'll never forget the moment I placed my hand on hers. It was surreal, one of the most significant moments of my life, overwhelming me with emotions of love, joy and awe. She was fair in complexion and blue-eyed, with wisps of blond hair framing her delicate features, but even at birth she had eczema.

The following day, exhausted, in pain and heady from the drugs, I noticed Elisha wasn't in my room.

'Where's Elisha?' I asked the nurse.

'She's in the nursery. She had a fit and turned blue,' the nurse replied, looking flustered.

'Is she okay?' I stammered.

'The paediatrician is assessing her now.'

Suddenly there was a whirl of activity. The doctor came to clarify the situation. Elisha had suffered two fits. They didn't know what had caused this. The best course of action was to send her to the Royal Children's Hospital where they could properly assess and monitor her.

It was a most bizarre feeling seeing Elisha, barely a day old, being wheeled away by the Newborn Emergency Transport Service (NETS). Already weak and disorientated from significant blood loss during my caesarean surgery, I went into overdrive, worrying about what could potentially be wrong with my child. Did she have a serious illness? Would she be seriously disabled? Numb with shock, I called my mother.

'Mum, I'm so worried about Elisha. Something really serious could be wrong with her.'

'Just take a day at a time. Try not to worry too much. Hope for the best.'

'Yes, that's good advice. Thanks.'

That night when Grant came into visit me, he looked visibly distraught.

'We just have to hope for the best. She's in the right place,' was all I could muster.

~

Family and friends kept our morale up and transported my breast milk. It was a difficult separation having only just given birth to her. Thankfully, after many tests, Elisha recovered and was returned to me at the hospital. They were unable to find a cause for the fits; it was just one of those things that occurred in newborns without a reason.

All this stress, added to the overwhelm of coming home with Elisha. I recall walking through the front door thinking what to do first, where to start? I'd never done this before.

The early weeks were a blur of feeding, sleeping, nappy changing, trying to establish a routine, and sheer exhaustion. Unfortunately, Elisha continued suffered from severe eczema, and whenever she was teething, it would flare up. This, in turn, disrupted her sleep because of the intense itching.

At one stage, I took her to a mother and baby sleep school, hoping to regulate her sleep patterns. At the time, the popular method of dealing with sleep issues was a method called 'controlled crying'. I found limited success with this because poor Elisha's eczema flare ups made her irritable and simply unable to sleep. I would also soon learn she had a strong personality. Later, as a toddler, if she didn't want to sleep, she stubbornly refused. I was to spend many a night sitting at her door, trying to get her to sleep.

When Elisha was three months old and Grant was away on business in Sydney, I developed a chest infection that caused a severe asthma attack. The previous months had been stressful – a difficult pregnancy, Elisha's illness, lack of support from Grant – negatively impacting my health. As the evening progressed, my breathing deteriorated to the point I was passing in and out of consciousness. I tried to keep checking on Elisha, but with my condition worsening, I had to call an ambulance. The ambulance officers were wonderful. Before I knew it, I was on a stretcher and they'd found a carrier for Elisha. Once in the ambulance, they gave me an oxygen mask and administered a drip with steroids. The relief was instant. I was transported to Box Hill Hospital, but I soon recovered, albeit shaken.

## Fiji

In August of 1998, our family took another trip to Fiji. Elisha was about to turn two. This time we stayed at The Fijian on an island near the coral coast. We had a wonderful time swimming, snorkelling and enjoying the fresh food and fine dining. The Fijians have a relaxed attitude to life and are wonderful with children. One tour, we took a river taxi to a village in a mountainous region. To our delight, the villagers treated us to a kava ceremony, a delicious spread for lunch, and beautiful singing and dancing. They made such a fuss over Elisha, being blue-eyed and blond, spoiling her with love and attention.

## Jacinta's birth

We were keen to have a second child, but sadly, I had several miscarriages. Then I had another significant dream – that I was pregnant, and the birth was going to be caesarean. Soon after, I was delighted to discover I was pregnant again.

Meanwhile, Grant started renovations in our laundry. With a new baby on the way, he wanted to make improvements in such a utilised room – add shelves, paint, change the light fittings and replace the flooring. Whenever he worked on the house, it was done to perfection, so I was really pleased with the end result. Though while he'd been doing the floor, there were open holes and some sneaky rats raided our house. I came home from shopping one day to find a rat squirrelling around in our living room. My response was to scream, grab the girls, hop in the car and escape.

My pregnancy progressed well, and on 31 March 1999, my waters broke. But after being examined at the hospital, I was told to come back the next morning at eight o'clock. I had made plans to go out with the mother's group for dinner, so with my doctor's approval, I continued with my plans for an evening out. Some of my family were shocked that I still went, but I couldn't see why not. I had a fabulous time, enjoying delicious Italian food.

As we left the house the next morning, I was emotional and crying. This was the passing of another stage of our lives, another baby, becoming a family of four. Grant, on the other hand, was excited about the imminent arrival of our baby.

We arrived at eight, and my labour progressed slowly. My cervix wasn't dilating, so I was given oxytocin to encourage dilation. No luck. It would have to be a caesarean birth. By now, it was ten in the evening.

As with my last pregnancy, I decided to have a general anaesthetic; however, one of the nurses was challenging my choice, saying I should have an epidural birth. Upset, I argued with her while I was being prepped in the theatre room; I was terrified at the thought of having a needle stuck in my spine.

So, on 1 April 1999 at 11:44 pm, Jacinta Hannah Junor Lamont was born. April Fool's Day and also Holy Thursday. Our Easter child.

I was still groggy from the general anaesthetic when I met Jacinta for the first time. She had blue eyes, fair skin, thick hair and delicate features. Even in my altered state, the excitement and love I felt was overwhelming.

In the foggy distance, I could hear the anaesthetist arguing with the theatre nurse. Later, I found out the reason for this – evidently, they'd given me too many opioids, and my breathing rate was eight breaths per minute. Narcan was administered to reverse this. I thank God for the nursing staff in recovery who were monitoring me, my guardian angels.

Coming home with Jacinta, I again felt all the apprehension of having a newborn – the inevitable exhaustion, lack of sleep and Grant's anger and insomnia causing further stress. Yet, one of my treasured photos is proudly nursing Jacinta on our verandah while Elisha, aged two years and eight months, was having a major meltdown at the reality of her new sister. I hasten to add they are now the closest of siblings.

# Cracks

## 1999

### Tasmania

When Jacinta was six months old and Elisha three years old, we took a trip on the *Spirit of Tasmania*, leaving in the evening and arriving in Devonport in the morning. Since we took our car on the ferry, it was a complex effort boarding the ship. I had the girls with me on the dock while Grant drove the car onto the ferry. He then joined me and went ahead with Elisha while I managed Jacinta in the pram. Elisha was feeling frustrated and started to cry. Grant tried desperately to pacify her by buying a toy, but she couldn't be consoled. By the time I caught up with them, Grant was visibly stressed and angry and Elisha was crying uncontrollably. Travelling with young children who can't cope with a change in routine is challenging, but with a father who also has a low tolerance, it's even more challenging.

The first place we stayed at was Stanley, a corner of the beautiful, rugged north-western coast, famous for The Nut – the remains of an ancient volcanic plug. We were staying in a lovely, renovated bed and breakfast. Once again, with the change in routine, Grant reacted in extreme manner and jumped in the car driving through night-time, coming back just before breakfast. While he was gone, I felt alarmed, abandoned, panicked (was he going to crash?) With him having the car and being alone with the girls I felt extremely vulnerable. Grant returned just before breakfast.

'Where have you been? I was so worried about you?' I exclaimed.

He shrugged. 'I don't want to talk about it.'

He settled down after this and the holiday continued without further incident.

We continued on through the port township of Strahan, then reached Cradle Mountain. This is a glacially formed mountain that rises above Dove Lake and Crater Lake, near the township of Cradle Mountain. The mountain was named because it resembles a gold-mining cradle. It's a most majestic place with the razor-shaped mountains as a backdrop, thick tufts of grass and plenty of walking tracks. The weather changes very quickly – cold, wet and cloudy one day, blue skies and sunshine the next. Next, we visited Queenstown, an early 1990s town of copper mining and mass logging. The terrain is a surreal rocky moonscape, quite an eerie sight.

Tasmania is a treasure trove of interesting places to see, and the girls were good travellers – sleeping a lot in the car when they needed to. They enjoyed riding on a mini railway and getting up close and personal to wombats in an animal sanctuary. Grant took a lot of pleasure in doing these activities with them.

We continued through to Hobart, then Port Arthur – a well-preserved convict settlement. To me, the place had an eerie feeling about it. I could only imagine the incredibly harsh conditions and suffering that occurred there. When you walk through, it leaves you with an incredibly cold and haunted feeling, a shiver down the spine. What makes this place more sobering is reflecting on the tragedy of the Port Arthur massacre, where a gunman killed thirty-five people.

For the remainder of the trip, we explored Bruny Island, Bicheno and St Helens before taking the ferry back to Melbourne.

## Sleep deprivation

Jacinta, like Elisha, was an unsettled sleeper, leaving me sleep deprived, exhausted and running on empty. Eventually, I returned to the mother and baby sleep school again. The midwives were wonderful in their care, advice and support, but just like with Elisha, their methods were ineffective with Jacinta. In hindsight, I think she simply didn't like being alone, needing company for comfort.

To add to this stress, Grant was a chronic insomniac, so during the night, I was always on high alert to tend to the children in case they woke him and set off an angry response. This is where trying to implement the controlled crying method was impossible. I couldn't let the children cry and risk Grant exploding. I ended up spending a lot of nights on a mattress next to the girls' beds. I felt it was critical for them to have that support and nurturing.

There is a proverb, believed to have originated from an African culture, that says it takes a village to raise a child. This means that through every stage and aspect of a child's life, their community should provide support and positivity. While some within our village were supportive, others were not, unwilling to give us the love and support we needed. This had a tremendous impact, placing more stress on all of us. The help we so desperately sought just wasn't there.

By now, the cracks in our marriage were widening. It was almost as though I had married a man with a one personality, then something inside him switched, like a Dr Jekyll and Mr Hyde.

It seemed Grant had a limited capacity to cope with living in the everyday world. Yet, to his credit, he managed to function at work and was still successful in his project management career. But when he was home, he had no energy left, so he would just sit, leaving me to do all the domestic work. He would spend whole weekends watching television or sitting at the computer with the blinds down.

Meanwhile, I would be constantly walking on eggshells, trying to keep the girls and the dog quiet, trying to keep the peace and cook a meal. Then he would get distracted and forget to eat the meal I'd cooked. It was his way of escaping from reality. He was still a chronic insomniac and now suffered from debilitating irritable bowel issues. Often in the mornings, he would go to work without even saying a word to me. That really upset me. It was horrible emotionally, leaving me feeling isolated and abandoned.

The cause of his behaviour was complicated. I'm sure there were factors in his childhood that contributed to low self-esteem and his difficult personality and behaviour as an adult. I'm aware he was bullied at school. In his twenties, Grant had been diagnosed with depression. Of course, in hindsight, I can now recognise the manic episodes of heightened activity followed by the depressive lows when he literally could not get out of bed. I believe he had a dependant personality and was most likely attracted to my empathetic and caring nature, feeling secure and unthreatened with me. This, combined my own financial dependence on him, made for an imbalance in the marriage, adding pressure.

However, I felt his issues were even more complex than that, mentally, emotionally and socially. I do believe he had Asperger's syndrome – now referred to as autism spectrum disorder. Though highly intelligent, he showed the classic signs of difficulties with both social interactions and non-verbal communication, along with restricted and repetitive patterns of behaviour and interests. His desk was meticulously tidy, everything lined up. He was also compulsive in his behaviour – if he was working on fixing his computer for example, the focus was so intense that he wouldn't eat his meal. Strangely, one of the ways he did connect with people was fixing their computers. He would spend hours doing this. At times, I felt he was taken advantage of.

Sadly, as time progressed, Grant became increasingly isolated and social events became more of a challenge. When Jacinta had a birthday party in a hair salon, he found it impossible to stay. In the later years, I ended up having the girls' birthdays in a park because he couldn't deal with the social interaction of people in confined spaces.

Often, I would end up going to events with just the girls and had to explain his absence. At one event he didn't attend because of his mental state, a person argued with me. They were furious at Grant not attending. I lost my temper; how dare they hurl their anger at me and Grant. Couldn't they have some compassion? What gave them the right to take this attitude? And where was the support for me, while I struggled to cope with Grant's illness and look after the girls with minimal help. I was furious and let my feelings be known.

# Breaking Point

## 2000

Grant's behaviour became more erratic. Highly agitated and anxious, nothing seemed to calm him down. One night, I was in the kitchen preparing dinner when I heard him pick up the car keys. The door slammed, and my heart sank as I listened to him reverse down the driveway. There was no use running after him. I never knew where he was going.

An hour later the phone rang. I knew it was him. My mind raced, panicked. What could I possibly say to him at his most vulnerable time?

'Hello?'

'I want to end it all. I can't go on like this,' he said, desperation in his voice.

'Grant, the girls and I love you very much. Please come back home. Taking your life isn't the answer.'

'I don't know. I can't see a way out.'

'Please, please come home. We need you.'

He hung up.

I had no idea if he would come home or if there would be a policeman knocking at my door. This was to happen on many occasions.

When he returned home, of course I was relieved, but it was hideous to see him in such a desperate state, lying on the floor in foetal position. It filled me with helplessness and inadequacy. But also a nagging fear – would this keep happening?

It did.

Thus, began my own descent to breaking point. Sleep deprived, exhausted and unable to eat, I began having panic attacks. Some mornings, I'd wake up vomiting. I'd stand, face pressed against the front screen door, looking outside, feeling as if I were living in a prison. Why was no one helping us? How had my life got to this point? I was effectively a single mother caring for three children – a three-year-old, a twenty-two-month-old and a broken soul.

One morning, desperate to escape, I fled with the girls to Flinders Ocean Beach. We arrived around eleven. The weather was sunny, thirty degrees, with a strong offshore breeze. We climbed down the steep incline to the wide beach, which had a strong current, and walked to the water's edge. One moment, the girls were both by my side, and the next, Jacinta was gone. I flew into a panicked hysteria. Had she drowned? Had someone snatched her? I started screaming out that my child was missing. Thankfully, people were quick to help me scour the beach as I desperately clutched Elisha. It seemed an eternity, but perhaps was only five minutes. She was found higher up the beach about thirty metres away. I gave her the biggest hug. She was quite calm, but I've never forgotten the feeling of sheer terror that I'd lost her.

It's hard to put into words what it's like to go through a mental breakdown. There are the obvious symptoms of extreme anxiety and depression, totally irrational fear, inability to function in everyday tasks and loss of interest in food. My whole perception, my thinking, was distorted and fear based.

This couldn't go on. I went to my doctor. Fortunately, I had a wonderful practitioner who had an excellent grasp of mental health issues. I sat in his office and gave him an honest account of how I was feeling – the anxiety, depression, inability to function – and Grant's fragile mental state. He listened attentively. I was raw, not pulling any punches about the precarious state of my mental health. He asked if I had private health insurance. I did – this would end up being the time I most appreciated having it.

~

January 2001, on a hot summer's day, plants in the garden beds parched and brown, I stood outside the clinic. Despite my apprehension about leaving Grant at home with the girls, I knew this was the right decision.

I was led to a four-bed room. It had that antiseptic smell reminiscent of a hospital.

A nurse greeted me. 'You're very fortunate to be getting help. Many others with mental health issues don't receive the support they so desperately need.'

I pressed my face against the window, looking out at inner-city Melbourne – miners' cottages, a park, factories, shops – a world away from my life for the next two weeks.

A doctor gave me a physical check-up, including a blood test. He seemed distanced and made little eye contact. I got the feeling he was overworked. I left his room overwhelmed and demoralised.

My stay was an education. The patients here had incredibly varied issues. Gayle, a prison officer had suffered an injury from a prisoner and now had post-traumatic stress disorder. Wendy had suffered a mental breakdown when her daughter was raped by a family member. Another patient, Sally, had gone to the local pharmacy, purchased paracetamol and overdosed on it. Her stomach had been pumped. Afterwards, she'd begged her doctor not to tell her children, as she felt so guilty for her actions. Another young woman, Alison, was suffering ill effects from a failed operation for epilepsy.

Sometimes, patients came in screaming and strapped to a bed with a police guard. Jeremy, a patient in his seventies, was admitted for depression. He was discharged, only to return a week later. Fiona, a single woman with multiple sclerosis, was suffering depression from the impact of her disease. Jack, a country man, sunk into depression when he was forced to take a factory job in preference to a job on the land. This made me reflect on Grant – how only within the confines of the workplace was he able to function reasonably well.

Quite a few patients who were suffering from depression were admitted for electric current therapy (ECT). Other patients were admitted to allow time for their body to withdraw and adjust as they changed from one antidepressant drug to another.

Sonia, an accomplished pianist who was sexually abused as a child, was unable to sleep on a bed, as it brought back memories of her abuse. Sofia, an Italian woman, was being treated for chronic pain management. Sadly, the drugs she was given did not interact well, and she died as a result. Sam, a man in his twenties, was studying medicine when he fell ill due to chronic fatigue, resulting in depression and dependence on a wheelchair.

Jane, a physiotherapist, suffered a breakdown when her marriage dissolved. Her children went to live with her sister, as she was too unwell to care for them. Later, when I saw Jane in a shopping centre, her face gaunt and anxious, it shocked me. Still so unwell and unable to look after her children, she perhaps brought up a subconscious fear of mine – being too ill to look after my own children.

Eating disorders, drug abuse, pain management, post-traumatic stress disorder, sleep disorders, stress from workplaces and family disputes, it was all here. The patients with anorexia were the most confronting, as they looked like walking skeletons.

My schedule included individual and group therapy sessions, relaxation, craft and cognitive behaviour programs. In the mornings, after breakfast, we had a group walk. The programs were well run. A lot of emphasis was placed on ways to improve our health on all levels – physical, emotional, mental and spiritual – plus subjects such as time management and personal organisational skills. I have always had an interest in these areas, so I found it easier to relate to the themes of the programs.

I recall one group session when a patient discussed how he felt more attention was given to people suffering from cancer than depression. In another session, I was confronted to see someone suffering so much that he'd covered himself in self-inflicted wounds. At one stage, the three people I shared a room with were all having ECT. I found this disquieting, as I understood this therapy was not prescribed lightly, more a last resort when all else had failed. Anyone who's seen the movie *One flew Over the Cuckoo's Nest*, with Jack Nicholson playing a patient having this therapy, would understand the intense feelings around this subject.

Occasionally, we were given opportunities to leave the clinic, and I relished these despite my mental fragility. Retail therapy was a pleasant distraction from the intensity of being a patient at the clinic. One evening, a group of us got on a tram and visited Southbank. It was lovely to get out and feel 'normal' again. Often the discussion among fellow patients was comparing anti-depressants, waiting for the medication to kick in.

In the middle of my stay, I had weekend leave to go home. I did, but the contrast was vast – as if I had come from Mars. At the time, Elisha was three years old and Jacinta was twenty-two months, obviously too young to appreciate the situation. I was relieved that, despite his own issues, Grant made a genuine effort to make my time at home as positive as possible.

People's reactions to my illness were varied. Some were comfortable to visit or send me flowers and cards, while others found it too confronting – while disappointing at the time, I now take into account that it was twenty-one years ago, and mental health did not have the profile it has today, so my situation may have been too overwhelming for some people to deal with.

The theme of therapy at the time was Cognitive Behavioural Therapy (CBT), the emphasis on: challenging unhelpful thought patterns, stress management, time management, goal setting, communication skills, assertiveness skills and building self-esteem. The program I participated in focused on reflection of problems in my life; how responses may become habitual and unhelpful; and learning behavioural and cognitive techniques for adjustment, coping and change. Sessions on styles of what they called 'distorted thinking', I found particularly useful, as it helped me to challenge my negative thinking habits. I felt fortunate to be in the care of a doctor who was up to date with the latest research.

After two weeks at the clinic, it was now February, and I felt ready to go home. My stay had given me essential time to rest and recover. I said my goodbyes to the patients and staff I'd become friendly with, then sat in Dr Lam's office to discuss the details of my discharge. Fragile and vulnerable, I was concerned about the future – not just for my mental health but Grant's too. Would our marriage survive?

Dr Lam agreed to take me on as his patient, sparking a twenty-one-year relationship, which is still ongoing. It's been an amazing journey, and I feel incredibly grateful to have him as my doctor. He's one of the most gifted psychiatrists – humble, insightful, intelligent and smart. His calm and down-to-earth demeanour has guided me through some of the most challenging and horrendous times in my life.

Time and time again, I discussed different aspects of my life, whether health, relationships, career, travel or goal setting, he'd listened intently and give sound practical advice. He has a knack of teaching me problem-solving skills that give me a sense of self-empowerment in my life.

I am an emotional and passionate person. In the past, if a person or event upset me, I found it difficult to move on from that point. From all the work I've done with him, I'm now better able to process my reactions and move on, rather than get stuck. In my lowest points, when anxiety and panic completely overtook me, I'd ring him for reassurance.

Back home, Grant was on sick leave for the remainder of 2001. He continued to busy himself with the project of creating an attic room with a pull-down ladder. At the time, both of us were in quite fragile states, so in a sense, I think each of us were coping as best as we could. But soon I was in survival mode again – looking after him and two young children while maintaining the household exhausted my immune system. I suffered from cellulitis, ear infections, and by the end of the year, I had pneumonia and pleurisy.

# Western Australia

## 2001

In the winter of 2001, we did a driving holiday to Western Australia, Elisha was three and Jacinta fourteen months – a challenging age to take a driving holiday but also easier because they were young enough to sleep a lot. This was a critical time as Grant and I were both recovering from our nervous breakdowns. Grant was on extended sick leave, so he suggested the idea of doing this trip. Given past experiences, I was initially hesitant; however, after discussions with my psychiatrist and putting strategies in place, I agreed.

Our trip went through Horsham, where we spent the night in a BIG4 holiday park cabin. I'd never been a camper, but on a practical level, a cabin was ideal for a family with children.

The next stop was Hahndorf, a small German-themed town in the Adelaide Hills settled by nineteenth-century Lutheran migrants. This was one of my favourite places in South Australia. We stayed in a beautiful bush setting with ducks, sheep and kangaroos roaming around. The area was a smorgasbord of wineries and had a chocolate factory, where we indulged our sweet tooths.

The first night, we dined in the holiday park's restaurant. Jacinta kicked the champagne bottle over, then Elisha knocked her head. I quickly picked up the bottle while Grant scooped Elisha up and comforted her. The start of holidays is always an adjustment in routine, and as with other trips, I felt hesitant about Grant's mental state. It had been a long day of travel, and we were all weary, so it was a hasty trip to bed.

For the next leg of our journey, we headed to Port Augusta but got lost in Adelaide peak-hour morning traffic while trying to find the correct highway. Grant was driving at the time, and I had the map, trying desperately to give him accurate directions. A tense hour later, to my relief, we eventually found our way. It was a blessing that, given we were travelling long distances – up to five hundred kilometres a day – the girls were surprisingly well behaved.

Ceduna was our next stop, the name said to originate from an Aboriginal word *Chedoona*, meaning 'a place to sit and rest'. We then started our journey across the flat and arid Nullarbor – from the Latin terms *nullus* and *arbor*, meaning 'no trees'. The expanse is the world's largest single exposure of limestone bedrock, covering 200,000 $km^2$. The road, which stretches straight without a turn for 146.6 kilometres, is also known as the 90 Mile Straight.

I had a pre-conceived notion that this would be a boring trip, unlike my own childhood family holidays in Rosebud, where Dad had built a simple fibro house on some land inherited by my mum. Originally, we had a kerosene fridge and porta gas cooking. The forest had native Xanthorrhoea plants, known by the rather racist term 'blackboys', and we found rabbit skulls and echidnas. We were always on the lookout for brown snakes or croaking frogs in the swamps. In summer, the carnival would arrive with dodgem cars, a Ferris wheel, train rides and a merry-go-round.

But I was wrong about this trip being boring. We saw whales in the Great Australian Bight; rugged, spectacular cliffs; and varied vegetation, despite the lack of trees. Rabbits scurried, kangaroos hopped, emus ran, foxes darted, and we watched eagles soar high above.

Just over the border, along the Eyre Highway, is Eucla, which means 'bright'. It has the remains of the Old Telegraph Station – a landmark building now mostly covered by sand dunes. At one stage, Grant had been a radio operator, so this was of particular interest to him. Our next stops were Balladonia, then Kalgoorlie-Boulder. This town lived up to its reputation as the 'Wild West' – with its wide, dusty and deep guttered roads, I almost expected to see a cowboy come riding a horse down the street. Although there were quite a few pubs, the locals were not at all friendly. When we went into a local shop to ask for directions, we got a terse response, and on the main street, people didn't smile or acknowledge us.

The next day, we took a trip on the rail loop and visited an open-cut gold mine. The rail ran along the edge of the mine, which dropped five hundred metres – an awesome sight not visible from the road. Within the massive hive of activity, trucks carried huge loads of soil, though from our high viewpoint, it looked like a Legoland.

We moved on through Northam until we reached Geraldton, a coastal city nearly five hundred kilometres north of Perth. We had been travelling continuously for a week, driving all day, staying only one night in each place. By this stage, we had developed a routine: we got up early, had breakfast, packed the car, found a place to buy our picnic lunch, then off we headed for the day.

To keep the girls entertained, we had video screens, books and toys. Of course, being with each other 24/7 was challenging, and at times, the girls would be upset, which angered Grant. There I was, caught in the middle of trying to comfort the girls and pacify Grant. But even though it was sometimes a stressful juggling act, with the benefit of hindsight, I'm so grateful we experienced the trips as a family. Waking up with a sense of adventure, with anticipation of new sights and explorations, was so exciting.

We continued to stay in cabins in caravan parks, as they were spacious and more pleasant than motel rooms. When we drove into the BIG4 caravan park in Geraldton, we were delighted they had a mini cottage available. After seven days of continuous driving, feeling cramped from long days in the car, it was a pleasant change. We had space!

The busyness of our days determined whether we'd cook our own meals or eat out. In places like Geraldton, a fishing town, of course we bought fresh fish. So while Grant attended to the barbeque, I prepared salads, and the girls would help set the table. In milder weather, we ate outside next to a campfire. It also gave us the opportunity to chat with fellow travellers over a glass of wine and hear their experiences and travel tips. Geraldton is renowned for its breezes and, therefore, a popular spot for windsurfers. It was certainly windy on our visit; I have a photo of myself with that windswept look.

We continued up the north coast, passing through Kalbarri until we reached Denham, which is close to Monkey Mia. This is a marine park and world-heritage-listed site, famous for bottlenose dolphins that have been coming close to shore for over fifty years. One of the highlights of our trip was feeding these dolphins. Grant stayed on the beach with Jacinta while I tried to encourage Elisha to give fish to a dolphin as I took photos. It was a highlight of the trip to be so close to them. Midges – annoying little sand flies – made it impossible to stay on the beach for long due to their bites.

Another interesting spot was Shell Beach – a sixty-kilometre stretch, ten metres deep with shells. It was an extraordinary sight, though a bit too sharp to walk on with bare feet. We searched the beach and collected some of the more beautiful shells.

Our next stop was Carnarvon, a sub-tropical agricultural hub. We then passed through the Tropic of Capricorn before reaching Coral Bay. This was another of the highlights of our trip – idyllic weather, white sand, warm water with a beautiful reef to explore. Being winter at the time, it was delightful to swim in warmth and soak up the sun.

The farthest we travelled north was Exmouth, before we turned back south and retraced our path. By then, the scenery had become the same monotonous arid landscape, day after day, until we reached the Pinnacles just above Perth – an impressive expanse of limestone formations, reminding me of a moonscape. By the time we arrived at Freemantle, the weather had turned wet with gale-force winds. I loved the character of Freemantle – alfresco dining, lots of historical places to visit, an arty old-world feel. The scenery in this south-western corner of Australia was some of the most beautiful I'd seen in our travels.

Busselton was another highlight with its nineteenth-century jetty – nearly two kilometres long and featuring a train. It had survived a cyclone, storm and fire to retain its status as the longest wooden-pile jetty in the southern hemisphere. What fun we all had on such an unusual train ride along a jetty. The artificial reef under the jetty has gained worldwide recognition for its beautiful coral and over three hundred species of fish. It's also known for its seasonal humpback whale population. Ngilgi Cave, with its stalactites, stalagmites, helictites and amphitheatre, was a sight to behold. Although, as an asthmatic, I found breathing challenging in its humid atmosphere with a high density of carbon dioxide.

Pemberton had the most stunning forests featuring tall karri eucalypts and beautiful waterfalls, which can be viewed via a tramway that extends through the forest. Catching trout in the dam and enjoying them on the barbecue that night reminded me of my own family holidays at Rosebud. One of the few activities I did with Dad was fishing. We would board the boat *Julie Ann* at seven in the morning, returning with a hessian bag full of flathead, which we ate every way you could imagine: steamed, fried and baked. The bones were very small, and if you swallowed one the wrong way, there was a desperate clutch for bread before the bone got stuck in your throat

Walpole had a treetop walk with a suspended walkway, its highest peak rising forty metres above the ground. Although I'm not usually great with heights, I enjoyed it because of the bird's-eye view of the trees and the feeling of being a bird soaring high above.

We then ventured to Albany – originally a convict settlement and whaling station – at the south-western tip of Australia. It was a rainy grey day on the rugged coastline, but a beautiful rainbow formed over the sea. On to Esperance, a town known for its goldfields, agriculture and fishing. Cape Le Grand National Park was one of the most spectacular marine parks I'd ever visited – turquoise waters, white sands, granite rocks, wildflowers and rolling heathlands. It truly was a place of unspoilt natural beauty.

Our trip home led us back along the Nullarbor. It had taken two months, and we'd clocked eleven thousand kilometres. What an epic journey. I had hoped the holiday would rejuvenate Grant, but once back home, things returned to their usual bleak state. Again, I felt alone, trapped, exhausted and totally overwhelmed. As the year wore on, Grant's depression and moods became progressively worse. Finally, I put my foot down and insisted he see a psychiatrist.

Grant was highly anxious and agitated as we arrived at the psychiatrist's rooms.

'I don't want to go to this appointment,' he exclaimed.

'We are going to this appointment,' I responded defiantly.

It was a stressful and awkward meeting – Grant anxious and hostile, and me stressed and desperately in need of advice on dealing with his mental health issues. The session covered generic issues regarding Grant's life, health, childhood, attitudes and, of course, our marriage. Plus how this was all affecting me.

Grant was placed on medication for anxiety and depression. This was in 2001, and CBT was the buzzword term for treatment. Grant, somewhat reluctantly, accepted the help.

# Darwin

## 2002

In winter of 2002, we took another driving holiday. This time to Darwin. Given our fragile mental states and our young children, it was a brave decision, challenging. However, it was another wonderful opportunity to truly experience our vast country. Grant and I had always enjoyed travel, adventure and exploring new places, so I still believe it was the right decision, since it removed us from our everyday stress and gave us something more positive to focus on.

Initially, we retraced the route we'd taken on our Western Australia trip, passing through Horsham and my favourite town of Hahndorf, then Port Augusta, before branching north-west to Coober Pedy. This name is thought to have come from the Aboriginal term *kupa-piti*, meaning 'whitefellas' hole'. Known as the opal capital of the world, Cooper Pedy has a landscape akin to a moonscape – flat and uninspiring with mounds of red dirt from the opal mining. Because of the intense heat, many dwellings were carved out below ground, the sandstone being ideal for underground homes. We stayed in an underground hotel reminiscent of a cave, the temperature constant. This unique town boasted a diverse population of fifty nationalities, some a bit rougher than others.

The trip from Coober Pedy to Uluru was the longest day's travel of the trip – seven hundred kilometres of monotonous scenery. I can still recall the excitement of seeing The Olgas and Uluru on the horizon. Since there's nothing to obscure the view, they stand out all the more. The amazing rock formations, so quintessentially Australian, are a sight to behold. I felt in total awe of their beauty.

Uluru is a giant red monolith, cast into ever-changing colours with sunrise and sunset. Standing at 348 metres, it has a circumference of 9.4 kilometres, with steep valleys. What makes it so significant is its desert surroundings – the flat red-sand landscape in the middle of nowhere – and its unique animals. I also found it fascinating and important to learn about Uluru's spiritual significance, and why certain places are so sacred to the Anangu people – the Yankunytjatjara and Pitjantjatjara traditional landowners of Uluru. Many of the Dreamtime stories relate to this place. Grant chose to climb Uluru, while I took a short walk around its base with the girls. At that time, it was less controversial to climb the rock. However, in October 2019, the rock climb was closed due to its spiritual significance to Aboriginal peoples Australia-wide. There were also environmental and safety concerns – the initial path is steep and slippery, and people have been injured or died attempting the climb.

At Kings Canyon, we stayed at a lovely hotel that had a delicious buffet. I remember how much I enjoyed the meal while sipping champagne. Outside, the setting sun intensified the red of the desert, shadowing patches of shrubs, below a vivid blue sky. For some reason, that picture has stayed with me – the middle of our country epitomising Australia's unique beauty, filling me with a deep sense of satisfaction after a long day's travel.

Our next stop was Alice Springs, where we spent a week as it had so many places to explore. One of the highlights was visiting Adelaide House in the Todd Mall. Originally the first hospital in the Northern Territory, built by Reverend John Flynn who started the Flying Doctor Service, the building is now a museum. I was thrilled to see it housed some photos of my father, who was in a working party to restore Adelaide House, while he was doing some voluntary work at a church in Alice Springs some years before.

The West MacDonnell Ranges have some of the most spectacular scenery in the outback. They have been described as the jewel in the crown of Central Australia, and I think rightly so. Standley Chasm Angkerle Atwatye, meaning 'gap of water', is a three-metre wide, eighty-metre-high gorge with jagged cliff faces, ghost gum trees and natural flora and fauna. Depending on the time of day the sun changes angle creating beautiful contrasts of light and shadow. Further along the road there are gorges, waterholes, and ochre pits. These ochre pits consisting of multicoloured layered rock are traditionally used by Aboriginals in ceremonies. We got to see meteorite cranites, sieve for garnets in Gemtown and visit an old Lutheran mission. As we travelled the country, I loved seeing the changing colours throughout the day. One of the lasting impacts of this trip is it ignited an interest and passion for all things crystal. I now have a beautiful display of crystals in my house.

We continued further north, coming to the Devils Marbles – a collection of massive granite boulders. Another interesting place is Wycliffe Well, famous for visitors of the extra-terrestrial kind. Two green model aliens sit out the front of the holiday park. Since World War II there have been many sightings in the night sky in this area, even the Royal Australian Air Force has investigated.

Tennant Creek to Katherine was an exhausting seven-hundred-kilometre drive. But once we arrived, it was well worth it. We did a boat trip along the Katherine Gorge in the Nitmiluk National Park where jagged cliff faces have some of the oldest Aboriginal rock art. The hot springs were absolute heaven, all of us floating around enjoying the warm waters. There were warning signs about saltwater and freshwater crocodiles, which left me feeling apprehensive, but given it was the dry season when the crocs are supposedly less active, and lots of other people were doing the same, it was worth taking the risk.

Finally, we reached Darwin, where we got to experience more hot springs. We took a boat cruise on a billabong, and among the water lilies lurked plenty of crocodiles. One snapped when we got too close. We also got to see wallabies, wild pigs, Brahma cows with their camel-like humps behind their necks, and a wide range of birds. Litchfield National Park featured huge termite mounds, hot springs, spectacular waterfalls, and Komodo dragons. We ended the day with delicious seafood and champagne while watching the sunset. This had been a wonderful adventure, and we'd all enjoyed the many experiences. A welcome reprieve from the pressures back home.

# Counselling

Back home, the strain of our relationship returned. We couldn't continue like this. I insisted that we start counselling. So, with a psychiatrist who specialised in couple counselling, we started therapy together. It was challenging, each of us sitting at either end of the lounge – awkward, painful, hurtful, embarrassing.

As we drove Grant back to his work, we would both be silent, his anger simmering. I came to dread the sessions, but we continued for three years until the psychiatrist suggested we stop as he believed the issues within our marriage could not be resolved. In hindsight, I don't think any type of therapy would have helped us.

As a part of my rehabilitation after my clinic stay, I was given the opportunity to take part in a return-to-work program. This was a wonderful opportunity for me to re-establish my confidence and upgrade my skills so I could get another job. I studied bookkeeping, marketing and running a small business. A psychologist got me to draw a picture of my ideal job. I drew a community centre–craft shop, as I believed this represented the essence of any work that I would enjoy – being creative and social, and teaching others new skills.

I started a business called Crafty Fingers and taught craft classes at a local Salvation Army church. I loved the freedom, variety, and creativity of the job. I did everything from card making, scrapbooking, candle making to creating dream catchers and Christmas decorations.

Creativity is an essential part of my self-expression; it relaxes me, it's meditative, social and one of the best forms of therapy. When I'm in that creative flow, it takes me to a place of Zen, where I'm relaxed, de-stressed and detached from everyday issues.

## Grant's Asperger's

By this stage, I started to believe Grant was on the spectrum – specifically Asperger's syndrome, considered the milder form of autism. Currently, the model is to group all the different types of autism under the same umbrella called 'autism spectrum', but I am using the description of Asperger's syndrome, to give greater clarity. The three hallmarks of autism are: difficulty communicating; problems with social development; and obsessive, narrow developments.

A person with Asperger's may be very intelligent and able to handle daily life. They may be focused on topics that interest them, but struggle socially. Anger is a symptom of autism because people on the spectrum experience higher feelings of nervousness, emotional upset and anxiety than those not on the spectrum. Also, these feelings are brought on by frustration in social or communication situations that create sensory overload and difficulty in processing. I did my homework – I went to Autism Victoria to get relevant articles and presented my case to him. He was speechless and neatly filed the articles away in his desk.

This began one of the biggest conflicts in our marriage. One that never resolved. Grant was angry, defensive and resentful that I'd brought the subject up. He felt victimised, discriminated against and unfairly labelled. He resisted having a professional assessment, as he felt if he wasn't on the spectrum, he couldn't be responsible for his anger. It was a no-win situation. I would bring the topic up with my psychiatrist Dr Lam and our counsellor Dr Field (also a psychiatrist) but it wasn't taken as a legitimate concern. Yet from my perspective, him being on the spectrum was a major contributor to the issues in our marriage. This scared the hell out of me. Anger was ever present in our marriage, toxic to live with, a suppressing negative energy in the home.

# Gold Coast

## 2006

Life rolled on and we took another family holiday while the girls were in primary school – a driving holiday to the Gold Coast. We took the inland route going along the New England Highway, finding a beautiful spacious cabin overlooking the water in Southport.

I felt a mixture of anticipation and apprehension as always with holidays. Would the change in routine cause a flare up in Grant's behaviour?

We took full advantage of all the theme parks, with fabulous water rides of every description. Swimming has never been my strength, but I did enjoy a wave pool, which held 3.1 million litres of water. I wasn't keen on rides that were excessively fast, claustrophobic or high. These criteria limited the rides I chose to go on, but despite this, I managed to find plenty. For Grant and the girls, the higher and faster the ride all the better. I watched them getting strapped in ready for a ride that had 360 degree turns and I felt physically sick at the thought of what this would entail. While they joked about my hesitation with rides, they accepted my feelings. My favourite feature was Tiger Island, watching those beautiful creatures was amazing, so majestic, fierce looking, mighty creatures with much power and strength. I had to admire the courage of the handlers.

After a wonderful holiday full of fun activities, we drove back along the Pacific Highway, considered one of Australia's most dangerous roads for accidents and fatalities – not surprising with the way the road twists and turns. It was a stressful drive for me, being tired and struggling with anxiety. We stopped at Coffs Harbour to visit a marine park, where Elisha got to scrub the teeth of a dolphin. The seals were so personable, waddling up to us and letting us shake a flipper. It was an awesome experience to be up close and personal with such beautiful animals.

We continued down the highway until we reached Port Macquarie, where we found a lovely cabin in a caravan park. Jacinta had developed a cough, which was getting progressively worse. She coughed continuously throughout the night. At first light, I heard the distinctive laugh of the kookaburras. At six o'clock, feeling weary from having been up most of the night, I failed to see anything to laugh about.

We went to Tamworth Base hospital, where she was x-rayed and diagnosed with pneumonia. They admitted her as a patient, thus delaying our return home. I stayed at the hospital with Jacinta while Grant and Elisha explored the sights of Tamworth.

Once sufficiently recovered, Jacinta was released. Unfortunately, both Grant and Elisha started to feel unwell and developed coughs. Once home, Grant had a chest infection and Elisha was hospitalised with pneumonia. Strangely, Jacinta's pneumonia was viral, yet Elisha's was bacterial.

Meanwhile, the tension continued to build regarding Grant being labelled an Aspie – as he called it. Being a practical person by nature, I sought out information and assistance. I consulted a psychologist, Leanne, who specialised in autism. Firstly, she confirmed that, in her opinion, Grant was on the spectrum. This was a relief because I'd been having trouble convincing others, including close associates, that Grant was indeed on the spectrum. Doctors, professionals and other people in our lives had been non-committal, hesitant to make any judgements, questioning if it would make any difference to our situation. I was constantly coming up against a brick wall, and it was incredibly frustrating.

As I look back now, I think if Grant had been officially diagnosed – and he'd accepted this diagnosis – then strategies could have been put in place to alleviate some of the pressures on us and our marriage. I think too, without him being diagnosed, I felt I wasn't being heard, wasn't validated, and this created more anxiety for me. I recall Grant mentioning to a close associate, the possibility of him being on the spectrum. The person replied they didn't know the answer. I felt like screaming. Why didn't they encourage Grant to be professionally assessed and find some definitive answers, rather than giving such a wishy-washy answer? If there is one thing I have learnt in my life, it's to have a pro-active attitude to problem solving.

Meanwhile, I continued to manage the girls, do the housework and work part time, all while struggling with depression and anxiety. It was tough, and having little physical back up with the children made the situation a lot tougher. I would look at other parents who had a lot of support and feel quite envious and resentful.

# Working in Aged Care

## 2004 – 2010

I was relieved when both girls were finally in primary school, as this meant I could get a job and spend time away from the house and the unrelenting anxiety. I took a job as an activity worker for Uniting Care, where I met a wonderful person, Valerie. We worked together really well, and to this day, I still cherish her friendship. Valerie is a petite woman with vivid blue eyes and ash-blond hair, who shares my interest in cooking and craft. She has a caring and compassionate nature, and was very understanding and supportive during my challenging times. Together we ran activities in a day centre for aged people with dementia. We did craft activities, music therapy, quizzes, had theme days, cooked lunch and went on bus trips.

Dealing with dementia had its challenges. Some clients had epileptic seizures, others had diabetic seizures, often requiring an ambulance. I have always admired paramedics; I think they do an amazing job, given the daily pressures of their work.

Geoff, an eighty-year-old, sometimes became verbally abusive and physically aggressive, and it took careful management to placate him while keeping all the other clients calm. Patience was a necessary skill, since short-term memory could be an issue with the elderly, and we found ourselves repeating the same message frequently.

Soon, I changed direction to work more out in the community, helping clients with basic needs such as housework, showering, personal care and cooking or shopping. I enjoyed the role and found it more fulfilling helping people to stay in their homes rather than residential care. But while I appreciated the interaction with clients, I was still waking up with feelings of anxiety and sadness and would often be crying on the way to work. All I could do was focus on emotionally surviving the day. I honestly couldn't see what the future might hold for me or my marriage, what lay past the present mental and emotional pain. Every day, I felt more pessimistic about the possibility of ever being free of the anguish.

Community aged care presented its own unique experiences and challenges, giving me insight into people's lives and teaching me so much on many levels. I developed tolerance, patience, empathy and a good sense of humour. I always tried to be reasonable and fair; however, if I felt a client was treating me as a servant, not on equal terms, I wouldn't continue with them. The following was one of those cases.

~

My client's apartment was located on one of Toorak's most prestigious roads, and already, I felt out of my comfort zone. This was a luxurious apartment building, so my client was obviously wealthy. I pressed the intercom buzzer and introduced myself. I was met by Eva, the client's wife – Jewish woman immaculately groomed, coiffured hair, polished nails and adorned with expensive gold jewellery.

'Hello, I'm Yvonne, from MECWA.'

'Good morning,' Eva replied. 'I will show you the bathroom.'

The apartment was like a picture from Home Beautiful magazine, exquisitely furnished with stunning décor, no expense was spared.

There were two bathrooms and a huge room with wall-to-wall storage of clothes and shoes. Isaac, my client, emerged from his bedroom and barely acknowledged me with a grunt. I always made the effort to be friendly, and if this wasn't reciprocated, I could occasionally be brusque. This day, I already sensed the frostiness, which set me on edge. They obviously viewed me as subservient, and there was no rapport, no warmth. In all honesty, I would have liked to have run out the door right then. Arrogant people undermined my confidence and ability to perform my job.

Isaac took off his robe and sat on the shower seat. His nakedness didn't bother me, as I was used to showering clients by now. I ran the water, waiting for it to become warm, then positioned the hose over his back. It was an awkward angle, and just as I did this, the hose fell apart. I was horrified, sick to my stomach and embarrassed. How was I going to get out of this one?

'How could you be so stupid to break the hose!' Isaac berated me.

Speechless, I finished bathing him as best I could, then quickly dressed him. With burning cheeks and eyes brimming with tears, I grabbed my bag and dashed out the door. As soon as I got home, I burst out crying, humiliated and angry.

~

Hoarding was another issue I came across in my work, now recognised as a mental health disorder. Patricia, aged fifty and single, lived in a unit in Hawthorn. She had worked in the army. It was a hot day, and I was sweating profusely by the time I climbed the stairs and reached her door.

'Hi, Patricia. I'm Yvonne.'

'Lovely to meet you. Please come in,' Patricia replied. 'Sorry it's a bit tight in the hallway.'

'Tight' was an understatement. I could barely squeeze past all her piles of boxes and stuff. I was already feeling the effects of the heat, poor air circulation and, worst of all, no air-conditioning. Being asthmatic, I struggled. We went through the kitchen, again squeezing through mountains of stuff. Every single room we passed was the same.

'The main area I need help with is in my bedrooms,' Patricia said.

'It's got so out of control.' She explained she needed help sorting out and disposing of some of her clothes. It was literally standing room only, nowhere to sit, just rack upon rack of clothes. She seemed quite embarrassed and apologetic, so I tread very carefully and sensitively.

'So, Patricia, where would you like to start?'

'Could we begin in my second bedroom?'

'Sure, you show me which rack we begin on.'

This job was not only a health and safety issue but also a potential fire hazard; quite literally, there was barely any space to move. Even the bathroom was overflowing with stuff. I don't know how she was able to use her kitchen or bathroom, as they were so crammed full. We did some sorting of her clothes and managed to clear out some bagfuls. It is confronting and horrifying to see someone living in such circumstances.

~

Tensions sometimes ran high with clients, particularly with couples where one was coping with the impact of their disability, and their spouse felt the pressure of being a carer. Such was the case with Rodney and Rosanne. Rosanne was a feisty Jewish woman, small in stature, but with a fierce and dominating personality; however, underneath this show of strength was a caring and likeable person. When I first met her, she showed me her *mezuzah* – a scroll affixed in the doorway of a Jewish household, used as a type of protective blessing. She coped with her stress by going on clothes-shopping sprees, and her wardrobe was full of clothes with labels still attached and never worn. On the other hand, Rodney, was a friendly and easy-going man who had travelled the world while working in the navy.

I arrived one morning to find them in full combat mode.

'Rodney is being totally uncooperative,' Rosanne yelled as I entered the house.

I sighed inwardly at entering their war zone.

'Hi, Rodney. How are you feeling today?' I asked.

'Not well. Rosanne's been nagging me all morning, and I'm fed up with her.' He sounded rather depressed.

'Okay, I can see how upset you both are. Let's get you showered and ready for the day.'

For the remainder of the session, I relayed messages between them like a diplomat.

On another visit, while I was showering him, he lost his balance, slipped and fell on the floor. Horrified, I comforted him, covered him with towels, got a cushion under his head and kept him safe until the ambulance arrived. I felt terrible and responsible that he was in a lot of pain, but there was nothing I could have done to stop the fall. It didn't help that Rosanne blamed me. Rodney's accident caused him fractured ribs, resulting in a hospital stay.

~

Maria, a single woman in her seventies, suffered from multiple sclerosis. I helped her with showering, shopping, cleaning, and de-cluttering. She had led an independent and fulfilling life as a midwife, so being struck down by this disease was devastating for her – physically, mentally and emotionally. Although she preferred to stay in her own home, she was effectively a prisoner due to her limited mobility and opportunities to socialise.

She often had gems of wisdom to offer from her midwifery days, such as: 'When women are in labour, their honesty was at its greatest, revealing the truth about relationships.' She also thought a great number of women were not in happy in their relationships. This certainly resonated with me.

Helena, a seventy-five-year-old Australian woman, was married to Jean-Jacque, an eighty-year-old Swiss man who had worked with the United Nations. Jean-Jacque had dementia and, as can be the case, had reverted to his first language of French, so communication was challenging. The couple had worked extensively throughout Africa and

Southeast Asia, and their unit held an eclectic mix of art and mementos from their adventurous life – some unusual and interesting pieces.

Jean-Jacque came from humble beginnings, and was the first person in his family to go to university, where he studied languages. Helena became a nurse, and through mutual friends they met and later married. They had a son, Phillipe, and a Vietnamese adopted daughter, Annie.

I had been working with Jean-Jacque for a year, when sadly, he passed away from pneumonia. I continued to assist Helena with paperwork, doctor's appointments and shopping. We enjoyed coffee and delectable croissants at Laurent – one of our favourite cafes – and frequented the botanical gardens, observing the passing parade of people and bird life.

While sipping our cappuccinos, we had lovely chats about her travel experiences. 'We were living in Morocco,' Helena said. 'It was 1971, and Jean-Jacques was as a diplomat. He was invited for afternoon tea at the palace to celebrate the king's birthday. There was an attempt by military rebels to assassinate the king. Royalist troops took over the palace and defeated the rebels. Jean-Jacque came home bloodied from being caught in the crossfire.'

Another time, I asked her about Jean-Jacque's qualities.

With teary eyes, she reflected, 'He had a dry sense of humour and a good strength of character and kindness. Every time I had an operation, he would bring me a thoughtful gift such as jewellery or perfume. When Philippe took his life, Jean-Jacque was my tower of strength. There was never any blaming each other.'

Life has its ironies in that I ended up in a similar situation with Grant taking his life. Helena was incredibly understanding and empathetic. It was like we both belonged to a club we didn't want membership of.

Helena had a friendly and generous disposition, and despite the adversity and sadness in her life, she maintained a resilient attitude; she never became the victim. She said she put make up on to not only look good on the outside, but to make her feel better on the inside. If she wasn't using make up, she was giving up on life. That is true courage to me.

Even when Helena was in palliative care, in her dying days, she remained steadfast and positive to the end. I always admired her upbeat attitude, despite the many challenges of her life. Helena always took an interest in my life whether it was about my girls or the antics of my spoodle dog, Rosie. She was an unselfish and giving person, and her outlook on life profoundly influenced me.

The last time I saw her, she was sitting upright in her hospice bed, surrounded by bunches of flowers.

'Hi, Helena.' My voice quivered, tears filling my eyes.

'So lovely to see you,' she replied. 'How are the girls and Rosie?'

'Doing well, thanks.' Tears kept streaming down my cheeks.

'I'm not afraid of dying, of what lies beyond the veil,' she said, matter-of-fact. 'I've had a good life.'

'That's so good to hear, Helena.'

I said my goodbyes as best as I could and left knowing it was the last time I would see her. Though I was grateful for their nurses' kindness – taking me aside, listening to my grief – I sat in my car, held my head in my hands and burst into tears. A sobering moment.

Helena once told me Buddhism was the closest thing to her spiritual belief. After she passed away, I was given a photo of her and one of her Buddha statues, which to this day, I still treasure.

A cousin of mine who was working in palliative care once commented to me that, in her experience, it was sometimes the case that people who were highly religious had the strongest resistance to their death, while people who had lived rich and fulfilling lives were more accepting of their passing and unafraid of death. Our existence is finite, brief, in the scheme of things, and our mortality is but a reminder of what really matters most. At the end of my life, I hope I will have maximised the contribution I was able to make to society and been a positive and kind influence on the people I shared my life with. I believe that the success of anyone's life isn't necessarily what they achieved in their working lives, but in the humanity they expressed and how they enriched other's lives.

## Mum's death

On 27 March 2008, my mother passed away at age eighty-nine. In recent years, she'd had knee replacements, which had compromised her mobility and independence. Inevitably, she needed to go into a nursing home – a decision we dreaded, as do most people when it comes to their parents.

It was heartbreaking on the day, to see her anger and resentment. She stood in front of the nursing home, suitcase in hand, determined to go home. I stood with her, feeling her pain and anguish, wishing there was a better solution, yet knowing sadly, this was inevitable. Even though I was experienced with aged-care situations like this, today was different. This was my mum. It was heart wrenching to see her decline and suffering. Although she was an introvert and quite shy, she wore the pants in our family and wasn't going to accept this without a battle. A battle she, unfortunately, was bound to lose.

My daughters and I were at her bedside when she passed away. A memorial service was held at the Uniting Church in Heidelberg. Throughout the service, I kept thinking how very blessed I was to have had her as my mother. She'd left school at any early age to start work, until she became a stay-at-home mum. Like my dad, she was of the generation of missed opportunities and would have liked to have furthered her education. Despite this disappointment, she displayed all the qualities of love a mother could possess: kindness, patience, compassion, empathy, practicality, spiritual depth and strength.

The service was going smoothly, albeit punctuated by the noise of strong winds outside, when suddenly, there was a huge cracking sound. In the church yard, a sycamore tree had been completely uprooted. The sycamore has significance in the bible, being noted as one of the Plants of the Bible.

At the end of the day, as the sun set, grey clouds featured as a background to a spectacular rainbow. My mother had a fitting send-off.

# On the Spectrum and Separation

## 2008 – 2009

In 2008, I completed my Certificate IV in Training and Assessment. I really enjoyed the course, learning new skills and meeting people from diverse backgrounds. I continued my sessions with Leanne the psychologist, sometimes taking the girls to see her. This was still a bone of contention with Grant. I read the book, *Alone Together: Making an Asperger Marriage Work*, by Katrin Bentley and Tony Attwood. Grant's comment was, 'Instead of asking all these other people how to get on with me, why don't you ask me directly?' If only it were that simple. He still felt victimised and angry that I was broadcasting to people that he had Asperger's syndrome.

Leanne was very practical; I would describe an incident that occurred with Grant, and she would interpret it for me from an Asperger's perspective. Basically, teaching me to think like a person with Asperger's. I learnt how to plan family events to prevent potential pitfalls and minimise stress as much as possible. Despite this, we would still have our dramas and meltdowns. When I worked weekends, I would often get a call from the girls telling me that Grant wasn't coping, that he was angry and breaking dishes. The girls obviously found this distressing and were worried about their dad.

This unrelenting stress continued to take a toll on my health. I was chronically anxious, always on edge, crying a lot or, at worst, barely functioning. There were times when I couldn't sleep and panic overtook me, desperation making me pace the floor. I'd send messages on my phone to my friends and family asking them for prayers of healing. Sometimes mornings, before the day had even begun, panic would set in. I would ring a family or friend, just to have someone to help calm me down. They were wonderful in their kindness and sent messages of hope and encouragement to help me through my lowest points. I will always remember those who steadfastly supported me. They were the times I truly felt on the edge of sanity. I wouldn't wish that on anyone. It was hell on earth.

Being ever practical, I formed a support group for people with families or friends on the spectrum. We would meet in a cafe and chat about our experiences and situations. An interesting phenomenon occurred when one of the mother's children was diagnosed as being on the spectrum – the mother recognised the same attributes in the child's father.

One woman in the group had an eight-year-old son on the spectrum who was so depressed he was giving away his toys. He couldn't see any future. That case was extreme but, nevertheless, very sad. In another case, a husband with a wife who was on the spectrum rang me. His wife was struggling in her role as mother and needed a lot of support from him. I found a sense of camaraderie with him. A woman who was isolated on a farm, would ring me to feel a sense of relief in discussing her feelings and frustrations around her husband who was on the spectrum. Living in the country limited her opportunities for support, and from my own experience, I knew that social interaction was often difficult for people with partners living on the spectrum.

One suggestion Leanne made was to make a poster representing my concept of family life. I chose a photo of Olivia Newton-John and her husband, John Easterling. I have the highest admiration of Olivia's values, personality, achievements and tenacity. Her marriage to John represented the meeting of two people with the highest principles, values, love and healing ability. I had red hearts for love, white doves for peace and a verse from Ecclesiastes 3:5, 'A Time For Everything'. To me, this verse is so poignant and true of life; there is a pattern to our lives, where timing is so imperative. I placed this poster on what I called my 'manifesting board' – a bit like a wish list for my life – where I have lots of quotes and pictures representing my deepest desires.

In 2009, I took on a job as a trainer for aged care courses with a private training company. At the time, I wanted to expand my skills and experience, and this was a challenging role for me with a steep learning curve. I enjoyed the interaction with the students, but I didn't like the culture of the organisation. The staff weren't friendly or helpful, the training I was given for the role was insufficient, and my immediate manager was a bully.

After six months, my contract was discontinued because I wasn't prepared to increase my hours. At the time, I was upset, but in hindsight it was a blessing.

# Separation April

## 2009

The decision to separate was one of the most painful and difficult decisions I've ever made. It certainly wasn't made in haste – on so many levels, I still held a resistance. Loyalty, persistence and determination were some of my strongest traits, so giving up was contrary to my core beliefs. I was also concerned about Grant – how a separation might impact his dependant personality and ability to function. This weighed heavily on me.

But by Easter of 2009, emotions reached a boiling point between us – a point of no return. We'd had three years of marriage counselling, but ultimately, it hadn't resolved the issues or moved us forwards as a couple. The psychiatrist ended our sessions, stating there wasn't anything more that could be achieved. Such a slap in the face. And after all my sessions with Leanne, attempting to understand and live with Grant's Asperger's, he was still angry and hostile at the mere suggestion that he was on the spectrum. Something had to give.

The practical considerations of a separation were starkly real – how could we afford two houses? I certainly didn't have great earning potential, and there were the girls to consider. At age ten and twelve, they were old enough now to feel the impact. How would they deal with this change? I tried contacting a person, close to us to ask if they could accommodate Grant in light of my decision to separate, but they refused. I was absolutely gutted, angry at my greatest hour of need, that they were not there to support us.

My mental health was fragile, precarious. This was a crossroads in my life; there'd been so much water under the bridge, and every avenue of hope had been well and truly exhausted. There was nothing further to give, and nothing could save our marriage. And so, it was with all these considerations whirling through my mind and a heavy heart, I made the decision.

It was Easter Saturday, a beautiful sunny day, not a cloud in the sky. The girls were playing outside while I was hanging clothes on the line. Grant was working in his shed – his man cave. It had been a tense morning. We had argued when I'd asked him help in the house, and he'd declined. Both of us were still angry.

I put down the washing and headed over to his shed. He was drilling some wood. Standing in the doorway, I took a breath and said, 'Grant, I want a separation.' The words came out so abruptly, I felt sick to my stomach.

He didn't speak, but the look of shock and disbelief on his face told me this was completely unexpected. He stormed past me, went and grabbed the car keys and drove away. My heart sank. Were my worst fears about to be realised? Was he really about to take his life?

Around six o'clock, I was preparing dinner when he returned and headed to the backyard. Agitated and pacing, he refused to come inside.

'I don't want to keep living if we're separating.'

There it was. The inevitable. What was I to do? How should I react?

Without making it obvious, I attempted to ring the Crisis Assessment and Treatment Team (CATT), a service for people in mental crisis, but they weren't available to attend. Terrific, I thought, in my hour of greatest need they can't come.

In desperation, I called the police. They came immediately, followed by an ambulance and a fire truck. Grant was now out at the front of the house. As Joseph, one of the police officers, approached, Grant told him, 'My wife has just separated from me. I don't want to go on.'

Joseph responded with empathy, seeming to understand how desperate Grant was feeling. 'Would you be prepared to go to hospital?'

There was a lot of discussion and negotiation between Grant and the officers, but eventually, with eyes downcast, he agreed to let the ambulance officers take him to Box Hill Hospital.

Once Grant had been removed, the police officers and I went to the shed where Grant had planned his suicide. We found a mattress with photos of loved ones surrounding it, a helium tank, a mask and a tube. The police officers wisely advised me to hide the helium tank to prevent a possible suicide when he came back.

Finally, with all the drama over, the girls and I collapsed into bed, anxious and exhausted, and fell into a fitful sleep. At midnight, we were awakened by banging on the front door. The hospital, in their wisdom, had released Grant. I was shocked and horrified. How could they release someone in that mental state?

The next morning was hideous for us all. Exhausted, anxious and fragile, I sat in the car crying as Grant and I took the helium tank back. It was such a roller coaster of emotions, and I felt flooded with sadness and helplessness.

On the Monday, I took Grant to our family clinic. I stayed in the waiting room while he had a long discussion with the doctor. It was decided he needed to go into Delmont Hospital and was admitted as a patient for three weeks.

While Grant participated in the hospital's programs, the girls and I visited him. We tried to make these visits as upbeat as possible, bringing him in cards, photos and chocolates. The girls loved to tell him what was happening at school and with friends.

Grant was under the care of psychiatrist Dr Goldman, and I would sometimes join the last ten minutes of his sessions. This felt reminiscent of our couple counselling sessions, again raising our unresolved issues of his anger at me labelling him as being on the spectrum and my frustrations with his lack of support as a husband. I was left feeling even more anxious, trapped and without a sense of hope for the future.

He soon returned home, and a black cloud hovered over us, refusing to dissipate. His mood was fragile, and at times he seemed to be more withdrawn. There was no more talk of separation, and I tried my best to keep the home as stable and harmonious as I could.

In an attempt to lighten things up for the family, in August of 2009, we took another holiday. This time to Gippsland Lakes. We hired a boat that had comfortable beds and a well-equipped galley. We loaded our food supplies and belongings and set sail from Metung. Each morning, we plotted our course for the day. I loved the challenge of navigating Lake Victoria and Lake King, steering the boat between the red and green marker buoys. One night, we moored the boat to the jetty at Raymond Island. Another time, we moored the boat close to Bairnsdale and enjoyed a pub meal. When we visited Paynesville, we got to see all the beautiful pelicans and black swans. We had a lot of fun, exploring all the lakes and learning the skills of navigating.

I now have a particular fondness for these memories because this was the last holiday we had as a family of four.

Once again, when we returned home, there was a noticeable decline in Grant's mental state, and his body language showed signs of depression, his shoulders sunken. He commented that his boss had also noticed his demeanour had changed. It was a sad day when we went shopping to look at camping gear and Grant realised camping was now beyond him. Yet, he still wanted to reminisce about his previous camping days. I could feel his depression from being in this debilitating condition while still at this relatively young stage in his life. But it was beyond him now.

## Loss and Christmas misery

In December, Peter, a close friend and work colleague of Grant's, passed away from cancer. Grant found it too confronting to visit him before he passed away. Peter's death was a great shock to him and further affected his mental health. Whether the guilt of not visiting Peter before he died added to Grant's sadness, I don't know. Peter had a wife, Liz, with whom I got on very well. As a foursome, we'd shared many happy social times together.

I saw Dr Lam before Christmas. He checked how my mood was, if I was eating and sleeping well, how the girls were going and whether I felt supported. Every year at this time, I would try to have a plan of action to cope with the coming holiday period. Like a lot of people, I found Christmas had so much emotion attached to it, and hearing Christmas songs like 'It's the Most Wonderful Time of the Year' created heightened expectations. I'd learnt from previous experience that Grant's behaviour could be exacerbated at this high-pressure time, and I had to walk on eggshells. When the girls toddlers we were driving to my sister Joy's place for Christmas, and we had a huge argument. I was so annoyed that I pulled over and got him to walk home. It ruined the day; the girls were obviously upset that we had argued and that their dad wasn't joining us.

On the last Christmas we had (in 2009) For a combination of reasons, Grant did not join the girls and I when we went to Christmas lunch, so the day became a juggling act. This Christmas, in hindsight was poignant, we opened our presents first thing in the morning, then I set up for his family to have Christmas lunch at our place while the girls and I went to my family. I cried a lot, deeply frustrated at not being able to resolve the situation, no matter what I tried. Even as I reflect on those times, I don't think there was much I could have done differently to alleviate the pressures on this holiday period.

Christmas over, we rolled into January. Here, Grant's mood became particularly bad, suicidal again.

# Grant's Death

## 2010

That Monday morning at seven o'clock, with the birds singing and the blue, blue sky streaked with orange, I stood outside Grant's shed, dread in my heart. In an instant, my life had fundamentally changed. At age forty-nine, nothing would ever be the same again. My husband was dead.

Before I knew it, the police and ambulance were there. Our neighbours took me and the girls in while the authorities and medics attended to the scene. Another neighbour, a police officer, kindly identified Grant for me, saving me the horrific task. Later on, he and his family would take away the shed. I was so grateful for such kindness, for such supportive neighbours who were caring and ready to lend a listening ear. It meant a lot to me at such a vulnerable time.

I have no recollection of how I told the girls. I think my mind went into autopilot. The day and those that followed were a blur of people coming and going, writing the notices for the papers, arranging the memorial service, flowers arriving. A lot of phone calls to friends and family – Grant's parents, sister and her three children.

We decided on having a memorial service at our beloved Uniting Church in Heidelberg. It was a lovely gathering of people – friends, family, relatives and workmates – and both the girls and I spoke. There were heartfelt tributes, flowers, kind gestures. His work had made a beautiful memory album full of lovely photos and anecdotes, a generous and thoughtful act.

## Post Grant's death

The year following Grant's passing was very busy and full of new challenges. Because Grant's death had been a suicide, it required a police report and coroner's inquest. I gave my statement to the police, and this was given to the coroner's court. We had a will, so that made the legal process much simpler. I think 2010 was the 'year of paperwork'. It seemed to go on forever, along with the endless phone calls. I often started each day feeling overwhelmed at the tasks that lay ahead, but I tackled them one by one.

Fortunately, Grant had been an excellent manager of finances. He'd taken out life insurance and had a good superannuation fund. I was so grateful for these considerations, and never took this for granted. What he had done for us, in very difficult circumstances for him, was admirable. One of the most important decisions I had to make was to find a financial adviser. I took my time in deciding, as I felt this was a critical decision. I asked for recommendations and eventually decided on someone a friend of mine used. This friend was financially savvy, and I felt confident following her recommendation. This proved to be the right decision, and my financial adviser has been a steady and helpful support since. I started my own superannuation fund named, appropriately, Rainbows.

Soon after Grant's passing, I contacted Grant's psychiatrist, Dr Goldman, and notified him of Grant's passing. He expressed his condolences, saying, 'If only he had more time, the outcome could have been different.' While his intent was commendable, I felt this couldn't have been further from reality.

I took the girls to a psychologist. Many people suggested it was imperative that I do this. This psychologist was not a good fit for the girls – they didn't like her or the sessions – so I didn't continue with her. Instead, I closely followed the advice on my own psychiatrist, Dr Lam, and kept him up to date with how the girls were going. This gave me a sense of peace, knowing I could bounce ideas off him and make any appropriate changes.

It wasn't until April that I felt ready to deal with Grant's ashes. The burial site we chose was Eltham Cemetery. It seemed an obvious choice since my parents were buried there. It's still one of the most picturesque and peaceful cemeteries, beautifully laid out. We had a small ceremony with a minister, the girls and me. A simple but symbolic acknowledgement of Grant's life. The grief was still raw with a reflective mixture of emotions – sadness, emptiness, relief for the release of his suffering. It was a lovely sunny day, very still, barely a cloud in the sky, ducks waddling around the creek. I listened to the magpies warbling. The minister read Psalm 23, said a prayer, then we placed Grant's ashes in the grave. For me, burying his ashes was my way of processing his death.

# New Beginnings

## 2010

I understand it's thoroughly individual how each person reacts in a situation such as mine. The first and instant decision I made was that I wanted to move house. This was based on an emotional and practical basis – I simply didn't want to live the remainder of my life with a constant reminder of Grant's passing. Secondly, the house was ninety years old, weatherboard, and I wanted a fresh start in a house that would better accommodate us as a family of three, now that the girls were growing. My focus was on creating a happy and peaceful home.

The girls initially were resistant to selling the house, which in hindsight, I understand. Their lives had been turned upside down, and now I was selling their home. However, as the parent, I knew we had to move on, to make a fresh start and find a place that better suited our needs. So as much as I was sympathetic to their feelings, I made the decision.

In preparation for selling the house, we worked on the features most important to bring the house to a saleable standard. Our house was a 1921 weatherboard Californian bungalow. The location was in a prime position in Glen Iris, ripe for renovation or demolition. My feeling was it was going to be a demolition, since a lot of houses like ours were being demolished after sale. I've learnt to always follow my intuition; it's always been correct, and in this case, it was. I had a running bet with the real estate agent that this was going to be the case. Therefore, I based my decisions on this assumption. When the agent suggested spending thousands on painting the interior, I settled on only painting the entrance hallway. Why waste money on what would potentially be demolished? So, the girls and I de-cluttered, painted the deck, tarted up the garden and literally squeezed the excess of our belongings into the cubby and garden shed. On the days we had inspections, all of us cleaned the house, decorated with vases of flowers and set up the aromatherapy vaporiser with our favourite oils.

The day of the auction was a wet, grey, cold day in June 2010. The girls and I had got the house ready, and the aroma of lavender oil was flowing. When I felt we were under control, I told the girls I needed my regular cappuccino at my favourite cafe, E'latte, in Ashburton. Anyone who knows me knows how much this is a part of my daily routine. I seem to cope better with life having this daily habit. It had been an exhausting morning, cleaning and preparing, and the girls weren't happy, so I stormed out of the house, desperate for my caffeine hit. I don't think the girls appreciated how much I needed a breather from the stress and anticipation of the day. As I sat with my coffee, I reflected on the significance of the day, wondering what Grant might have thought.

The auction began, and I watched from the front room. Bidding was consistent, then it slowed down. Eventually, it came down to a couple in their fifties and a family with young children. The couple made the final bid, and so the house was sold. As I had expected, they planned to demolish the house. I signed the papers, popped open the champagne and celebrated the sale with family and friends.

The following Monday, I went to the real estate agent to place an offer on a town house that would be a perfect for us. After negotiating a price, my offer was accepted. It was truly an exciting time. A close friend, Meredith, was waiting at E'latte for me, an upon telling her the good news we clinked our coffee cups in celebration. We'd met through a mother's group, just after our babies were born. We clicked straight away and have since supported each other through all the ups and downs of our lives. By this stage, the girls had adjusted to the idea of moving and were excited about the many advantages of the new house, most notably, each of them having their own bedroom. They started making plans for furnishing their rooms.

The house was perfect for our needs: tri-level, three bedrooms, garage, two bathrooms and a garden I could manage. The most outstanding feature was that it backed onto Gardiners Creek, so we had a beautiful view of only trees, grass, and the creek. Plus, it was walking distance to a park. The other bonus was that the house had a pond, which would be a wonderful feature of the garden.

## Moving day

The day of moving ran as smoothly as could be hoped for, with lots of friends and family to help out. I couldn't have been more pleased about our new house, and I was determined to focus on making our home a happy and peaceful place for all.

While some people who find themselves single waste no time in searching for a partner, this was not on my list of priorities. First and foremost, my girls needed a stable home at this critical time in their lives. Secondly, I needed to process my own grief and feelings before I would ever consider having another person in my life.

Central to our happiness were our pet family: our guinea pigs, Emily, Heidi, Katrina and Sparkles; our cat, Gingertree; and our spoodle, Rosie. Our animals were not just part of our family; they *were* our family, our heart and soul. The comfort they provided, the reassurance and healing energy, their unconditional love, was precious to us.

We now had beautiful parklands at our backyard, with an off-lead area for our beloved Rosie. We'd had Rosie since she was a puppy in 2006. Like most animals, she was sensitive to what was happening around her. If any of us were upset, she had a way of snuggling up to us, giving doggy licks and being so comforting. She's still the most loving and loyal dog, with a huge personality, and I credit her for being such a comfort and source of healing in our lives.

Gardiner's creek has an amazing array of birds. On my daily walks, I noticed groups of magpies in the same spots. Evidently, magpies can stay in the same area forever. Maybe this explains why they become so territorial in spring. Today, I see currawongs with their beautiful yellow eyes and distinctive bird calls. I love hearing their lovely gurgling sounds as they settle for the night. Other birds include rare black cockatoos; kookaburras with their distinctive laugh; noisy miners, which are also territorial in spring; wattlebirds; swallows with their soaring and darting motions; and wrens with their distinctive blue feathers. The wetlands are also home to frogs, moorhens, and herons who like to check out the fish in my pond.

The girls settled in well. We bought new furniture to suit their bedrooms, painted their walls and organised lots of sleepovers. Elisha was passionate about animals, so we visited animal sanctuaries and zoos, undertook animal communication courses, and at one stage, she fostered kittens for adoption. Jacinta enjoyed gymnastics and dancing, so she became involved those types of clubs and activities. As they progressed through their teenage years, like all sisters, they had their disagreements, but each having their own room gave them the necessary space they needed.

I had the typical challenges a parent faces – the girls pushing their boundaries and seeking greater independence. Single parenting brought its own challenges too, and sometimes, I found myself second guessing the decisions I made. Was I being too lenient or too strict? Sometimes I felt lonely in my role, not having a partner to talk things through with. At social functions, being the only single parent, I was often the odd one out.

At one point, someone asked me if I would consider a future relationship. I replied, "Not at this stage of my life." This was a critical point in my girls' lives, and I didn't want to complicate it by bringing in another person. I felt they deserved my undivided love and attention.

I focused on their needs and happiness. I was philosophical – if, when my children were adults, a relationship came my way, well, that would be a blessing for me.

## Soul work

As part of the healing process of this new stage in my life, I did a huge de-clutter, making endless trips to opportunity shops. I tried my best to dispose of anything that no longer served me. I found this process cathartic. It made room for new things to enter our lives, and it was lovely to find recipients who were happy and grateful to receive.

I think there's some value in the principles of feng shui – an ancient Chinese practice that charts the balance of energy or *chi*. The goal of feng shui is to invite positive chi into your home so that your life feels both energised and balanced. It's a meaningful yet simple way to improve the vibes of your home.

On a general basis, I try to follow the principle. I'm a systematic and organised person by nature. If my home and garden are orderly and not cluttered, then my life seems to run a lot smoother. Whenever possible, I try to periodically de-clutter, reducing the unnecessary stuff in my place. It helps me focus on what's most important in my life, plus there's a bonus – I sometimes find things I've lost.

## Friendships lost

It's interesting to note the shift in some people's behaviour towards me after my change of circumstances. Some seemed threatened, as if they were more comfortable with my previous situation. Some, who were in abusive or unhappy marriages, seemed envious of my new single status. Others were incredibly rude about my increased finances with the payout on Grant's life insurance policy. 'Gosh, you did well financially,' they said. Never mind all the trauma and stress I had experienced during the marriage, let alone losing a husband under such horrific circumstances. And disturbingly, there were people who didn't like the fact that I was less easily manipulated – perhaps they'd previously had a greater sense of control over me than I realised.

Some people made comments like 'you're at a greater risk of theft' or 'you're at risk of flood' or 'is it a good idea to move from such good neighbours?' I recall showing someone my new townhouse, I was so excited to be able to move and start the healing process. To my shock and dismay they couldn't muster one positive comment, only compare the value of properties in the east of Melbourne to the western side, green eyed!

Some of these friendships were soon lost, but I didn't waste tears over them because obviously they were not true friends. It taught me something quite fundamental: people who are happy, stable, loving and generally have their act together tend to be the supportive and loyal ones in your life. Others who have their own agenda, that is, are egotistical, unhappy or have unresolved personal issues, can tend to project this and sabotage you.

Even years down the track, the ugliness still raised its head. I'd made considerable changes to the garden, taking out trees, putting in new garden beds, adding decking and updating the pond. My vision, hard work and creativity had made this garden beautiful, and I felt so proud of my achievement. Upon showing my efforts to a certain person, I was taken aback by their negativity – not one nice word to say about my garden. Although this left me angry, hurt and deflated, I understood they were not coming from a good place, and this was their way of putting me down so they could continue to feel superior.

My sessions with Dr Lam always left me feeling reassured with a sense of calm. Time and time again, I would relate scenarios and situations with difficult people, and he would give me his sage advice – strategies to deal with these circumstances without being unduly negatively impacted by them, ways to effectively communicate myself in an assertive manner. His advice was that we can only control and be accountable for our own actions. We are not able to control other people's actions or make them accountable for their actions.

I think, over the years, he has taught me to feel much more confident in my communication and expression and not be controlled by anyone.

## Turning fifty – reflection

By the time I got to my fiftieth birthday in November 2010, I fell in a heap, The combination of grief, anxiety and all the accumulated stresses of that year had taken its toll. The girls wrote me a poignant birthday wish, appreciating me as a mother and wanting me to enjoy my special day and not be sad.

It was taking me an incredible amount of focus and energy to get through each day. I think I was burnt out on every level. Many people asked us the same question: Could Grant's death have been prevented? All three of us gave an emphatic *no*. Firstly, he had been suicidal many times in the past, so this wasn't a rash decision. Secondly, both individually and as a couple, we had exhausted all avenues of treatment, without any resolutions. The marriage could not have continued; it was destroying us both.

Years later, when I was going through my papers in preparation for writing this book, I came across a letter Grant had written to me. He described the sadness he felt for the way things had been between us and the affect his behaviour had on me and the girls. He expressed his love for me and the girls and the effort he had gone to to provide a lovely home and lifestyle for us as a family. He described the difficulty he experienced in his role as husband and father, that he couldn't meet my expectations and needs. He shared his feelings of guilt at what he had put me through and concern about his relapses. Grant felt he would never be free of the feelings of depression.

I sat and cried when reading this – the lost dreams of a happy life together, Grant's despair at never fulfilling my expectations. The letter helped to remind me that he loved me and the girls yet, for so many complex reasons, couldn't express or live it. A sense of forgiveness transcended all the hurt, anger, and trauma I had been through, leaving me with a sense of healing, peace and closure.

For some people, suicide is still quite a taboo or contentious subject to talk about. Whenever I mention that my husband died by suicide, I almost brace myself for the reaction. Most people are empathetic and kind, while others show pity – truly, I don't feel sorry for myself, so why should they? One even said with a sideways glance, 'You look so normal.' Well, what was I supposed to look like?

I'm cautious about making generalisations about suicide here; my comments reflect my own personal experience. In a sense, I'm a voice for Grant. Despite his many mental, emotional and psychological challenges, he achieved a significant amount in his life. He didn't die due a lack of trying; he gave it his best shot and, in his view, was 'tired of living with depression' and couldn't see any hope of his situation changing.

At his memorial service, there were friends from his diving club days who commented, 'If only Grant knew about all the people here at the service who cared about him.' While these sentiments were genuine, even if Grant had been aware of this, it would not have changed the outcome. I think people need to be more sensitive about the judgements they make about suicide – mental or emotional illnesses can be just as debilitating as physical illnesses.

In the past, there has been so much shame attached to suicide. People sometimes insinuate guilt on those left behind, querying whether they could have done something more to prevent it. The suggestion of guilt has been raised with me several times. Without a shred of doubt, I reply, "I have none whatsoever." I'm satisfied that I left no stone unturned in my quest to help Grant. People need to have open and honest discussions around this topic, rather than making uninformed assumptions.

Perhaps if there is any lingering hint guilt I feel, it's that Grant didn't get to enjoy the fruits of his labour. But, in truth, this is more a feeling of sadness than guilt. He suffered so much yet managed to provide for his family under extremely difficult circumstances.

# Healing

## 2010 – 2014

### Port Douglas and Bali

As part of our healing process, the girls and I took a holiday up to Port Douglas in winter. It was delightful to escape Melbourne's grey winter. This was a significant time of adjustment in all our lives. Though we were flooded with a collective sense of relief that Grant's suffering was over, we were sad he wasn't with us to enjoy the holiday, since he relished travel experiences.

Temperatures were pleasant in the high twenties, and the sea water was twenty-four degrees. We loved canoeing with sea turtles. We hired bikes, rode horses on the beach and went rafting. Naturally, we got to explore the delights of the Daintree Rainforest – the largest continuous area of rainforest in Australia. It's also one of the oldest rainforests in the world. We took a boat trip up the Daintree River, which featured plenty of crocodiles. These ancient creatures line the river, live around waterholes and the ocean. I understand there's an average of two fatalities a year from crocodiles in Far North Queensland.

We later took another holiday, this time to Bali. I'd always been curious about the island, considering so many Australians holiday there. The moment I stepped off the plane, I was enveloped in the distinctive aromas and high humidity – a challenge, as I'm an asthmatic. We stayed in a lovely resort, enjoying swimming, shopping and delicious tropical fruit. Unfortunately, Jacinta contracted a stomach bug, which meant she spent most of the holiday in our hotel room. However, we still managed to do various trips, including rafting, which was a lot of fun. We did a cooking class that included a visit to the market early in the morning. I found the combination of heat, humidity and strong smells a bit overwhelming. The class itself was a lot of fun, and we learnt how to make traditional Indonesian dishes, including satay, nasi goreng and tempeh – a dish made from fermented soybeans. A tour around the island took us to Buddhist temples, rice paddies, mountains and rugged coastlines. I'd read that Bali's beaches were a highlight of the island; however, I was quite disappointed with what I saw.

## Chocolate shop

At this time, I was unsettled in terms of work. I'd left aged care and was unsure what direction I wanted to go. I was still struggling with anxiety and panic attacks, so returning to paid work was going to be a challenge. For a while, I did voluntary work in the creche at the local YMCA. I enjoyed working with the children, loved their honesty. With assistance from a return-to-work program, I got a job in a chocolate shop. Apart from the obvious benefit of sampling the best quality chocolate – one strange combination they sold was 'bacon and chocolate', and yes, people did buy it – I didn't enjoy the job, as I was still not well.

This situation wasn't helped by the shop's manager being a bully and berating me for any mistake I made. So much so, that I came to hate the job. One of the shop owners was also a difficult person. She was all smiles when sales were going well, but when sales were down, she treated the staff like children who needed to be scolded. So humiliating. She was so controlling that she would sit in a cafe directly opposite to spy on us and ensure we were offering samples to customers. Any staff who did not comply were told off. This job did little to help my fragile self-confidence, and anxiety and panic attacks left me no relief.

I've always believed in using both orthodox and alternative forms of medicine. I was on the highest doses of appropriate medicines and had made significant progress in therapy with my psychiatrist. Still, even with the excellent work I did with Dr Lam, I needed a complimentary therapy to address my deeper issues. I sought alternative approaches to healing anxiety. I tried hypnotherapy; kinesiology, which deals with the mechanics of movements of the human body; emotional freedom technique tapping (EFT); and attended healing services.

## Joy's death

On the 12 May 2014, my sister Joy passed away from a brain tumour. At age fifty-five, she left behind a husband two daughters and a son. Her diagnoses had come as a complete shock as she'd been otherwise healthy, had a good diet and didn't smoke or drink alcohol. The diagnosis had been eighteen months prior, so her decline was rapid. Joy loved being a homemaker, was a talented knitter and dressmaker, like our mother, and her home was warm and inviting. When my daughters were born, she knitted them beautiful baby blankets. I treasured these and have kept them for future grandchildren.

I will forever be grateful for the love and support she gave me through my most difficult times; she was my absolute rock, particularly with all the mental and emotional stress I endured. When my life lacked stability, Joy was my constant source of strength, always backing me up. When I turned fifty, she gave me a crystal vase, and every week I put fresh flowers in it, and each day I light a candle to remember her. I miss her terribly

## New counsellor

In 2014, my naturopath recommended me to a counsellor, Jan. This recommendation was to again change the course of my life. Upon meeting Jan, I was struck by her piercing blue eyes and caring, compassionate nature. She had a wealth of knowledge and experience, a deep wisdom and authenticity. A true healer. From the moment I met her, I clicked straight away, knowing she was the person who would help heal my anxiety.

She explained that Eye Movement Desensitization Reprocessing (EMDR) was one of the techniques she used. EMDR was first developed by Francine Shapiro in 1988, initially for the treatment of post-traumatic stress disorder. It's a technique in which a traumatic experience is recalled while doing bilateral stimulation, such as side-to-side eye movement. This enables the experience to be correctly processed. The principle behind this psychotherapy is that negative thoughts, feelings, and behaviours are the result of unprocessed memories. The treatment involves standardised procedures, which include focusing simultaneously on:

a. spontaneous associations of traumatic images, thoughts, emotions and bodily sensations.
b. bilateral stimulation, most commonly in the form of eye movements.

Obviously, the significant part of my trauma related to the issues I dealt with in my marriage to Grant. However, I also needed to address issues in my childhood and within the wider circle of my family.

When I was born, my mother and father were forty-one and forty-six years old respectively. I was an unexpected surprise and a struggle for my parents on their limited income. My father's commitment to his church activities – bible study, committees, missionaries, lay preaching and Rechabites (non-drinking society) – was overwhelming, and his family came second. Although I always felt loved by my parents, I never doubted that my personality – a questioning mind, rather rebellious attitude and a wider perspective of spiritual matters – caused further struggle. My wider belief system began at an early age and continued throughout my life, sometimes making it difficult for me to find my own belief and value system, particularly in relationships.

So, a major part my personality did not fit into the values and expectations of a morally conservative and religious family. This left me feeling quite squashed, controlled and restricted, obviously creating inner conflict for me. From this situation, I then went into a marriage with Grant that was ultimately also restrictive and controlling. So, for a major part of my life, I struggled to find my voice and be authentic.

Because there have been dynamics on both sides of my family that have been detrimental to me, Jan said, in simple terms, my therapy would be like peeling back the layers of an onion. Step by step, she would take me back to my core and deal with my issues, helping me to resolve each one before addressing the next.

Jan and I would begin with discussing a particular issue that had caused me distress – for example, the times when Grant would hop in the car, drive to the country and ring me in a suicidal state. Jan would describe the scenario then move a wand – a small stick – in different directions in front of my eyes. When she stopped, I would close my eyes, breathe deeply and relax. I found this process quite easy to accept, it seemed to make sense to me. She repeated this process until I felt I had processed the issue and released it. Sometimes when I saw Jan, I would just talk through the relevant issues.

I wish to stress that the success of EMDR is dependent on the quality of the counsellor and their relationship with the client – whether they click together.

Gradually, I began to feel a sense of release, and bit by bit, I let go of an accumulation of issues causing me anxiety, anger and distress. In the process, I learnt that anxiety was sometimes an emotion stemming from anger. In my early family life, being the youngest of four in a strict religious family was not the ideal setting for expression of my wants and needs. I wasn't able to express who I truly was. Then of course, I entered a marriage with Grant who had many underlying complex needs – a precursor for disaster for me emotionally.

Grant's needs were high, verging on 'dependent, but with a moody and unpredictable personality', at times there was volatility with outbursts of anger. With someone displaying these characteristics, I was in survival mode trying to pacify him and keep the family going. Deep down, of course I felt angry and resentful of this situation, yet at the time, I couldn't articulate this. Therefore, it came through as anxiety and depression. As simple as this explanation now sounds, it made perfect sense to me – truly an 'aha' moment – as I connected the anger causing me anxiety and depression.

Through my treatment, I learnt the processes of letting go and forgiveness, not an easy progression for me. But once I could identify an issue, process it, genuinely let it go and forgive, it was liberating and empowering. For me, this was a critical part of my healing. Once I started to release a lot of pent-up resentment, the anxiety started to dissipate.

At my most critical and vulnerable times, there were people close to us who failed to support Grant and me. But through my work with Jan, I was finally able to release that anger and be open to new and wonderful opportunities in my life. Holding onto that resentment was only hurting me and hindering my healing process. Ultimately, we are all accountable for our own actions and conscience. The most I can do is to try to live my life to the best of my ability. As a mother, I'm very conscious of what example I give to my girls, and sometimes actions speak louder than words. In the words of Michelle Obama, 'When they go low, we go high.'

## Assertiveness

My belief system is similar to karma – what you give out, you get back. Slowly, my confidence grew, and I began to assert myself in surprising ways. As Jan described it, 'When we learn and grow in new ways, we often challenge ourselves and put our new confidence to the test.'

For me, one of those challenges came in the form of Joanna, a new neighbour who truly pushed my assertiveness skills. She'd built a new unit next to my house and wanted me to change my existing house number.

'Hello, Yvonne. I've got my plans to show you, with the new house numbers,' she began.

'Oh,' I replied unenthusiastically.

'Our unit will be 1a now, and yours will be 2/1.'

'Well, I am not making any commitment,' I said tersely. I didn't see why I should have to go through all the inconvenience of changing my address – mail redirection, my driver's licence, my household bills, medical records etc. Besides, there were other units in our street with a similar mailing address i.e. 8a instead of 2/8, illegal but not challenged.

But my neighbours were persistent, and a few days later, as I pulled into my driveway, stopping to collect my mail, Raymond, Joanna's son, pulled up in his car, got out and approached me. It was a stifling hot day, and I was tired from work, so not in the mood for a neighbourly altercation. Raymond struck me as being highly intelligent, arrogant and used to getting his way and, therefore, quite irritated at having to deal with me.

'Can you please change your number?' he demanded.

'No way!' Indignant, I stormed off.

I wrote to my councillor and put my argument forwards. He was empathetic to my plight and forwarded my details to the postal manager. I kept contacting the planning department to protest at the unfairness of the situation. However, the legal situation was simple: if I didn't change my address, I was going to face a two-hundred-dollar fine.

During this process, these neighbours received one of our parcels and returned it to the sender instead of giving it to us. I then received one of their parcels and left a note in their letterbox saying they could come and collect it from me. I was nervous but determined.

The doorbell rang.

'Raymond,' I began, 'don't ever send one of our parcels back to the sender.'

'Maybe,' he replied with a smirk.

I flushed with rage and totally lost my temper. 'You f**cking arsehole!'

I threw the parcel, hitting his ear. I'm not sure who was more surprised, him or me. It was so cathartic.

Ultimately, I accepted that I had to change my address. I was okay with this because I had worked through the process. Even though it might sound trite, there are some situations where it's imperative to make a stand, assert yourself and express anger, while other situations require a different approach, where you don't sweat the small stuff. I hadn't meekly given into my neighbour's demands without a fight. To thine self be true! If I hadn't taken these actions, the anger would have festered within me and given the wrong message to the neighbours. When I recalled this saga to Jan, she roared laughing.

But I'm also aware that both anger, or lack of it, can be detrimental. Grant, unfortunately, had a lot of anger – one of the most difficult aspects of living with him – which was unhealthy for both him and those close to him. My mother was at the other extreme, she had the patience of a saint. Perhaps typical of her generation, she was the peace-keeper in the family and a dutiful wife; however, I don't believe that it was healthy for her to have played such a submissive role either.

One of the critical things I learnt in my sessions with Dr Lam and Jan was to be in touch with my feelings and to respond appropriately. We all face challenges and situations that cause us distress and anger, but how we choose to respond is what's important. If we don't find ways to effectively deal with this, then it creates emotional blocks in us, stops us from healing, forgiving and moving forwards.

I think this aspect was my stumbling block and biggest challenge to overcome. The times I was under the greatest stress in dealing with Grant and bringing up the girls, there were people in my 'village' who failed to support me. I was angry and aggrieved at this situation for a long time. It took many sessions and a lot of work on my behalf to consciously forgive these people of their negligence and failure.

Once I reached that point of genuine forgiveness, it gave me a greater sense of ease and ability to move on from the past, enjoy the present and make plans for the future. I am now able to appreciate what these people have taught me about how I live my life – I'm the opposite to them. I'm a nurturer and caregiver to myself and others.

During this phase of healing, I came across Oprah Winfrey's Super Soul Sunday series, where she was discussing the topic of forgiveness. I found her interpretation of the definition to be quite interesting. To her forgiveness is 'giving up the hope that the past could be any different'. I could relate to that interpretation. In the past, so much of me was vested in an ideal of what marriage and family life was going to be like. I held a dream and assumption.

I think too, I'm challenged in forgiving myself. I have reflections of my past and wish and wonder what I could have done differently. I still ask 'Gosh, could I have chosen differently?', especially at critical stages in my life. Ultimately though, I wouldn't be the person I am today without the choices I made in the past.

# Aged Care

## 2015

In July 2015, I started work in a forty-five bed residential aged care facility in the inner east of Melbourne. My role was an activity worker. This facility had a high standard, and in hindsight, I wish my parents had been in a place such as this.

With the manager, Fleur, we ran an excellent program with lots of activities, including: exercises, musical entertainment, craft, aromatherapy, massage and gardening. Quizzes were always popular and some of the residents' families and friends became quite competitive. Happy hour on Fridays was a lot of fun, those who were alcoholics were always trying to get extra drinks.

We did lots of theme day celebrations. One of my favourites was Chinese New Year, where we decorated the lounge with red lanterns and animal symbols and, of course, had Chinese food. Wherever possible, we tried to celebrate the nationality of residents. One resident was Spanish, so in October on the National Day of Spain, we put up posters, flags, quizzes and food all relating to Spain. This creative part of the job was what I enjoyed the most; I loved researching ideas and coming up with innovative ways to decorate the facility. The bonus of the job was that I was always learning and increasing my knowledge on so many levels – I learnt a lot about human nature, family dynamics and facilitating events. Each day presented its own challenges, unique moments and funny situations. It also highlighted the need to look after my own health because I didn't want to end up in residential aged care myself.

Halloween was so much fun. Fleur and I went to a lot of effort to give the place a spooky feel, dressing as witches and using palm tree branches as our broomsticks. We had ghosts, black cats, bats, witches, spider webs and pumpkins, all giving a ghoulish feel. Even if it was the day of a bus outing, Fleur and I would still set off in our witch outfits.

~

These bus trips provided Fleur and me with some light relief from some of the more serious aspects of the job. We visited a vast array of cafes, which the residents appreciated. Montsalvat in Eltham with its cafe and art gallery was always a popular place to visit. An artists' community, it has an old-world charm with lots of birds, including magpies, ducks, geese and peacocks. The Heide Museum of Modern Art and its associated cafe in Bulleen was another place we frequented; the cafe overlooked sculptures in a heritage-listed park.

We also took a trip to Flemington Racecourse, just after the major racing events, and were given a tour around the racetrack, stables and, of course, the spectacular rose garden. We were lucky to bring home bunches of roses, as the gardeners were pruning them. We learnt that the roses are planted and pruned to a strict timetable, each plant being recorded on a computer program to ensure they bloom at race time. Being a gardener myself, I loved the opportunity to view such a vast and beautiful array of roses.

~

Opportunity shops were another favourite place the residents loved to visit. One particular visit was memorable for all the wrong reasons. Florence, who was eighty-five, had dementia. She had quite a strong personality and was very social. She was chatting away to the ladies working in the store, while the other residents were content exploring the wares of the shop. I looked at Florence and, much to my horror, saw faeces running out of her pants.

'Fleur!' I called, beckoning. 'Come quickly. Florence has had an accident.'

'Oh my god,' she replied, horrified. 'What should we do?'

'Maybe we should get everyone together quickly and make a quiet exit?' I suggested.

Just as I started to round up the troops, a woman came with a bucket and mop to clean the floor. Meanwhile, Florence was still chatting away, oblivious to her accident.

'Florence, time to go now,' I said, calm but firm.

Florence was in full conversation. She looked at me, annoyed at being interrupted. It took some persuading, but we nudged her onto the bus, loaded up all the residents, then made our hasty exit never to return.

~

Margaret was another challenging resident. Aged ninety-four, she had dementia plus obsessive-compulsive disorder (OCD). When she was in her fifties, her husband came into an inheritance and left her; he couldn't cope with her disorder. It would have been unusual for a marriage to end in those times. Margaret could be charming but also forceful and aggressive. When being showered, she would scream 'get away from me' and physically lash out at the staff. Her screams could be heard throughout the facility. Her anxiety levels were high, and she was emotionally dependant on her son, so much so that she would stand at the entrance door waiting for his return. One time, Fleur took her into a supermarket, and Margaret didn't have her continence pad on. She urinated on the floor. Fleur was mortified!

On another of our bus trips, we went to an apple orchard and cafe in Warrandyte. It was blue skies and sunshine, quite warm. We had enjoyed afternoon tea with scones, and everyone was relaxed. Magpies were happily feeding off the crumbs that fell from the tables. Fleur and I have our system of unloading and reloading the residents and their walkers down to a fine art; safety and prevention of falls were paramount to us.

I unlocked the bus, opened the rear door and started to let the residents in. Normally, I wouldn't have left an open rear door unattended, but on this occasion, I did. To my horror, Margaret fell out the rear door and landed on the ground. Luckily, she was wearing pants and a skivvy.

'Fleur!' I yelled, trying not to sound too panicked.

'Oh my god. Margaret, are you okay?' Fleur exclaimed.

'Yes, I'm okay. I'm not in any pain,' Margaret replied, quite calm.

Fleur and I quickly jumped into action mode, and I suggested, 'Fleur, you look after Margaret. I'll ring the ambulance and take the residents back to the cafe.'

Understandably, the residents were all concerned for Margaret but realised we had the situation under control. We got blankets from the bus to support Margaret, gave her some water and held up an umbrella to protect her from the sun. Within twenty minutes, an ambulance with two paramedics arrived.

'So, Margaret, are you causing some trouble here?' one of the male paramedics joked. 'How are you feeling?'

'All the better for seeing you,' Margaret quipped. She had a flirtatious nature when it came to men, so I think she was secretly relishing all the attention.

The paramedics assessed her and, as a precautionary measure, took her to hospital. Her son picked her up from the hospital later than evening and reported she'd suffered no injuries but was still flirting and giving cheek to all the staff.

~

Nasib was a ninety-two-year-old Indian man with dementia, who had led an extraordinary life. Born into an impoverished family in Delhi, India, his parents were determined for him to have a better life and supported him to further his education. He would study by kerosene lamp, and he knew when it was four in the morning because the kerosene ran out then. His doctor warned him to stop this, as it would ruin his eyes. The wall in his residency room was covered with his many qualifications and life achievements. He had studied and lectured at the most prestigious universities around the world. He'd been a scientist at the top of his field, and at one stage, had worked with Einstein. President Truman requested him to work on the atomic bomb; however, Nasib pulled out of the project when he realised its potential for killing people. He had a rare combination of great intelligence and a wonderful sense of humour. He was successful yet humble.

Nasib came on one of our bus trips when we went to the tulip festival in the Dandenongs. We set out on beautiful but hot day with a group of ten residents. Whenever we took a group out, we had to plan ahead and ensure there was: suitable parking, so they didn't have to walk too far; toilet facilities accessible for aged people; walking paths accessible for walkers and wheelchairs; sufficient shade; and tables and chairs they could easily get in and out of.

Well, the tulip farm scored badly in most of these areas. Firstly, the paths were mostly uneven or on a slope, which made it difficult to manoeuvre walkers and wheelchairs. Secondly, the toilets had steps and were cramped. Lastly, the outdoor tables and chairs had no shade, which was a problem on a twenty-eight-degree sunny day. We unloaded everyone off the bus and of course, some of the group needed to go to the toilet straight away.

'Fleur,' I said, 'how about I take this group to the toilets while you take the others and start setting up lunch?'

'Yep, that's a great plan,' she replied.

Poor Nasib grabbed onto the handrails as he struggled up the steps to the confined toilets. While I assisted him and the others, Fleur set up our picnic lunch on the tables. When I returned, she had distributed hats, so at least we had some protection from the sun. We made sure everyone consumed plenty of drinks and tried to finish lunch as soon as possible. We still had a lovely day, but it was exhausting. Just as we were putting the residents back on the bus, I saw a man in a wheelchair rolling down the hill.

'Oh my god! Did you see that?' I asked Fleur.

'That was terrible. Thank goodness he wasn't one of ours.'

So, we got everyone safely in the bus, amid a lot of chatter about the day.

'Can we call Susan when we get back?' Nasib asked.

'Yes, of course we can, Nasib,' I replied.

A few minutes later, he asked again. 'Yvonne, can we call Susan when we get back?'

I got the giggles, then I looked at Fleur, who started laughing too. Because of Nasib's dementia, he would repeat this question about his daughter five minutes later, forgetting he'd already asked. Nasib noticed both of us laughing and joined in.

Working in aged care exposed me to a wide spectrum of people, behaviour and situations. People like Nasib leave left a significant impression on me, an example of the most important qualities in life to aspire to. While Nasib displayed many outstanding personal qualities from very humble beginnings, other residents showed very different personality traits.

~

Trevour, a man aged seventy with alcoholic-related dementia, had come into care with extremally poor health and was not expected to live long. His life was a stark contrast to Nasib. Trevour was Caucasian, born into a family of wealth who sent him to the most expensive private school, Geelong Grammar. He'd been married and divorced twice and had children from both marriages. Whenever we had happy hour, he was always trying ways to get extra drinks. Sometimes, our bus trips would visit shopping centres, and on one occasion, Trevour came along, requesting to visit Coles.

As I was bringing the residents back, I noticed Trevour coming out of the Liquorland store. I was horrified, as his walking appeared slow and wobbly. I looked into his walker and discovered a bottle of vodka, half empty.

'Trevour, what the hell do think you're doing buying this?' I exclaimed. I walked over to Fleur. 'Trevour has just drunk half a bottle of vodka.'

'Oh god! Just what we need,' Fleur moaned.

'Let's get everyone on the bus, and we can get rid of the bottle when we get back,' Fleur suggested.

When we returned to the facility, we took extra care to ensure Trevour avoided any falls, thus, not alerting management of the incident. It wouldn't have been a good look to return to the facility with a drunk resident. We got him inside safely and quickly confiscated the bottle. Unlike Nasib, Trevour didn't have many visitors, and eventually passed away with little wealth.

~

Relationships and sexuality were an 'tread carefully' area in residential aged care. Generally speaking, we didn't interfere as long as both parties were willing participants. Kevin, an eighty-five-year-old widower with two children, had vascular dementia – which is caused by problems with blood supply to the brain, usually involving a stroke. When his wife died, he came out as a homosexual and started a relationship with Hans. Obviously, in his earlier life, he'd not been able to be true to his sexuality.

It was lovely to see Hans come in and show his love for Kevin, making sure his needs were met. Often at happy hour, they would enjoy a drink together. When his children visited, it appeared they'd accepted their father's sexuality, as did all the staff and most of the residents – I only remember a couple of negative comments. This all made me appreciate how much progress society had made.

~

Warren and Theresa were a couple in their nineties who'd been married for seventy years – a platinum anniversary was quite an achievement. Warren was a jovial and social man, while Theresa was introverted and very demanding of Warren – the main reason they'd come into residential care. Theresa whined and complained a lot, which, after seventy years of marriage, nearly drove Warren mad. Another resident, eighty-year-old widow Annette, was attracted to Warren. she would sit next to them and hold Warren's hand, much to his embarrassment. Eventually, Theresa passed away, much to Annette's delight. Warren was all hers now! Annette kept making advances, which Warren grew tired of, though he joked that he still in demand at ninety-seven. One year later, Warren passed away.

~

Annette could be a little fraught, in that she had frontotemporal dementia (FTD), which affects behaviour and can result in an increased interest in sex. Hence, her frequent inappropriate sexual comments about men. We had a young male manager, good looking, twenty-five years old with a great physique. When he walked past, Annette made suggestive remarks. 'Oh, I'd like to get into his pants.' One time, when she was using her iPad, I was shocked to see her on a pornography site. I advised the nurse in charge who discretely took the iPad and blocked access to the site. With Annette's dementia, I'm not sure if she was aware of the site being blocked.

Annette's fixation on sex was discussed with her geriatrician. He queried staff about these incidents, and we all had a bit of a giggle at the funny side of the situation. It was the geriatrician who was going to have to broach the subject with Annette's family.

~

Betty, a woman in her seventies, had a heart of gold She was kind, beautiful and gracious with a great sense of humour. One of my favourite clients. In her youth, she had lost a baby soon after birth and had also suffered serious injuries after a car accident. Her husband, though quite intelligent, was an alcoholic, he had died many years ago. At one stage, they had lived in Coober Pedy, where her husband mined for opals. She had a stunning opal ring from one of his finds.

David was a ninety-year-old widower who came into the facility with dementia. He was catholic and had eight children. Betty and David struck up a friendship, which turned into a physical relationship. It caused some awkward moments when staff, myself included, walked in unannounced and found them in bed together.

'Oh!' I said, shocked. 'So sorry.' I could see their heads just above the sheets. I quickly retreated and left them to it.

They continued to enjoy their liaisons. David was quite besotted with her; however, their romance was short lived. One day at lunchtime, Betty was sitting at her usual table, and David went to sit next to her.

'I don't want you at my table!' she scolded.

David looked crestfallen and confused. Staff quickly directed him to another table. The sad part was that, due to his dementia, David continued to pursue her, having continually forgotten her rejection.

~

Financial abuse was rife in aged care, due to the greediness of families, but it was so difficult to prove. I recall one Spanish woman, Marina, whose daughter would come in and announce to her mother that they were making a trip to the bank to sign some cheques, it was known among staff that the daughter was taking large sums of money out of her account.

Another woman, Veronica, was an eighty-year-old widow who came into the facility with dementia. She had two sons who were lawyers and were comfortably off financially. One of her sons became obsessive about her expenses – how much was being spent on hairdressing, newspapers and minor expenses. It never ceased to amaze me the attitude some relatives had with regard to money and their parents. Sometimes, it seemed the people with the most money were the most unscrupulous and mean.

~

When it came to dementia, it was curious how some people's persona changed. While some personalities remained much the same, others changed completely, becoming angry and violent. To be honest, some residents were less likeable than others.

Sophia was a case in hand. A ninety-year-old Polish woman, physically incapacitated and with advanced dementia, she was one of the most difficult residents I ever had to deal with. She had two children who, I suspect, spoilt her and gave into her every whim. She constantly and loudly demanded attention, and the whole facility heard it.

Three o'clock in the afternoons, we often ran quizzes as part of our program. This time of day could be a challenging time due to the sundowner effect – a phenomenon where people with dementia experience increased confusion, anxiety and disorientation, beginning at dusk and continuing throughout the night. Usually when I did the quiz sessions, I would sit at the front of the lounge to enable everyone to have the chance to participate. However, with Sophia, I sat in front of her seat because she was so agitated.

'Suri, Suri,' Sophia yelled to one of her favourite carers, waving her arms at him.

'Yes, Sophia?'

'Come here.'

'Sophia, I'm busy and Yvonne is doing the quiz.'

'I need you now!'

Meanwhile, I kept running the quiz and answering requests from other residents and their relatives. But it was hard to concentrate with Sophia so agitated, as we had to be careful, she didn't fall out of the chair – restraining residents was deemed unacceptable and illegal. As such, staff would try to place her in a slightly lower chair that she was unable to fall out of. Nevertheless, Sophia would continue yelling, trying to get attention. At the end of quiz session, I was exhausted.

What a contrast Sophia was to sweet Veronica who, as her sundowner time kicked in, stood quietly with her suitcase at the door, expecting her sons to take her home.

We tried everything to pacify Sophia – activities, diet, different drug regimes, adjusted sleeping patterns – and specialists in geriatric care assessed her. Management kept pressuring us to find solutions, but nothing worked. At night-time, she cried out continuously, much to the annoyance of the other residents. When she passed away, there was a collective sigh of relief.

Another case was Christine, a ninety-six-year-old woman, thrice married with four children. She too had dementia plus a personality disorder bordering on paranoia. She was dominating and unpredictable and could, in a flash, ram you with her walker or physically lash out at you. Staff had to tread carefully with her, as she was mostly distrustful of people.

Everyone knew when she was on a rampage, as she would become obsessed about a particular subject and keep asking everyone the same question. However, I couldn't help having a soft spot for her. Underneath, she was kind and authentic, just very high maintenance.

~

Aged care certainly highlighted the need for residents to have nominated their financial and medical power of attorneys. Timothy, a ninety-year-old Irish man who had dementia, was being treated for pneumonia. He was given course after course of antibiotics, obviously with the aim of prolonging his life. It was horrible to watch his decline and suffering, especially when he openly begged, 'Could someone come and shoot me?'

Timothy had two daughters who didn't get on. While one daughter supported prolonging his life with antibiotics, the other wanted to hasten his passing by stopping them and, instead, focusing on medication that would alleviate his symptoms and hasten his death.

Eventually, he passed away without undue suffering. It can't be underestimated just how important it is for people to express their wishes to loved ones.

~

On a sad note, two years after I left my position, the facility was closed and placed in administration due to debts of millions of dollars. When I worked there, the staff knew the two owners of the business had previously been charged with animal cruelty and declared bankrupt, so we were suspicious and wary of them running this business. The management certainly put on a glossy front, using aliases, dummy directors and a family trust to conceal their involvement. They siphoned funds from the business to pay for their mortgages, holidays and luxury cars.

It's beyond comprehension how their greed and selfishness caused so much suffering, with staff losing their jobs and all the residents having to be relocated. Investigations are still undergoing, but it's hoped the truth will be revealed and justice will prevail. In hindsight, I'm grateful I left in time to receive my entitlements and not be made redundant with all the associated complications.

# Cruise

## 2016 – 2017

Now that the girls were older, I felt comfortable leaving them to their own devices while I went on a cruise to the Pacific Islands, including Noumea, Lifou, Fiji and the Isle of Pines. I was feeling a lot calmer and more settled within myself, so it seemed like an opportune time. It was my first encounter with a cruise, and I was curious to experience such a holiday. The ship was enormous, carrying two thousand passengers – a floating hotel – and provided a huge variety of activities and entertainment. I enjoyed scrapbooking, mini golf, gym workouts, the spa and reading.

One of the highlights for me was enjoying fine food and wine at the end of the day. I opted for a la carte dining, which offered a sophisticated dining experience. There were many live performances, and it was lovely to finish a meal, walk to a show, then crash into bed. I tended to avoid the buffet, where some people piled their plates up, determined to get their money's worth.

One of the onshore excursions was a visit to a farm that cultivated vanilla. Being in the tropics, the bush was lush and green. It was quite an education learning how vanilla is pollinated and cultivated – a skill passed onto the island's inhabitants by missionaries in 1860. The plants are actually an orchid, and when they flower, they're pollinated by hand. Once the pods mature, they're also harvested by hand and soaked in hot water to stop their maturation. The drying phase is next, followed by being placed in sealed containers. It was lovely to purchase some vanilla pods directly from their source.

For something a bit different, I did a trip to a hot spring and mud pool in Fiji. Kava was offered, but I politely declined because I found the taste too much like the mud I was smearing all over my body. It was an unusual feeling, a squishing sensation, and took a bit of getting used to. The mud temperature was quite warm, and it was a funny sight, seeing all these people plastered with mud.

Once the mud dried, I washed it off in a thermal pool, then moved to another thermal pool where I washed off anything I'd missed. Lastly, I was given a massage and some refreshing fruit. While I'd felt hesitant walking into a muddy pool where I couldn't see the bottom, overall, it was an invigorating experience.

Though I enjoyed the cruise – certainly I loved the dining, entertainment, leisure activities and onshore excursions – I found I felt quite lonely. The size of the ship, with its thousands of passengers, wasn't conducive to me to finding people I could connect with. What irony to be on such a large ship with so many people yet feel so lonely. In contrast, the European bus tours I had done with around fifty people provided more opportunities to connect and befriend others. I would still consider another cruise, but it would be on a much smaller scale.

## Phuket

Elisha turned twenty-one in 2017, and instead of having a party, she opted for a trip to Phuket, Thailand. We relished daily walks on the nearby beach, swimming in the pool, massages, shopping and enjoying the local food. I love Thai food, and I particularly liked mango with sticky rice. Simply delicious. We also enjoyed fresh coconut water; the nuts literally cut open to drink. Divine. The local transport consisted of

Tuk-Tuks – a small minivan with seating in the back. I was surprised how many Russian people were in Phuket, with many restaurants offering special menus catering for them. Given how cold the Russian climate is, I can appreciate their attraction to the warmer climate of Thailand. On one occasion, Elisha had gone to a restaurant by herself. Having anaphylactic allergies to nuts and eggs, she had to be cautious when ordering. Unfortunately, there were traces of a nut she had an allergy to and reacted immediately with nausea, vomiting and swelling of the lips. It was in the middle of the day with burning sun, high humidity and little shade, and poor Elisha had to drag herself back to our room, exhausted. Even when the best precautions are taken, this situation still arises for Elisha.

We took a cruise northeast of Phuket to Khao Phing Kan islands, which are limestone tower karst – vertical rock structures. One of the smaller structures, an inverse needle-shaped island called Ko Tapu, is unofficially known as James Bond Island because it appeared in *The Man with the Golden Gun* – a movie from 1974. Twenty metres tall, with a diameter of four metres at the bottom and eight at the top, it was an impressive sight and well worth the visit. All the boats in this vicinity carried the James Bond 007 logo.

We swam at the Phi Phi Islands where the water was turquoise and beaches white, sandy and warm. With both of us having fair complexions, we were fully protected with hats, sunscreen and rashies.

Another part of the cruise was visiting Koh Panyi, a fishing village on stilts. With a current population of 1,685, the village was established by two seafaring Muslim families from Kedah, Malaysia, more than 200 years ago. As we explored the village, we learnt it had a school, mosque, a floating football field and a health centre.

We enjoyed lunch in a restaurant equipped with high ceilings and fans to help to reduce the stifling heat and humidity. The view from the restaurant was beautiful, overlooking the Andaman Sea, but whenever a speedboat went past, the restaurant foundations shuddered from the waves. With the buildings packed so closely together, it was easy to forget we were walking above water until we caught a glimpse of discoloured water through the gap of an alley. I was shocked to find out they had only started receiving fresh water and electricity supply four years prior.

There were a lot of stray animals in Thailand, and as Elisha was training to become an animal behaviourist, she took a particular interest. I also struggled to see these animals suffering in such vulnerable conditions. We visited the Soi Foundation – an organisation dedicated to assist in the welfare of dogs and cats – and I was so impressed by the wonderful work they do to alleviate animal suffering.

Dogs in Thailand seemed to take on a more protective role in the household, rather than family pet. This made me reflect on Rosie's role in our lives. Rather than protector, she's our comforter and healer of anxiety and stress, motivator for exercise, and a focus for social interaction on walks when we meet the neighbours and community. The girls and I have been so blessed to have her; she's brought so much joy and happiness.

Next, we visited an elephant park – the absolute highlight of the trip. We got to feed and walk with the elephants in the jungle. It was pure delight to watch them in the river, to be up close and personal, and looking at them eye to eye was magical and spiritual for me.

We did this trip on the last day of our holiday and unfortunately, I was exposed to too much sun. A couple of hours into the flight, I developed a headache, felt faint, fatigued and nausea, I experienced waves of pain that left me debilitated, but all I could do was walk up and down the aisle and keep drinking water until, eventually, it began to subside. It was an unpleasant reminder to be more careful about heat in the future.

## Europe

At the age of twenty-three, Elisha qualified as an animal behaviourist. By now we had settled into our home, and again I felt comfortable taking another trip on my own. So in May 2017, I took my first trip to Europe – a lifelong dream. This journey took me through Scotland, England, France, Belgium, Netherlands, Germany, Switzerland, Austria and Italy. In particular, I wanted to explore Rosemarkie in Scotland, where a significant part of my ancestry lies.

The flight was uneventful with stopovers in Abu Dhabi and Dublin. At Dublin airport, I had never seen so many red heads in the one place. Nearly every direction I looked, there was another redhead! Finally, I made it to Inverness airport; however, my luggage wasn't there. I had hired a car, which turned out to be a manual Ford Fiesta. I hadn't driven a manual for over twenty years, so it was a bit of shock. I'd also booked a bed and breakfast (B & B) in Nairn, so with a map in hand, I found my way. The couple who ran the B & B were a lovely English couple who made my stay an absolute delight. The next day, having slept fourteen hours, I woke up relatively refreshed and happy that my lost luggage had been delivered to my door.

Visiting Rosemarkie on the Black Isle was a dream come true. Both my sisters and brother had already visited this place. It's an ancient village, with one of its outstanding features being the parish church built in 1821. As I drove down the narrow road through the village, I felt overcome with emotion – anticipation, excitement, happiness and curiosity. It was a picture-perfect day, blue sky and sunshine.

The graveyard overlooked the sea, and since it was springtime, hyacinths, jonquils, daffodils and bluebells provided a beautiful setting. I carefully examined all the gravestones, many of them with my surname. Some were so weathered, it was difficult to read the words. For a moment, I closed my eyes and reflected on my ancestors, trying to sense their spirit. I stood in awe of the history of this place, where so many of my relatives lay – a moving and spiritual experience for me.

Findhorn is a spiritual community, learning centre, ecovillage and charitable trust. I had read many stories about this place and was thrilled to be able to visit it. It had begun over forty years ago in windswept and barren sand dunes, which sprouted miraculous gardens. With guidance from God and listening to their small inner voices, the occupants used faith in the art of manifestation to create an alluring centre that now draws people from all over the world. They were able to contact and co-operate with the nature spirits, known locally as 'devas', to create these amazing gardens.

The style of the gardens was predominately cottage, populated with fences that displayed messages such as 'listen' and 'be still and know'. While there were large trees, the pathways were lined with daffodils, roses, daisies and bluebells. Other areas featured organic fruit and vegetables, plants from every climate, including tropical, and a pond of black, speckled and yellow goldfish. The exquisite buildings seemed to blend in harmony with the landscape.

It was one of the most stunning and inspiring places I had ever visited, peaceful, natural and harmonious with perhaps a touch of magic. Being a gardener myself, I was in awe of its beauty and found I resonated with the philosophy and beliefs of this community.

While in Findhorn, I reflected on my own beliefs about religion and spirituality. I had been raised in a strict Presbyterian tradition, but I'd struggled within the confines of its structured belief system. For me, the religion failed to answer some of life's bigger questions. I don't reject religion outright – there are truths and aspects that are relevant – but from my perspective, I found it limiting. Despite my reservations, I respected and admired my father's devotion to religion, particularly when he petitioned to keep the Heidelberg Presbyterian Church.

Instead, I find its *spirituality* that resonates with me. It provides a sense of peace and purpose, and I incorporate this into my everyday life. It may be while I'm sitting in the morning, enjoying my cappuccino, that I ask God/the universe for help in solving a problem. It might be while gardening that I sense the spirits of nature and connect with them.

I have a strong affinity to psychic energy. This may take the form of having a precognitive dream. It could be as simple as having a sixth sense about a person, whether to be wary of them or embrace them. I've learnt to follow my intuition – sometimes a random thought will come into my mind and help solve the simplest of problems or have a profound impact on course of my life.

Some of the philosophies of religion I find limiting include their rejection of the concept of reincarnation and mediumship – contacting souls who have passed on. The basis of my belief system is that we are a soul having a physical experience. We choose our pathway –who we are born to – and our souls grow through our experiences while on earth.

So, inspired by Findhorn's style and grace, I incorporated some of its ideas into my own garden back home. It shaped the concept of a garden being a place of beauty, reflection and introspection.

~

I then flew into London, where I had two days before I started my tour. It was a nice surprise to find it was light at four in the morning and didn't get dark until ten at night. Usually, I struggle with reduced sunlight in winter. I decided to use the double decker buses to tour the city. They were a fabulous way to see the sights. I had a good sense of direction, but I sometimes struggled with finding where the bus routes started and ended. I'm never hesitant to ask for directions though, so with map in hand, I set off.

My initial reaction to London was adjusting to the size, (compared to Melbourne), it struck me as a city segmented with different area's. I visited a lot of the typical tourist spots, enjoying seeing Kings Cross Station, as featured in the Harry Potter movies. I was fascinated by its architecture and curves and couldn't resist visiting the Platform 9 ¾ display and having a picture taken with the iconic scarf. It was a lot of fun, trying to impersonate one of the characters.

I crossed over London Bridge and viewed Buckingham Palace, continually reminded how steeped in history this city was compared to Australia's younger history. Harrod's was an fascinating retail experience, showcasing the finest of wares. I settled for a high tea, which I thoroughly enjoyed, typical for such an occasion I had English breakfast tea, scones jam and cream. To me, one of the delights of travel is the opportunity to walk. I was surprised by the size of Hyde Park and loved seeing the *Diana, Princess of Wales Memorial Fountain* – a beautiful tribute.

Finally, with great excitement, I joined the guided tour I'd booked. We were led by Gerald, a New Zealand man who was like a walking encyclopedia and full of practical advice on the history and highlights. Some people can be judgemental about tours, but for someone like me who was travelling alone, it was the ideal way to go. Tours have lots of advantages: everything is taken care of; the operators know the best places to take you; you often avoid the queues; and it's a lovely way to meet other people and not feel lonely on a trip, whether you're sharing a meal or chatting on the bus.

I often had people comment that I was brave travelling by myself, but I didn't think this was the case. Part of me enjoyed the freedom of being open to so many unique opportunities and experiences when travelling solo.

~

As we crossed the English Channel on the ferry, the Cliffs of Dover came into view – an impressive sight. With a sense of excitement, the passengers became chatty, busy taking lots of photos of the cliffs. Finally, we reached Amsterdam. I really enjoyed this city that, like Venice, is often described as the City of Canals. And I could see why. Of course, the bike paths were another feature – one I had to adjust to when crossing pathways and looking out for cyclists. This is one of Europe's major contrasts to Australia – cyclists are well catered for and given priority.

A visit to Amsterdam wouldn't be complete without walking down the Red Light District. It was a strange sight with such graphic displays in the shop windows, but we were given strict instructions not to take photos. Overall, I found the Dutch to be very friendly.

Our tour continued through to Cologne, famous for the impressive Cologne Cathedral – the tallest Roman Catholic Cathedral in the world – then we cruised down the Rhine River, viewing the hillside wineries and castles on our way to Munich, a well-laid-out Bavarian city.

Crossing over the border into Austria, we stopped at picturesque Innsbruck with its cobbled streets lined with shops selling traditional crafts, and snow topped mountains in every direction we looked. It had a lovely small-village feel and a stunning eighteenth century baroque cathedral called the Cathedral of St James (St Jakob in German).

We then journeyed along the alpine highway, reaching Venice, the capital of Italy's northern region. This city is made up of a hundred small islands in a lagoon on the Adriatic Sea. I was so excited to finally visit this famous city and ride a gondola. These flat-bottomed boats are such an iconic symbol of Venice, so I was so excited to experience one – a dream fulfilled.

Venice is one of those places featured in movies a lot, so it felt a bit surreal, though I was surprised how dirty the water was. I sat eating ice cream on St Mark's square, watching the huge number of tourists passing through – one of my pleasures of travel is taking in the sights and smells while people watching. The plentiful bridges and Gothic style of architecture are another feature of Venice – it's easy to get disorientated among the labyrinth of streets and forget the route you have taken. I very nearly got lost, realising just in time that I needed to pay better attention to where I was walking.

The furthest south we travelled was Rome, a city truly etched in history, culture, religion and surprises – one moment you're looking at modern buildings, the next, a historical site thousands of years old. The Colosseum with its incredible history was a sobering experience for me. As I walked around the impressive building in it thirty-degree heat, sweaty and hot, I couldn't help but reflect on all the tragedy and suffering that had occurred there.

That evening, a group of us from the tour had delicious Italian food in a restaurant close to the Colosseum. We had just finished our first course when a man serenaded us with a piano accordion. He played it with such passion. The next course was served while a beautiful Italian woman dressed in a black evening gown entertained us with opera. Her voice was stunning. Afterwards, we took a group photo in front of the Colosseum. Truly a night to remember.

The next evening, I sat in a restaurant in the Piazza Navona with its beautiful fountain called Fontana dei Quattro Fiumi, which translates to Fountain of Four Rivers. I ate typically Italian – pizza, salad and white wine – as I sat observing the tourists and absorbing all the culture and history of the city. Later, of course I visited Trevi Fountain and threw the obligatory coin in. I wished for good health and a safe trip. It was a bit of fun and nice to do.

Vatican City was remarkable on so many levels – religion, art, history and culture. The highlight was seeing the Sistine Chapel, its beauty, symbolism and grandeur totally captivating, let alone its spiritual significance.

As we drove into Florence, I viewed the outskirts of the city and reminisced about, years ago, watching the movie *Room with a View*, which was filmed in this city. I had dreamt of the day I would visit this captivating city, and here I was. Florence is known for its art, culture, architecture and monuments – we stopped at a bronze replica of Michelangelo's David, an amazing statue. I enjoyed shopping for clothes and handbags, purchasing a black leather handbag and beautiful silk scarf. Years ago, my sister Joy had visited Florence and brought back a handbag for me. I still treasure that gift today

While exploring, I was so absorbed in my surroundings that I got lost. We'd been given a meeting place, and as it got closer to the time, I became anxious that I couldn't find it. Panicking, I walked in circles, alone, without any means of communicating with my tour leader. I didn't even have the details of our accommodation on me for that night. Eventually, I approached a couple of local police. Communication was a challenge, but somehow, I was able to let them understand my situation. They took me to the police station where they contacted the head office of Trafalgar, who in turn contacted my tour leader. They gave the police the name of the hotel where we were staying, and the police officers kindly escorted me to the taxi stand. They were so friendly and helpful in my stressful situation. When I arrived at the hotel, I got a mixed reception. Gerald greeted me with open arms and a look of relief that I was okay. But a tour member made a sarcastic comment that I'd kept the bus waiting. Florence is forever etched in my memory.

We then drove through the Apennine Mountains, crossing the Swiss border then heading into the heart of Switzerland, Lucerne. The scenery was breathtaking with snow-capped mountains, winding roads and long tunnels. Our tour leader let us know how many minutes it took to travel through each tunnel. Lucerne, of Roman origins, is a picturesque town located on a lake. As expected, it had plenty of watch and chocolate shops. Of course, I tried out the local cafes and enjoyed many chocolate delights.

We stayed in a typical alpine-style resort, and I enjoyed walking down the road to the local pizza restaurant, where I could view the beautiful mountain scenery with snow on the peaks and experience the bracingly chilly but pure air.

Mount Pilatus, with an elevation of 2,132 metres, is one of the most legendary spots in central Switzerland. On a clear day, it has a panoramic view of seventy-three mountain peaks. Fortunately, the day I visited was picture perfect with blue skies, and the scenery was spectacular. From the viewing point, there were also a series of caves. The cogwheel railway that takes you to the top is the steepest in the world.

The last part of our trip was Paris, truly one of the most romantic cities in the world – a city of beauty, art, culture, cuisine, parks and famous buildings and monuments. We arrived at a hotel that was ten kilometres from the city centre. So, after we briefly checked in, our first experience of Paris was taking a cruise down the Seine. It was ten o'clock at night, and Gerald pointed to the Eiffel tower at the very moment it was lit up. A sight to behold!

I enjoyed a meal in an outdoor bistro just down from the Arc de Triomphe, which had surprised me with it underground walkways. I sat there savouring my delicious meal of grilled fish, sautéed vegetables and white wine, pinching myself that I was in Paris. It was a warm evening, and I soaked up the ambiance, enjoying watching the passers-by. Notably, a lot of the people seemed to be dressed more formally than in Australia.

I only knew a few words of French; however, most French people spoke English, so communication wasn't an issue. The Eiffel tower gave the most spectacular view of Paris, giving me an appreciation of the size of the city. Notre-Dame's architecture, history, beauty and religious significance had me in awe. It's one of the most beautiful and inspiring cathedrals I've ever seen. I sat there in a reflective state, calm and peaceful, appreciating the cathedral's majestic qualities. It was devastating to see the fire of 2019 cause significant damage. I was fortunate to have seen it when I did.

~

My first trip to Europe certainly whetted my appetite to explore other parts of Europe. It also motivated me to discover my DNA profile. The results were not surprising – I have Scottish, English, North-Western European, Irish and Norwegian ancestry.

My next trip took me to Scandinavia, Denmark, Norway and Sweden. I was impressed not only by the beauty of the countries but also the friendliness of their inhabitants – a similar friendliness to Australians.

My flight was uneventful until I reached Abu Dhabi, where my connecting flight was delayed, which in turn affected my flight from

Frankfurt to Copenhagen. When I arrived in Frankfurt, I knew I had to update my tickets. It was a Sunday evening with minimal staff, and I struggled to find the correct service desk in the complex airport. Seemingly more lost than ever, I became overwhelmed. Here I was in a foreign place, knowing very little German and facing security guards holding semi-automatic guns. Eventually, I found the desk I needed, and put the experience behind me, knowing at the end of my trip, I would have a deep sense of satisfaction of what I'd achieved as a solo traveller.

~

Copenhagen greeted me with blue skies and sunshine. I really enjoyed exploring this easy to navigate city with its beautiful parks, interesting shops, canals and lots of eateries. As with many European cities, bikes were commonplace, and I had to be extra cautious when crossing roads. I ventured around all the canals, took a photo of the Little Mermaid sculpture, inspired by the Hans Christian Andersen tale, and tried out the eateries.

I was surprised how accessible the palaces were – certainly a more relaxed attitude to security compared to places like Buckingham Palace. Evidently, these palaces are connected by underground tunnels. While talking to a tour guide, I was told that Princess Mary – formerly Mary Donaldson – was sometimes seen riding her bike here.

No trip to Denmark would be complete without visiting the birthplace of Hans Christian Anderson in Odense – a quaint, old fashioned and picturesque place with cobbled streets. The house, which is now a museum, had a fairytale feel to it, with Andersen's statue featuring in the garden.

~

Out of all the Scandinavian countries I saw, Norway was the most impressive in terms of beauty, history and landscape. Our trip continued through Stavanger to Bergen, which is surrounded by mountains and known as the 'City of Seven Mountains'. I was fascinated to visit the Telavåg museum, where during World War II, a Norwegian agent and two Gestapo officers were killed, sparking a savage response by the German occupation. The Fjell Fortress was built by the occupation forces, with 450 metres of tunnels built into the rock with room for more than two hundred soldiers. It had an overwhelming eerie sense – I was walking where Nazis had been, as if stepping back in time. Dark and damp, the tunnels chilled me with their history.

One of the most spectacular and scenic drives was through Trollstigen, where the mountain peaks were covered in snow, yet at seventeen degrees Celsius, it wasn't cold. The road descending into the gorge was steep with hairpin bends. I held my breath every time we rounded a bend. We then reached Geirangerfjord, known as 'the pearl of the fjords'. Fifteen kilometres long and 260 metres deep, its mountains reach up to 1,700 metres. Its beauty is confirmed by UNESCO (United Nations Educational, Scientific and Cultural Organization) including it on the World Heritage List. I took a cruise and was awe struck by the majesty of its Seven Sisters waterfall, which comprise seven separate streams, the tallest free-falling 250 metres. How exhilarating to experience the mist and spray from the waterfall.

Just before the trip to Trollstigen, we were having lunch in a cafe when my passport dropped out of my bag. I didn't realise until we got to Geirangerfjord. After an initial panic, I was advised my passport had been handed in, so the tour leader organised a taxi to transport it to me.

We came to Lom, which had a stave church built in the eleventh century. Its timber frame and poles – 'stavers' in Norwegian – is an example of medieval architecture, unique to Scandinavia. I was fascinated by its unique decorations, which were a mixture of Christian and Viking symbolism, including runic inscriptions, paintings and carved dragon heads said to protect it against evil. Being made completely from timber gave the church a warm and inviting feeling. I had never come across a church that embraced both pagan and Christian beliefs and found it intriguing. An explanation for this combination was given in the book *Nordic Religions in the Viking Age* by Thomas A Dubois. He said that for centuries prior to Christianisation, and for the centuries thereafter, communities developed their own versions of religion. This included their own deities, rituals and worldviews that helped to explain their situations at that time. Perhaps some of our present-day religions could learn from that, to be flexible of other rituals, beliefs and religions.

Our last stop in Norway was Oslo, capital city and home of the Nobel Peace Prize. It was a beautiful city with lovely wide streets, ornate architecture and beautiful parks.

The trip across the border to Sweden was uneventful, with the scenery quite plain compared to what I'd seen in Norway. Of all the cities in Scandinavia, I enjoyed Stockholm the most. The city comprises hundreds of islands with interconnected bridges and walkways making it a joy for me to walk. Stockholm's beautiful architecture is enhanced by the water surrounding the islands, adding a lovely ambiance to the shops, eateries and well-designed parks. So many places to visit.

I took a boat ride to the summer palace, Drottningholm Palace, where the gardens were exquisite. The palace has three main styles of gardens: baroque, being symmetrical and formal; rococo, a more natural theme; and English style. One of the most surprising places I visited was the Vasa Museum, built around a Viking warship. The Vasa ship was built in Sweden in 1628 but sank on its maiden voyage due to design issues with its centre of gravity and stability. Lying in the shallow waters of the Baltic Sea, the wooden vessel survived, preserved by the salinity of the water. It was discovered in 1956 and salvaged between 1959–61. This maritime museum boasted the only intact seventeenth-century vessel ever salvaged and displayed many artefacts that were both educational and impressive.

The other significant place of interest I visited was the City Hall. Built in 1923 from nearly eight million dark-red bricks, its architecture is described as 'national romanticism'. Of course, this is the venue for the Nobel Prize banquet held every 10th of December. The size, scale and artefacts within this building were impressive, especially the Golden Hall with its mosaic walls. It was certainly befitting the grandeur of the Nobel Prize banquet.

One of the more unusual experiences I had was the Ice Bar. This original and permanent ice bar had its interior theme redesigned by a skilful ice sculptor every April. The staff provided us with oversized coats to keep warm, and we sipped a cocktail in a glass made from ice – most bizarre and a lot of fun sharing drinks with my fellow tour friends. The attention to detail in the ice carvings was impressive.

## Hong Kong

In February 2019, Jacinta and I took a trip to Hong Kong, a place I'd always wanted to visit. When we arrived, it was Chinese New Year, celebrating the Year of the Pig, so the city was adorned in beautiful decorations. Hong Kong is a cosmopolitan city with a colonial past and an East meets West culture. Shopping was high on our priority – so many department stores and street markets, we literally shopped until we dropped. We did a lot of the tourist spots, including taking the tram up to Victoria Peak. The Peak has one of the best panoramic views, but on the day we went, there was only rain and clouds.

We took a sky rail with wonderful views to reach Tian Tan Buddha – the Big Buddha – one of the world's tallest statues of a seated Buddha. Climbing all the steps was tough but well worth the effort. A sight to behold, the bronze Buddha stands thirty-four metres high. The statue, which was completed in 1993 and is near the Po Lin Monastery, symbolises the harmonious relationship between man and nature, people and faith. Besides being a tourist attraction, it's the major focus of Buddhism in Hong Kong.

It was special to experience a symbol of such importance to many people's spiritual belief. As we approached the monastery, I could smell incense, and I appreciated this holy place's aura of peace and tranquillity and its beautiful gardens.

For me, one of the attractions of going to Hong Kong was the chance to visit Disneyland. This had been one of my bucket list items. I loved arriving at Disneyland in the train with its Mickey Mouse windows. I had a ball on the rides I took, including the Jungle River Cruise, the Big Grizzly Mountain Runaway Mine Cars and the It's a Small World boat ride. Contrary to my daughters, I'm conservative about the rides I choose. I find anything too fast or that rotates three-sixty degrees makes me feel sick and anxious.

The Ocean Park Polar Adventure was another theme park we visited. Its sky rail gave us a wonderful bird's-eye view of the city, highlighting the incredible number of apartments that house some of Hong Kong's population of 7.5 million. According to the Borgen Project – an organisation dedicated to addressing global poverty – Hong Kong ranks as seventh out of ten of the most overpopulated cities in the world. However, despite its population size, Hong Kong has a highly effective and sophisticated public transport system. I found it to be very user friendly and it made it a pleasure to explore the city.

Still, on my return to Australia, I felt a renewed sense of appreciation for our wide-open spaces.

## Europe again

My third trip to Europe was to Austria, Slovenia and Croatia in May 2019. I began in Vienna, as I was curious to experience its cultural, musical and historical significance. Stefan, our tour guide, was born in Australia, but his parents were from Croatia, so he had a wealth of knowledge throughout our trip. Our group comprised people from Australia, New Zealand, Canada, the United States, South Africa and Malaysia.

As I was staying at the Hilton Hotel on the outskirts of Vienna, I decided to try to walk into the main part of the city and came across an Irish family. I explained I was wanting to get to the city centre, so they kindly helped me navigate the train system. These are the experiences of travel that stay with you – the kindness of strangers. Once I got my confidence with the train system, I explored all the different parts of the city. Having a sweet tooth, I couldn't resist some sachertorte – a world-renowned chocolate cake invented in 1832 by Franz Sacher, a sixteen-year-old Austrian apprentice cook. It lived up to my expectations and was one of my culinary highlights of the trip.

One of the most amazing nights I experienced was at the Marchfelderhof 'restaurant', Austria's most historical and traditional restaurant. As we approached the restaurant, a lollipop man stopped the traffic to let us cross. The doorman then unfurled a red carpet, and a brass band greeted us. Talk about a VIP welcome. Every wall was covered in musical instruments, artefacts and the names of VIPs who'd stayed there. Some of the famous people included Cliff Richard, Elizabeth Taylor, Joe Cocker and Plácido Domingo. The venue felt like a living museum. All night we were serenaded by violins and singing. This once-in-a-lifetime experience was the most unusual and entertaining dining experiences I'd ever had.

The next part of the journey was Lake Bohinj in Slovenia, to visit the Church of St John the Baptist. Built pre-1300, the building is a beautiful example of medieval architecture with styles from Romanticism to Baroque. Fresco murals adorn its walls, and to me, it had a warm intimate feeling about it. On the outside is a fresco of St Christopher the patron saint of the traveller. It's said to give good luck and protection for the day.

The Postojna caves was a most spectacular tour. Twenty-four kilometres long and two million years old, it has a train service that takes you through tunnels, halls, galleries and caverns. These caves feature many stunning displays of stalactites and stalagmites, with the Concert Hall accommodating up to ten thousand people for musical performances. Humidity was high at ninety-five per cent and the temperature steady at eight to ten degrees Celsius. I was in awe of the beauty and scale of the features in these caves. It was like travelling through a world of its own.

We had a brief stop in Slovenia's capital, Ljubljana, which was an impressive city with mixed architectural styles dating back to the twelfth century. I liked the layout of the city with plenty of trees, parks, canals and bridges – a touch of Venice. It was a well-designed city with many unique features making it a pleasure to explore. I had morning tea at a cafe, but unfortunately, what I ate did not agree with me, and I felt progressively sicker on the bus until we reached Plitvice Lakes National Park.

When the bus stopped, I bolted into the toilets and vomited, causing me to get separated from the tour. It was quite chilly outside, so I took refuge in a nearby restaurant. It felt wonderful to enjoy the roaring fire and the aroma of delicious , enjoying the cosiness and warmth until my tour leader found me and took me to the hotel.

We then travelled to Croatia's Dalmatian coast to the city of Split, famous for the Diocletian's Palace – built for the Roman emperor Diocletian as his retirement residence in 305 AD. I had a wonderful time exploring this vibrant city known for its history, architecture and markets, and I enjoyed some local cuisine by the harbour.

Following this, we took a ferry to the island of Hvar, described as the 'jewel of the Adriatic', with good reason – it was a beautiful island, with crystal blue water, natural attractions, beautiful beaches, culture, fine food and wine and an excellent climate. Hvar's history dates back to pre-historic times and the island has served many purposes, including a naval base and a source of agriculture, fishing, trade and tourism. One warm blue-sky day, I walked up a zig-zag path to reach the sixteenth-century fortress. The view was magnificent, and I spent the rest of the day walking the length and breadth of the island, finishing the day at a restaurant overlooking the bay. I enjoyed seafood, a tossed green salad and a glass of white wine while I watched the setting sun glisten over the sea. I had a lovely relaxed and satisfied feeling of physical tiredness, reflecting on a wonderful day's events with gratitude.

After a glorious time in Hvar, we went further south down the Adriatic coast to Dubrovnik, famous as a filming site for the show *Game of Thrones*. Founded in the seventh century, it's a majestic city with a stunning coastline. The architecture features a mix of Gothic,

Baroque and Renaissance. Many of the streets are cobblestone and the buildings have distinctive bright-orange rooftops. From every angle, it's a stunning and picturesque city.

I had the opportunity to do a day trip to Montenegro, to reach the Bay of Kotor. Part of the trip passed through Bosnia, and I reflected on the 1992–1995 Bosnian War, which was part of the break-up of the Yugoslavia. This conflict, between Serbian, Croatian and Bosnian forces, resulted in over one hundred thousand deaths. Throughout my trip, there were reminders of this war – one shop displayed a photo a destroyed building, and next to it, a post-war photo of the building repaired.

As I mentioned earlier, Stefan, our tour guide, was Australian with Croatian heritage. Throughout his life, Stefan had often visited Croatia, so he was able to give us a personal view of life during communist rule, times of war and post Tito. This first-hand account gave us an excellent insight into the country's history and stages of development.

The Bay of Kotor is described as Europe's southernmost fjord. It has steep imposing cliffs that plummet into a narrow inlet of the sparkling Adriatic Sea. Montenegro means 'black mountain', and the area features some of Europe's most rugged terrain, averaging an elevation of two thousand metres. It has a diverse cultural base, reflecting its geographical location, with ethnicities including Greek, Italian, Turkish, Austrian-Hungarian and Yugoslav. The town has cobblestone streets, and the architecture is a mixture of Gothic, Romanesque, Baroque and Ottoman.

I took the opportunity to go ona group tour to the town of Kumrovec, the birthplace of Josip Broz Tito, late president of Yugoslavia. It was a beautiful town, and being spring, daffodils, bluebells, geraniums and roses were all blooming. We had a delicious meal with fine wine, overlooking a vineyard. The weather was perfect and the view simply stunning.

At the end of the trip, I spent some time in Zagreb, the capital of Croatia. The upper area of the city – a historic district marked by beautiful, cobbled streets – was absolutely stunning, with medieval settlements on hilltops. The lower section contains the parliament buildings and cathedral. Like most European cities, Zagreb offers a diversity of cathedrals, museums, and shops.

There was also a passionate focus on food – understandable as the town had an abundance of fresh, healthy and cheap food with plenty of restaurants to choose from. In the warm weather, it was delightful to enjoy my meal outside in the balmy evening. I also took delight in enjoying a cappuccino in a cafe overlooking the city square while watching the passing parade of locals and tourists. One day, a cohort of students jumped into the fountain, celebrating their last day of school.

A bonus for me were the lush, green parks located on the perimeter of the city. I spent many happy hours exploring them. I also visited the Stone Gate. Built in the thirteenth century, this sacred site is one of four main gates leading into the town. The shrine of Our Lady of the Stone Gate houses the painting of the Mother of God. This painting miraculously survived a seventeenth-century fire and is now protected by an iron fence. The square stone slabs are engraved with messages of the locals, mostly giving praise and thanks to the Virgin Mary. The Gate is regularly visited by people who come to light a candle and thank the Lady for protecting them. I certainly felt a sense of peace and tranquillity as I passed through this gate.

An interesting tidbit, I learnt while in Zagreb was that the Cravat tie originated in Croatia in the seventeenth century.

# Education

## 2020

My holiday gave me a chance to reflect on a desire to change the work I was doing. I had worked in aged care, in various roles, for several years and felt I needed a new challenge. After much research, introspection and discussion with my psychiatrist, counsellor, friends and family, I decided to apply for a course in education support.

To my delight and relief, I was accepted at Holmesglen TAFE straight away, and to celebrate, I booked a return trip to Scotland plus Ireland for July. At fifty-eight, I was excited to be making such plans for my future, in a job where my age would be considered an asset not a liability.

With great anticipation, I started my course in February. The course was practical, covering all aspects of education and learning including digital technology, legal and industrial issues, numeracy and literacy, developmental domains, first aid, supporting behaviour, cultural diversity and inclusion.

There was a wide range of ages of students from twenty to sixty, who came from a variety of backgrounds. Some were chiropractors, builders, shop assistants, traffic officers, plasterers, dancers, disability workers, traffic officers and former army officers. A lot of people were doing the course to upskill. Others, who worked in disability, hoped to complement and expand their work options, with this qualification being an asset.

Apart from the obvious benefit of enhancing my literacy and numeracy abilities, the course gave me a wide range of skills and knowledge, plus a renewed sense of confidence in myself. Maths had always been a struggle for me, and I also felt my skills in technology were lacking, so I welcomed training in these areas.

The course gave me a deeper understanding of the broad range of factors that impact people's ability to learn. I think both on a personal and professional level, this was the single most important thing I learnt – how complex the process of learning is. The most important aspect of teaching is to personalise learning for your student.

There are five developmental domains: language, cognitive, physical, social and emotional. We are all individual in our strengths and weaknesses in these areas.

Language is both spoken and written. Our verbal language includes para linguistics – how we communicate outside of the spoken word. For example: volume, intonation and speed. It's important when communicating that our verbal language should match our body language – that they are congruent, otherwise we are giving out mixed messages.

The cognitive domain includes mental processing – reasoning, thinking, working memory, being in the here and now, processing thoughts, auditory and visual processing.

The physical aspects are the way we interpret the world, including gross motor skills –whole limb movement and growth, and fine motor skills. Our five senses are a part of the physical, with the sense of smell being the strongest.

The social and emotional domains relate to how we experience, express and manage our emotions – how we react to situations and the ability to establish positive and rewarding relationships with others.

Cultural and religious factors also impact a student's ability to learn. In our western culture we consider it important to have direct eye contact when communicating with someone. However, with Aboriginal people, continuous eye contact is not expected or accepted as a courtesy of conversation. If unique qualities of cultures are not understood and accepted, it causes misunderstandings and impacts the communication and learning process. Similarly, with religious clothing and head coverings, if children are prejudiced and mistreated for their dress preferences or requirements, this will affect their ability to learn. Therefore, tolerance and acceptance of cultural and religious beliefs is an essential factor to be taught in the classroom.

Each of us have a preferred sense or style of how we learn – either visual, auditory or kinaesthetic. Visual learners prefer using visual objects, remember things better if they are written down and prefer note taking to getting involved in discussions. Auditory learners receive information through listening to the spoken word, their self or others and sounds and noises. Kinaesthetic learners require the physical experience – touching, feeling, doing, practical hands-on experiences. In recognising a person's preferred learning style, it helps to identify strategies that will help that person learn more effectively.

The course gave me greater insight into the role I would play in supporting the different needs of young people and how these considerations would impact their learning process. There needs to be inclusion, where no one is left out for reason of race, age, culture or disability. My role would be to have empathy, to be able sense other people's emotions and understand their situation. I needed to be able to listen, learn and observe. It caused me to reflect on my own attitude – my prejudices, presumptions and personality traits – and acknowledge how much that would impact the success of my role in education support.

As a part of the course, we did the Values in Action (VIA) personality test. I found it to be most illuminating. The test looks at twenty-four personality traits including: appreciation of beauty and excellence, bravery, creativity, curiosity, fairness, forgiveness, gratitude, honesty, hope, humility, humour, judgement, kindness, leadership, love, love of learning, perseverance, perspective, prudence, self-regulation, social intelligence, spirituality, teamwork and zest. The test results are then ranked in order of your strongest values. I was both surprised and intrigued by my result: love of learning, kindness, spirituality, love and curiosity. It was one of those 'aha' moments, when I saw my results in love of learning and curiosity. Suddenly, I looked back on my life and realised these were significant traits I'd overlooked about myself. Now I saw all the times I'd embraced learning – my love of reading, travel, courses and hobbies. I think I thrived on challenges and never rested on my laurels. Understanding my values gave me perspective to know what my purpose in life was. And now that I was clear about those values, I could easier align myself with opportunities that represented this.

So as a part of my course, I did a placement at a primary school that ran a Stephanie Alexander Kitchen Garden program. I had always admired Stefanie's work and social ethics and thought it was fantastic that she created such a program, initiated in 2001 at one Melbourne school. The program now operates in more than a thousand Australian schools. Stephanie, considered the 'grand dame' of the kitchen, has excellent credentials with a successful career in restaurants and writing. Her philosophy is that, by setting good examples and engaging children's innate curiosity, as well as their energy and their taste buds, they could be exposed to positive and memorable food experiences, which would form the basis of healthy lifelong eating habits. What I find inspiring is that she's authentic and lives her philosophy of food, gardening and living a healthy life.

Of course, with my cooking background and love of gardening, this was an ideal choice. So, I helped the students with all the gardening tasks: weeding, planting, mulching, harvesting and safety. The students loved their tasks and happily volunteered at lunchtime to help. And in the kitchen, I was impressed by how enthusiastic they were with cooking. It taught them so many valuable skills apart from cooking: teamwork, healthy eating, the joy of sharing a meal with friends and table manners.

Just as we completed term one, Covid lockdown came into effect, so our course went on-line. Like everyone else, I stumbled along with learning the techniques and protocols of Webex meetings. I would set myself up on the couch with my laptop, iPad and phone, Rosie next to me, and our cats, Lulu and Honey, hopping on and off at intervals. Often, at a critical moment when I was about to speak, Rosie would bark or decide it was time to chase the cats. By the end of the sessions, Rosie was tired and over me being distracted from her, so she let me know by incessantly barking.

## Studying autism

As a part of my course, we were asked to research a disability. I chose autism spectrum disorder (ASD) because Grant had been on the spectrum. Autism is a neurodevelopmental disorder characterised by difficulties with social interaction and communication and by restricted and repetitive behaviour. As I researched the history, I was alarmed to discover how people with this disability had been treated. My own perception and understanding of autism was initially limited, but now that I was working with students on the spectrum, I have a far deeper understanding and empathy.

The term 'autism' was first used by psychiatrist Eugen Bleuler in 1908. He used it to describe a schizophrenic patient who had withdrawn into his own world. The Greek word 'autos' meant self and the word 'autism' was used by Bleuler to mean morbid self- admiration and withdrawal within self. In the 1940s, Hans Asperger and Leo Kanner were pioneers in research into autism. Although they worked separately, there were similarities in their descriptions of the children they studied: difficulty in social interaction, difficulty in adapting to changes in routine, good memory, sensitive to stimuli, resistance and allergies to food, good intellectual potential, propensity to repeat words of the speaker and difficulties in spontaneous activities. Autism was first described as a form of childhood schizophrenia; then in the 1950s, a result of cold parenting; then as a set of related developmental disorders; and finally as a spectrum condition with a wide-ranging degree of impairment.

From the 1960s to 1970s the focus of research was on medications such as lysergic acid diethylamide (LSD) and electric shock and behavioural change techniques, which relied on pain and punishment. During the 1980s and 1990s, behavioural therapy and language therapy became the approach. Today, treatment for autism falls into four categories: behavioural and communication therapies, medical and dietary therapies, occupational and physical therapies, and complimentary therapies – for example, aromatherapy, art or music therapy.

My learning curve of autism began with dealing with my husband, reading, initial consultations with a psychologist who specialised in autism, then through a support group I helped to run.

There is currently a lot of discussion around the pros and cons of putting a label on someone who is on the spectrum. From a personal point of view, Grant was furious and never forgave me for labelling him as having Asperger's syndrome; he felt it victimised him. However, for me, it was a relief to have an understanding of his behaviour, given the pressures I was under at the time. Yet others, when given the diagnosis, are relieved and grateful to have some insight and understanding of themselves.

There are those who believe that, in some small way, we may all be on the spectrum, that we all have some of these characteristics, but some people are more towards the extreme end. This is a hotly debated subject, and I don't pretend to have a definitive answer here. I do, however, think it's important to have an honest, informative discussion, where the goal is for the higher good of those who are on the spectrum. Most importantly, there needs to be compassion, empathy, understanding and insight, and we need to listen to those impacted. This is why education is critical.

And I was so glad to be a part of this – finally returning to the classroom when lockdown was over and finishing my placement hours to complete my course. With all the challenges Covid had presented, I felt particularly satisfied with accomplishing it. I had gained new skills, confidence, friends, and along the way, it gave me the impetus to write this book.

# Health

## 2020

Now that I was studying, (my education support course) I had time to focus on my health. I'd had a couple of health scares in the last two years. One being severe abdominal pains, nausea and vomiting. Jacinta drove me to the emergency room at Cabrini hospital, where I was admitted, assessed and given appropriate medication so the symptoms became less severe, though I spent the night in the emergency department, getting very little sleep – an elderly man in another cubicle needed a catheter inserted, and it seemed the doctors were having difficulties. I heard every step of the procedure. It was painful to listen to, though the patient was stoic and took it in his stride.

I was discharged in the morning with a referral to a gastroenterologist. After many tests, it was discovered I had an ulcer in my stomach. I had several follow-up gastroscopies, and within two years, the ulcer healed. I believe the stress of the marriage was a contributing factor to causing the ulcer.

On my fifty-ninth birthday, I celebrated at an Italian restaurant with my family. It had been a lovely night, and we'd enjoyed the delicious food and wine. Later, I woke during the night with excruciating pains in my abdomen, followed by vomiting and diarrhoea. Again, Jacinta drove me to Cabrini hospital, but a bed wasn't immediately available. In my condition, the wait felt eternal, so when I was finally admitted I was so grateful and relieved.

I was given medication through a drip to relieve the nausea and pain but continued to have symptoms throughout the night. The conclusion was food poisoning, and I could only assume it was the prawns I'd eaten that night. The doctors made a formal report to the health department. I rang the restaurant but didn't get much of a response, not even an apology. Not the reaction I'd expected when I'd felt at death's door.

After a week in hospital and another gastroscopy to check on the stomach ulcer, I went home, weak and exhausted, but so relieved to have recovered.

As part of reviewing my health, I consulted an integrative doctor at the National Institute of Integrative Medicine (NIIM). An integrative practitioner is a healing-orientated physician who takes account of the whole person, including all aspects of lifestyle. Dr Pearsdale was a warm and engaging woman with piercing blue eyes. I liked her immediately. She took down a detailed account of my life, early childhood, relationships, environmental factors, stress and diet. She then ordered several tests, including blood, urine, faeces, and saliva.

The results helped explain several symptoms I had been experiencing. They showed a tumour marker for bowel cancer, gluten sensitivity and a thin gut lining. The most significant result was adrenal fatigue, and my cortisol, melatonin and progesterone levels were all too low. I also had elevated homocysteine levels, which can be a precursor to diseases such as diabetes, heart disease, cancer etc.

So, with the results in hand, Dr Pearsdale made her suggestions. Obviously, diet and exercise were critical factors along with appropriate supplements. She was pleased with the work I'd done with my psychiatrist and counsellor, as the adrenal fatigue was symptomatic from all the stress I'd endured during my marriage. Basically I'd burnt out.

I'd also done a lot of reading and research relating to health and diet. One of the most helpful sources was a book *What the heck should I cook?* by Dr Mark Hyman, a functional doctor. He has devised a 'pegan diet', which I found to be most helpful in navigating a healthier eating plan.

There are ten principles of a pegan diet:

1. Quality counts
2. Plants should be the star of your diet
3. Go gluten free or reduce gluten
4. Avoid or limit dairy
5. Avoid sugar
6. Eat fruit in moderation
7. Eat clean meat, poultry and eggs
8. Eat a lot of healthy fats
9. Vegetable oils are not a health food
10. Enjoy legumes occasionally

Because of Covid lockdown, I had a lot of time to experiment with new dishes. For breakfast, I now have a cereal made with almonds, seeds, a sprinkle of cinnamon – which helps with blood sugar levels, and a banana. My morning cappuccino is now almond milk. For lunch I have a banana waffle made with banana, egg, oats, cinnamon, a linseed sunflower and almond mix (LSA). For dinner I have barramundi on the barbecue, chicken, turkey, pork, tacos, rice dishes, roast vegetables, salad, steamed vegetables, and Thai dishes. For a snack to satisfy my sweet tooth, I'll have fruit or a nut, seed and chocolate slice. I include a lot of flavourings such turmeric, garlic, ginger, pepper and soy sauce. I have a vast array of home-grown herbs, including parsley, basil, chives, spring onions, marjoram, oregano, rosemary, tarragon and thyme.

With these changes, I've had significant improvements in my health. Giving up dairy has improved my sense of smell – a bonus. I continue to take anti-depressants; however, I've been able to reduce my anxiety medication to a small dose. At night, I take melatonin supplements and use a CPAP (continuous positive airway pressure) machine for sleep apnoea, so I now get a great night's sleep. I also take a number of supplements: vitamins A, B, C, D and E.

Stress management is a critical factor in healing adrenal issues, so I focus on my pets, walking, gardening, spending time with my family and friends. Another significant improvement – my homocysteine and cortisol levels are now at an acceptable level. I do have to pace myself, needing to sometimes stop and take a siesta; however, I can say that, in the last twelve months, I have more energy and feel a lot stronger within myself.

## Anne's accident

My sister Anne had an accident where she fractured her vertebrae and ribs. It was a huge shock, reminding me of the fragility of life – how our lives can change for better or worse in a flash. After a seven-hour operation to stabilise her spine, she spent a week in hospital recovering. She then went home, skipping a rehabilitation facility due to Covid. Her healing was a long and slow process, and I supported her in whatever way she needed. It was the least I could do, since she'd always been so supportive and encouraging in my most difficult times, particularly during my struggles with Grant and raising the girls. Fortunately, Anne made a complete recovery.

# Time to Reflect

## 2020

In November 2020, I turned sixty, and I was determined to celebrate this significant milestone in style. Throughout the year, I'd become obsessed – it was something to focus on through the monotony of lockdown.

Like everyone else's travel plans, my trip to Ireland and Scotland was cancelled, I was obviously disappointed but so grateful, with the benefit of hindsight, to have already done so much travelling when I could.

I reflected on the last decade and what had transpired in my life. Fifty had been such a turning point, re-defining who I was – a widow with two children to raise alone. For most, parenting presents its joys and challenges, but being a single parent, I sometimes questioned my judgement of how I raised the girls. My psychiatrist and counsellor were fantastic at giving me insight, perception and understanding of my skills as a parent.

After Grant died, I made the conscious decision to focus on the things that would bring us happiness and move us forwards both individually and as a family. The holidays we had at Port Douglas, Bali and Thailand were wonderful experiences to share. And I'd been able to focus on healing myself and find a pathway to happiness through self-development. I'd wanted to be the most positive example for my girls. Being a happy mum was the most important goal for me to aim for.

One of my proudest achievements was transforming my garden to feature a pièce de résistance – my pond. I removed trees, put in new garden beds, a vegetable bed, herbs and fruit trees. When I'd first moved in, the existing pond had been a struggle to maintain, and the design wasn't fantastic. I'd always dreamed of having a beautiful pond with goldfish, recalling the beautiful water features with every colour goldfish imaginable at places we'd stayed at. So I made the decision to find a professional who could achieve this for me.

With the help of Google, I found Philip, who came up with a brilliant design for my pond. Being a water feature expert, he understood what was needed, looking beyond the current pond and visualising a better design. With the help of his son, Philip produced a stunning result. I was delighted and took pleasure in introducing black, yellow, orange and speckled goldfish. This year, we had baby goldfish, such a thrill.

With the pond completed, it highlighted how ordinary the old decking now looked. Hence, the next step was to get a landscape gardener to replace the decking, retaining walls and fence. I also had gas connected to the barbecue to save the hassle of replacing gas cylinders.

Gardening is my Zen place. It gives me a sense of becoming one with the plants and the tasks at hand. In my travels, I was appreciative of the opportunity to have seen so many beautiful gardens. Of all the gardens I came across, Findhorn in Scotland was still the most impressive. Its spiritual basis was inspiring and fascinating, but the design of the gardens and buildings was perfectly integrated, blended seamlessly.

The other aspect of gardening I love is the plants I've been given by family and friends. They rekindle fond recollections. Gardening fulfils me on many levels: physical, emotional, mental, spiritual, social and also in a creative sense. It has taken eleven years, but now I have a functional and beautiful garden I feel proud to call my haven.

My fifties, though challenging, gave me incredible personal growth and transformed me in so many ways, shifting the core of my being, and I'm so grateful for the healing.

So, with family and friends, I celebrated my sixtieth at the Stokehouse in St Kilda – a restaurant that had burned down in 2014 and had been rebuilt. Perhaps there's a metaphor here – just like the phoenix rising from the ashes, this restaurant had been rebuilt, as too had my life. We had a luncheon limited to ten people due to Covid restrictions. The weather was beautiful – blue sky and sunshine, and the restaurant being next to the beach gave us a stunning view over the bay. I had a fabulous time; it was so lovely to celebrate with the people dearest to me as we came out of lockdown. Whatever else comes to pass in my life, it's my relationships – be they family, friends or pets – that I hold as the most important aspect of my life.

# Finding My Voice

## 2020

One of the most profound impacts therapy has had on me is dealing with difficult and challenging people. Most of us have had someone in our lives who have caused us considerable grief and anger. Sometimes it's a matter of not seeing a person's real personality until a conflict arises.

By nature, I'm an introvert, a sensitive and empathetic person with good listening skills, which at times, has worked against me. I usually try to have an open friendly disposition and expect the best of people, giving them the benefit of doubt, but in the past, I've let people take advantage of my good nature. Mostly, these people tended to be ego-centric or arrogant, and time and time again, I would listen, giving them my time and allowing them to take all my energy. If I was an upset with someone, I found it hard to verbalise my feelings, to stand up for myself, and it would only be later on that I would think of the perfect response, too late. However, in 2020, this all changed for me. I found my voice.

There were, of course, other people in my life who blindsided me. Confident people, who attended church, were non-drinkers or considered themselves of high moral standing. But I'm not going to give those people air space here. It's been a long process for me to arrive at this position in my life. If you had asked me years prior, then yes, I might have laid it all out bare here. But therapy and support from my doctors, counsellor, family and friends has taught me a lot along the way.

First and foremost, I can only control *my* actions in my life. I can't control other people's reactions. Secondly, by dealing with other people's negative energy on an emotional level, particularly in therapy, I've dealt with its impact on me, and it's freed me up to move on rather than being stuck with anger and frustration. Thirdly, I want to be the best example for my girls, and actions will always speak louder than words. I think too for me being in touch with my feelings and emotions, and working on my communication, assertiveness and forgiveness skills, plus focusing on my personal goals, has held me in good stead. Lastly, from a spiritual point of view, I believe we sow what we reap – what we give out, comes back to us. It may take time, but it does. Perhaps that's the Scorpio side of me speaking.

That doesn't mean there won't still be awkward moments for me to deal with. Like the time I was up the street and ran into a person who I used to be friends with. We'd parted on bad terms, with her expressing anger towards me. As we spoke, I realised I no longer felt any connection to her and hoped she wasn't wanting to rekindle the friendship.

The older I become, the more selective I am as to who I give my time, energy, friendship and focus to. Turning sixty, living through Covid and writing this book has given me time to reflect and appreciate the people who I want to be with. In my earlier life, I found it more difficult to assess people's character and deal assertively with people who behaved in an inappropriate way. Now I feel much more attuned and confident in understanding people and putting those boundaries in place. My younger self felt the need to be liked and validated by those around me, and had a sense of obligation to others. Now, I question those obligations and put my focus on people who matter the most to me.

# Working in Education Support

### 2021

I was now working in numerous school facilities – primary, secondary, catholic, special and specialist. A special school can include disability, chronic illness and mental health issues. A specialist school is for the specific needs of children who are: deaf, have physical disabilities or autism. I was shocked to learn how broad the autism spectrum is.

Two specialist autistic schools, in particular, caused me culture shock when I was challenged by the extremes of some students' behaviour. Suddenly a child might strip off all their clothes, another child might have an extreme emotional outburst, and yet another, a verbal and physical outburst.

Safety was the highest priority, and the staff were excellent in teaching me these skills. There were some heart wrenching situations. One case concerned twin girls who were both autistic. While one girl was happy in disposition, the other twin was depressed and tore at her clothes in expressing her anguish. It was heartbreaking to watch such despair. My heart went out to the families of these children. It's a tough and challenging journey for everyone.

Most teachers I observed did an amazing job. Their roles required considerable patience, resilience and strength. I only observed one occasion in a primary school where the situation wasn't satisfactory.

I was doing a casual shift and walked into the classroom where the other aide introduced me to the student I was supporting – a boy, Paul, ten years of age. The aide left the classroom, but the teacher didn't acknowledge me, so I introduced myself to him.

He had a specific spot for Paul to sit on, seemingly to segregate him from the rest of the class. He displayed no engagement, tolerance or empathy for the needs of this student who was limited in his attention span.

Sometimes, interacting with these students could be chaotic. Oscar, a nine-year-old primary school student, had oppositional defiant disorder. As the name suggests, this disorder is marked by defiant and disobedient behaviour – uncooperative and hostile to authority figures, peers and parents. Oscar was obviously a highly intelligent child, who liked to demonstrate his knowledge to everyone. He wasn't easy to communicate or negotiate with, as he believed he knew best. I watched with interest a session he had with a psychologist, who tried to use stamps and artwork to introduce new concepts to him. I spent most of the day either negotiating with or running after him. It certainly wasn't a boring day.

~

I had the opportunity to work with students completing the Victorian certificate of applied learning (VCAL) at a specialist school for students in years 11 and 12. The students had various disabilities, including autism, Down syndrome, cognitive impairment, cerebral palsy and attention deficit hyperactivity disorder (ADHD). The attention span of the students was limited, and anger could flare quickly.

At one school, the students were learning about occupational health and safety, and resume and interview techniques. They were taken to training facilities and visited potential places of employment. The program was highly successful as they had a high rate of employment for their students.

At another specialist school, I had the opportunity to spend the day with autistic students in a VCAL program called Make 'n' Bake. This is a food production non-profit business that creates delicious baked products, but also helps provide students with intellectual learning disabilities the opportunity to learn skills and gain employment. The training and practical experience gives them food certificates to gain employment. In the first part of the lesson students are given theoretical knowledge, and in the second part, they cook.

On the day I was there, they made almond biscotti. With my love of cooking, it was a delight to be a part of the process. It was impressive how each student knew their role, they were confident, enthusiastic, and enjoying themselves in the process. The staff who ran the program had excellent communication skills, were passionate about their work and instilled confidence in the students.

~

I found it refreshing to work with children at this stage of my life, enjoying their honesty and outlook on life. One of the best parts of the job was the range of subjects I got to do: English, maths, history, sex education, sign language, sports days, gardening, cooking, career guidance, languages, computers, swimming, woodwork, art, music and drama. Usually, I was only in a school for short periods of time, often just for the day, so the most challenging part of my job was to establish a trusting relationship with the students and teachers. I was acutely aware of the importance of communication, particularly my body language and being observant.

One of my most memorable classes was assisting a Grade 4 class in a specialist school. It had been a busy morning with a special birthday celebration for one of the students, so there was party food and decorations. In most classes, there was a mixture of challenges with the students – some were easy to manage, others were the devil incarnate. This day, there were some very disruptive students, and I was also struggling with the teacher, who wasn't good at communication and got frustrated when I asked for more instruction.

By now, my tolerance levels were low, so when one of the students hit me on my back, I protested to the teacher. All I got was a muffled non-committal response, before she continued with her sex education program. One child, Romeo, whose name suited him perfectly with his intense blue eyes and blond hair – almost an angelic aura about him – sat quietly trying to watch the program but was obviously feeling threatened by the disruptive students who were running riot around the room. What a fiasco.

~

The job appealed to me because it was challenging on so many levels, sometimes right out of my comfort zone. One morning, I arrived at a high school where I would be working with a student called Anthony – a thirteen-year-old of Iranian heritage who had an intellectual disability and cerebral palsy. Anthony attended a special school for part of the week; however, because he was in the local zone for this school, his parents wanted him to also attend this school, perhaps to give him a sense of 'normal'. The previous teacher's aide had left because the job was too stressful, and I'd heard that another support worker had needed to run out onto the road after Anthony. Obviously, my work was going to be cut out for me.

The assistant principal, Emmanuel, gave me a briefing: 'Apart from cerebral palsy, (he was able to move well) Anthony has limited cognitive ability with only rudimentary comprehension and processing skills, which can lead to frustration and outbursts of anger.'

When Anthony's parents dropped him off in the car park, I went out to meet them. I was surprised by his six-foot, heavy frame. 'Hi Anthony, lovely to meet you. I'm Yvonne. Let's get started. Say goodbye to your parents.'

I could tell he was reluctant, but he bade them farewell.

We headed into his allocated room, which had a whiteboard, iPad and other teaching resources. I started off by trying to engage him in some basic activities such as literacy and numeracy. Anthony wasn't interested. He stood and pushed the whiteboard to the ground, his height and build proving a formidable force.

'Where's Emmanuel?' he shouted, throwing his pencil case across the room. 'I want to see him now!'

I'd been told that Anthony was very attached and emotionally dependant on Emmanuel, but it was my job to assist the child.

'Anthony, he has work to do, and so do we. When it's recess, we can see him then.'

Anthony stormed out of the building towards the office.

'Emmanuel! Emmanuel!' he screamed.

I panicked, feeling embarrassed, threatened and totally out of control of the situation. Anthony charged into Emmanuel's office, and upon finding he wasn't there, went next door to the other assistant principal's office, shoved everything off her desk, then kicked the wastebin. The assistant principal had a look of sheer terror on her face, her body frozen in fear. I watched on, petrified myself, not knowing how to respond and fearing for everyone's safety. Hearing the commotion, Emmanuel came charging in.

'Anthony, I'm very disappointed in your behaviour,' he said. 'I'm calling your parents now to come and collect you.'

'No, Emmanuel, please don't call my parents,' Anthony babbled in a babyish voice. 'I want to stay here at school.'

Soon after, his parents picked him up and took him home.

I was relieved the harrowing day was over, but I still had more dealings with Anthony to come. Day two started on a similar pattern – I met him in the car park, took him to our room and attempted to start work with him. Nothing worked. He wasn't interested in engaging in lessons at all. Again, he stood and ran off.

'Where's Emmanuel? I want to see him now!' he demanded.

His physical strength was frightening – he managed to shove some wheeled steps with several students sitting on them. My training kicked in – safety lesson number one: do not confront or antagonise the situation further. Instead, I ran helplessly after him, unsure how to deal with this out-of-control situation. Terrified students and teachers ran in the opposite direction. The only action I could think to take was to call Emmanuel, who responded quickly. Again, he called Anthony's parents to collect him, as it was a health and safety issue. When they arrived, they were obviously embarrassed, so I broached the subject of recommending another specialist school.

'What's the curriculum like?' they responded.

Not an entirely relevant question in the circumstances.

'They run an excellent program specifically geared towards specialist needs for children such as Anthony,' I replied.

Unfortunately, his parents were in denial about their son's needs and his safety – for himself, the staff and the other students he was putting in jeopardy in this mainstream school. Emmanuel decided it was time to get Anthony assessed by a specialist and collect enough evidence to remove him from the school.

~

I had a similar experience with an eight-year-old boy in a primary school. Finn had autism, cognitive impairment, ADHD and was non-verbal. I met the school's principal, who was a warm and engaging person and appreciative of me accepting the job.

'When his mother enrolled him, she lied about the extent of his disabilities,' the principal explained. 'His parents thought enrolling him in a mainstream school would 'normalise' him, so I immediately employed an aide worker for one-on-one support. Unfortunately, he isn't toilet trained, and he smears his faeces.'

'Gosh, that must be difficult for the staff to manage,' I replied.

'It certainly has been. He should be in a specialist school, and we're having to spend eight thousand dollars extra out of our budget to have him. It's a ridiculous situation, but his mother is adamant she wants him here. She also has two more children with the same disabilities. The poor woman has no life.'

'Wow, that's a heavy burden to carry,' I replied.

'Well, here they come now. Don't expect any greeting from her,' Sharon quipped. 'And don't take it personally.'

I greeted his mother, then turned to Finn. 'Hello, Finn. I'm Yvonne, and I'll be looking after you today.'

His mother neither looked at me or responded.

Finn gave me a look of puzzlement as I took his hand firmly.

We had a huge classroom to ourselves, which I had set up with playdough, exercise equipment, books and art materials. Nothing sustained his interest for any length of time, and soon, he was climbing over all the furniture. Then boredom and overstimulation set in, and he began yelling and physically invading my space. Being alone in the room with no immediate physical back up left me vulnerable and feeling unsafe.

'Finn let's go to the playground,' I suggested. 'Remember to hold my hand.'

'Okay,' he grunted enthusiastically.

So, off we set. Unfortunately, he tore away from my grip and shot out of the school grounds onto the road.

'Finn, just stay there. Don't move,' I called, trying to sound calm, yet feeling horrified and panicked that this had happened under my care. Fortunately, there were no cars, and I was able to quickly persuade him back into the school grounds. I immediately notified the principal of the incident, who took it in her stride rather than blaming me, much to my relief.

When Finn's mother was told, she immediately attempted to record the conversation with me and the assistant principal, but the principal advised her she had no right to do that. The following day, the woman sent a letter from her solicitor threatening legal action over the incident. From that point, the school had to communicate through their legal department.

Inclusion of special needs children wasn't always so difficult though. And the focus of education has changed in recent years to be more inclusive of these children, providing more options for placements in mainstream schools where teachers give the students work suited for their level of development. I've worked in many situations where it was successful for the student and the school. Like the time I assisted James, a Year 10 boy with Down syndrome who attended a mainstream public high school. James had a passion for cooking, and he proudly showed me photos of his achievements. He was hoping to pursue cooking as a VCAL subject and eventually gain employment in that field.

Talish, a boy of Indian descent, was highly intelligent, very sensitive to stimuli, and autistic. Originally, he attended a mainstream primary school; however, it soon became apparent he wasn't coping and found this environment overwhelming. From the recommendation of the school, he changed to a special school. When I first worked with Talish, he needed to have one-on-one support, and he found the television and other students too overwhelming. Ever so slowly, the teachers were able to improve his tolerance until eventually he participated in the classroom with the television on.

There's still a lot of debate about inclusiveness and exclusiveness for children with disabilities. While inclusivity has merits and works in some situations, in other instances – as I've have described – it may not work or can become a safety risk for all concerned.

From my discussions with staff at schools, I was surprised to find out that schools have little control over a situation where a student is not suited and are unable refuse a student. I cannot understand why there isn't an independent arbitrator to advise and settle these situations where common sense should prevail. The focus needs to be on the highest good for the individual student, staff and school. In the case of Finn, despite funding the school received, they still had to pay an additional eight thousand dollars to support him.

To me, it was ludicrous that Finn was missing out on the benefit of a special school, where he could learn routine, boundaries and receive care specifically suited to his needs. Yet, Finn's parents refused to have him professionally assessed, further compounding the situation – a selfish position, to my mind, as he would have been entitled to additional support and funding. Quite frankly, I think he's a ticking time bomb, given his physical and verbal outbursts. As he grows and becomes older and stronger, he's at risk of becoming more violent. I certainly felt conscious of my safety being compromised because of the poor decision his parents made.

~

One of the most humbling experiences for me was working with sixteen-year-old identical twins, Alicia and Lin, in an inner-city mainstream high school. Originally from Vietnam, where their parents ran a restaurant, both had been born blind and shared a strong bond and wonderful sense of humour. They were like two peas in a pod, finishing each other's sentences and manoeuvring together with their canes. This was my first experience of working with blind students.

'Our father came to Australia as a refugee on a boat,' Alicia explained. 'Once he was settled, the rest of the family came. We were so grateful to come to this country, the land of opportunity, offering better disability support for us.'

'Our father later divorced our mother and remarried,' Lin chipped in, 'but that was okay because we were so grateful that he made it possible for us to come to Australia.'

I tried to support them in any way I could, while also encouraging independence where possible. It was a fine line trying to accomplish this. They're learning was through me giving them a running commentary of a program, while they used braille computers and their sense of touch.

Their maths class was on Year 10 geometry, learning about different shapes. Maths had always been my weakest subject, so I felt daunted at the prospect of helping them; however, I was surprised how easy the task was.

'So, Lin, what shape do you have?' I asked, handing her a piece of bent plastic.

'It's a triangle,' she replied.

'Can you tell me what type of triangle it is?'

'It's a right-angle triangle,' she stated confidently.

We went outside, and using string and a tape measure, we measured as many shapes as possible that we could find.

'Thanks for all your help today, Yvonne,' they both chimed.

'You're very welcome. It's been my pleasure.'

It had been a very satisfying day. I'd learnt so much about assisting vision impaired people.

These girls were fortunate to have the financial and physical support they needed. But other children weren't so lucky, with socio-economic factors having a huge impact on their access and ability to learn. Johnny, a six-year-old boy of Māori heritage, was one of nine children living in a two-bedroom house. His parents attended a Pentecostal church. Teachers had visited him at home and described it as chaos. None of the children had been to childcare or kindergarten, so their social skills had been affected. Yet, Johnny was a delightful child, though with a short attention span. To compensate for this, when he'd completed some work, we broke it up with some outside playtime. He often said he was hungry, so I imagine money for food was also limited within the family.

Working with all these children on a casual basis, in a range of schools, often humbled and reminded me of the many blessings in my life. The experience didn't only develop my professional skills, but also touched me on a very personal level, increasing my awareness of disability, enhancing my communication skills and expanding my empathy and understanding.

Many times, I reflected on Grant and wondered what difference it might have made if he'd been diagnosed early in his life. Perhaps he would have accepted it and had more support to live a more fulfilling life.

# Covid and Beyond

## 2021

By October 2021, it looked like were coming to the end of lockdown number six. In the past eighteen months, our lives have had fundamentally changed by Covid. This time was a critical one as we moved towards the magical eighty per cent vaccination rate – a figure that would afford us our freedom and a new sense of normality.

I chose the AstraZeneca vaccination and was fortunate to not have any side effects. It was a very changed world to navigate through – compulsory vaccination in the workforce, working from home, technology at the forefront with zoom meetings. And we now had the option of doctor appointments by phone.

Despite the tremendous negative impact Covid had on our lives, there were some silver linings. It gave people the opportunity to pause and reflect on their lives, to consider if they were happy with the way things were. Personally, I used the opportunity of those eighteen months to leave my former career, retrain, then begin a new career.

The other opportunity I took was to de-clutter my house and garden and spend more time with my pets. Some people loath de-cluttering, but I'm one of those people who love it. For me, it's a cleansing process, and my life seems to run more smoothly when I get rid of the crap. I find lost treasures and can locate things in my house much more easily.

It also gave me the opportunity to keep focusing on my health, with consulting my integrative doctor and experimenting with new food and diet ideas.

One of my Covid pleasures was walking Rosie in her pram twice a day. Rosie had previously suffered a slipped disc requiring surgery. Given her age of fourteen, it had been a risk, but we didn't have any choice. When I dropped her off for surgery, it was at the time of curfew with eerily quiet streets. Her operation was on a Sunday at midnight, and much to our relief, she came through the operation well. Then came six weeks of confinement in a crate, which was stressful for both her and us. This was followed up with hydrotherapy, a physiotherapist and a special exercise program.

Because her walking was initially limited, we got her a pram from a pet shop to take her to the nearby off-lead oval at Gardiners Creek, giving her a chance to exercise and socialise. My usual routine was to wheel Rosie to the park, leave her pram aside while we walked the oval, then put her back in and continue my walk.

Jacinta warned me that I should take the pram with me around the oval, but I thought no one would want to steal it. One day, someone did, so I had to carry Rosie home, frustrated and angry that someone had the nerve to do that. Off I went, back to the pet shop to buy a new pram. This one was upgraded with a more manoeuvrable front wheel, so that was a plus.

On the way home, I spotted a dog without an owner. Fortunately, the dog was friendly and let me pick him up. At Elisha's suggestion, I took him to our vet clinic so they could scan him and hopefully locate the owner. To top the day off, when I took Rosie for her evening walk, I found the original pram had been left in the park, so then I rang Jacinta to come and collect it. On reflection, despite being annoyed about the pram being stolen and dumped, good things had come out of the day – I got a better pram, I saved a dog and now I could donate the old pram.

I still maintain my walks to Gardiners Creek now and, where possible, include friends and family. The off-lead dog oval becomes very social as I catch up with the regulars. Of course, nature is so calming and therapeutic – I enjoy watching the birds and all the interactions of the dogs, while witnessing the changes of season.

My way of coping with the restrictions was to stick with a routine, so I continued to have my cappuccino and read the newspapers in the morning, though I did this in the car with my beloved Rosie. I took along lots of treats for her so she too enjoyed our time together.

My creative side was also a boon to getting through the lockdowns – sewing, knitting, calligraphy, writing, papercrafts, decoupage or scrapbooking. I've always found reading a wonderful pastime, so I invested in new cookbooks, autobiographies and self-help books. There's always something new to learn. And of course, gardening was, and still is, my best therapy, beneficial on so many levels. I receive so much satisfaction from creating beautiful flowers for my vases, plus herbs, vegetables and fruit to enjoy in my cooking.

Mental health issues were majorly highlighted during the lockdowns, with people being confronted with so much change and uncontrollable factors in their lives. For neurodivergent people, the changes, along with uncertainty and disruption to routine, were more challenging.

Like most people, I struggled with the restrictions – social isolation, travel, missing family and friends, and the loss of small niceties like going to my hairdresser, cafe or restaurant – but I also acknowledge that I was in a stable financial situation, my girls were in employment, and we were all in good health, so I surely counted my blessings.

When I saw my psychiatrist, early on during Covid, he asked how I was coping. I replied that overall I was doing okay, and he was pleasantly surprised. I explained that, while I felt frustrated with the situation, all the work I'd done in therapy, with him and my counsellor, had given me resilience, discipline, flexibility, adaptability, problem-solving skills and coping strategies to deal with life's challenges. For me, being able to talk through whatever issues were happening in my world, and being genuinely listened to and given strategies, was so empowering. All this work had held me in good stead.

# Epilogue

## Connecting the Dots of My Life

It's a glorious sunny day, not a cloud in the sky, when I arrive for my appointment with Dr Lam. As I pass the window where I was an inpatient all those years ago, I'm reflective in thought, noticing how much those trees have grown. So much has transpired.

I sit with Dr Lam, and we chat about general matters and my goals for the year ahead. I remind him that I've been coming here for twenty-one years and joke that I must be one of his longest-term patients. I tell him of my plans to write my autobiography, and his response is one of interest and understanding. He appreciates my desire to tell my story and help other people. He also understands it will be cathartic and healing to share my journey.

I express my excitement at beginning my business, Rainbow Connexions, with plans to start teaching craft classes – a long-held dream of mine.

Fast-forward to November, and I'm close to my sixty-second birthday. I've written the first draft of my memoir, but I'm struggling to encapsulate what the essence of my message is. A message that will reflect my life, what I've learnt, my truth, and be authentic to my soul's purpose.

Arriving at this stage has certainly given me many insights, strengths, skills and understanding about life that I couldn't possibly have known in my younger years – years when I couldn't possibly have seen how the dots of my life would connect.

Throughout my life and the changes that ensued, I was always left with a sense of 'where is this all heading to?' How could I have known the impact each experience would have on my future? But I had one of those 'aha' moments with connecting the dots when I chatted to Diane, a program co-ordinator in a neighbourhood learning centre. I was proposing some ideas for craft classes and theme days, outlining my suggestions as I showed her photos of my work. Diane was impressed and asked me about my life. As I relayed my life story, I was taken aback as it occurred to me how much all my experiences had mattered, bringing me to this stage of my life. The dreams I'd had earlier – of being an author, starting my own business, running craft classes and being involved in a community centre – were only now coming to fruition because all the dots had connected. Following my curiosity and intuition had proved to be invaluable for this new stage of my life.

You can't connect the dots looking forwards; you can only connect them looking backwards.

It's a matter of trusting in something – in your gut, destiny, life, karma, whatever that something is that you relate to. It's this belief – that the future dots will eventually connect – that gives you the confidence to follow your heart. Trusting this process, even when life takes you off the well-worn path, makes all the difference.

Being the youngest of four children in a family with modest resources certainly didn't allow me any illusions I wasn't the centre of the universe, but I was loved unconditionally, and that's what matters the most. I was blessed to have wonderful parents who taught me important values and instilled a grounded moral compass.

I survived my darkest times by a combination of luck, medication, determination, support of loved ones and excellent therapy from my doctor and counsellor. Not everyone survives major trauma in their lives – my husband being a case in point. I'm not going to sugar coat the trauma I experienced. It was horrendous, and for a long time, I was in a dark place, unable to see any way out. However, I did survive and eventually thrived, despite all the trauma I went through. I liken it to the mythical phoenix emerging from the ashes, reborn. I have gained insight, wisdom, empathy, understanding and growth as a person.

Finding your passions in life can be an ongoing process, each of us has particular things that excite us and ignite our energy. I love the feeling of waking up on a Sunday morning and anticipating my plans for the day – breakfast and papers at a cafe, walking Rosie, gardening, doing a craft project and enjoying a glass of wine with my meal at night.

Being absorbed in an activity we love is so critical for our wellbeing. Too much time dwelling in our own head space isn't good for our mental health. Being curious and open to learning not only enhances our mental faculties but helps us grow as a person.

Finding your life's direction and soul's purpose may not happen until later in your life. In my younger years, I used to feel envious of people who already knew the direction of their life. I've criss-crossed, trained, retrained and changed my career many times, seeking different and better opportunities. Throughout this process, I've been stressed, analysed and wondered where the hell my life was heading. I didn't have a big picture or grand design of my life, but that was okay.

There are times when we need to make decisions based on our intuition, to take a leap of faith that we're heading in the general right direction. Personally, it's only been in the last three years of my life that I've genuinely felt relaxed and content as to where I am and the direction my life is now heading. I'm just now coming into my own power and fulfilling my soul's purpose. Reaching this age has its benefits – wisdom, discernment and confidence. I've learnt to focus on the people who matter the most to me, the ones whose opinions I acknowledge as genuine.

Happiness is our own responsibility. I try to avoid the blame game or not being accountable. Now, if I feel I'm being judged unfairly by others, I know not to take it to heart. I now have faith enough to take life in my stride, coming from a place of strength, harmony and self-assurance. Giving, receiving and being a loving person are the most fundamental things in life. Nothing else equates to this.

So, my message to you is to look after your health and relationships because they are intrinsic to your happiness. Treat them as sacrosanct. Sometimes in life you get only one chance to get it right, so be authentic to yourself, because it's from this place of truth and honesty that you'll find your life's direction and soul's purpose. Your time and energy are your most valuable assets, so choose wisely where you direct them. Practice gratitude, count your blessings and look for the silver linings, and down the track, you might just find your own rainbow.

Milton Keynes UK
Ingram Content Group UK Ltd.
UKHW010907150823
426904UK00002B/186